All of a sudden, faster and faster…

Rhett was moving the crossbar, guiding their little airship toward stronger currents.

The hang glider smoothed like a gentle sail on calm waters.

This time, when Rhett glanced at Olivia with that elated grin, she was able to return it.

I've missed this. That feeling of movement without engines or traffic.

"Extend your arms," Rhett told her. "Like wings."

An eagle banked in a circle, catching air to fly above them.

"Extend your arms," Rhett hollered again.

This time, she did as instructed. She felt strong and powerful and free. Oh, so free. Like she had no cares, no fears.

No fear.

Tears filled her eyes and stung her nose.

There was nothing up here. No expectations. No roles to play. No people to answer to. There was only the warm wind and the man flying with her.

I could love him…

Dear Reader,

There are those in my family who love trying new things where their feet aren't firmly on the ground—parachuting out of airplanes, zip-lining over forests, rafting through the rapids. It almost seems as if they were born with the thrill-seeking gene. Me? That's not in my DNA. I'll stick to thrills on roller coasters with safety harnesses, which is why I enjoyed writing about Rhett and Olivia's heart-pounding experiences—my feet were always firmly planted beneath my desk!

Cowboy Rhett Diaz was born with the thrill-seeking gene. As a champion roper on the rodeo circuit, he discovered all kinds of ways to satisfy his need for an adrenaline rush outside the rodeo arena. You'd think racing sailboat captain Olivia Monroe would share his love of the thrill. Well, she might have if her boat hadn't capsized in her last race and her courage hadn't gone down with it. How low has Olivia's confidence sunk? In order to avoid fighting with her family, she's told everyone in Second Chance that Rhett is her boyfriend. No one is more surprised than Rhett, especially when she plants a big kiss on him!

I enjoyed writing Rhett and Olivia's adventurous road trip, one where they both get more than they bargained for. I hope you come to love The Mountain Monroes as much as I do. Each book is connected but also stands alone. Happy reading!

Melinda

HEARTWARMING

The Cowboy Meets His Match

Melinda Curtis

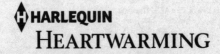

HARLEQUIN®
HEARTWARMING™

PLEASE RECYCLE • THIS PRODUCT IS RECYCLABLE

Recycling programs for this product may not exist in your area.

ISBN-13: 978-1-335-42663-5

The Cowboy Meets His Match

Copyright © 2022 by Melinda Wooten

This edition published by arrangement with Harlequin Books S.A.

For questions and comments about the quality of this book, please contact us at CustomerService@Harlequin.com.

Harlequin Enterprises ULC
22 Adelaide St. West, 41st Floor
Toronto, Ontario M5H 4E3, Canada
www.Harlequin.com

Printed in U.S.A.

Melinda Curtis, prior to writing romance, was a junior manager for a Fortune 500 company, which meant when she flew on the private jet, she was relegated to the jump seat—otherwise known as the potty (seriously, the commode had a seat belt). After grabbing her pen (and a parachute), she made the jump to full-time writer. Melinda has become a *USA TODAY* bestselling author, and her Harlequin Heartwarming book *Dandelion Wishes* is now a TV movie—*Love in Harmony Valley*.

Brenda Novak says *Season of Change* "found a place on my keeper shelf."

Jayne Ann Krentz says of *Can't Hurry Love*, "Nobody does emotional, heartwarming small-town romance like Melinda Curtis."

Sheila Roberts says *Can't Hurry Love* is "a page turner filled with wit and charm."

Books by Melinda Curtis

The Mountain Monroes

Rescued by the Perfect Cowboy
Lassoed by the Would-Be Rancher
Enchanted by the Rodeo Queen
Charmed by the Cook's Kids
The Littlest Cowgirls
A Cowgirl's Secret

Return of the Blackwell Brothers

The Rancher's Redemption

The Blackwell Sisters

Montana Welcome

Visit the Author Profile page at Harlequin.com for more titles.

THE MOUNTAIN MONROES FAMILY TREE

Harlan Monroe
(deceased)

Darrell Monroe
(Oil/Finance)
- Holden Monroe
- Bo Monroe
- Kendall Monroe

Carlisle Monroe
(Hotels/Entertainment)
- Shane Monroe (twin)
- Sophie Monroe (twin)
- Camden Monroe

Ian Monroe
(Yacht Building)
- Bryce Monroe (twin, deceased)
- Bentley Monroe (twin)
- Olivia Monroe

Lincoln Monroe
(Filmmaking)
- Jonah Monroe
- Laurel Monroe (twin)
- Ashley Monroe (twin)

PROLOGUE

ALL OLIVIA MONROE had ever wanted to do was sail, and sail fast, faster than anyone else.

And for a long time, she'd done just that, to the delight of her family, her sponsors and her fans.

But any athlete will tell you that success is fleeting.

One minute, Olivia had been on top of the world and ahead of the race with her fortunes on the rise. The next minute, she'd been thrown into the ocean and trapped beneath the surface with her life flashing before her eyes.

She'd come back to the living in a racing official's boat. She'd come back, but she'd left her sponsors, her racing yacht and her nerve at the bottom of the Atlantic Ocean. For weeks after the accident, Olivia had hidden away from the world, the press and, some might say, from herself. She needed an intervention.

One came in the form of an old sports psychologist named Sonny. His goal was to help her rebuild her life and reclaim everything she'd lost. She'd come to the remote Idaho mountains and the tiny town of Second Chance with Sonny in tow.

Why would a sailor come to a landlocked place like Second Chance?

Because Olivia, her siblings and cousins had inherited the small town—a little known fact—and no one in the racing world would look for her there. Heck, for the most part, the Monroe branch of the family left her alone in the capable care of Sonny.

She spent nearly two months trying to stow away her fear of the water and get back on a boat, even if it was only a dinghy and only on a small mountain lake. Two months of listening to Sonny encourage her to be honest with herself (she'd never *been* good at that). Two months of him guiding her into a solid meditation routine (she'd never *be* good at that). And two months of facing the broken internal parts of herself (she wanted to *be done* with that).

Admittedly, Olivia wasn't the best client, but she and Sonny had formed a bond. She trusted the old man, even as she dragged her feet through his recommended treatment. And just when it seemed there was hope for her, slim though it might be, Sonny suffered a heart attack and her family closed ranks around Olivia, determined to send her back home to Philadelphia.

Olivia wasn't leaving Sonny alone in Idaho or caving in on her determination that he continue to help her rediscover her backbone. But Olivia wasn't the headstrong, independent woman she used to be. The more her family argued, the more Olivia felt her resolve crumbling. Cornered and desperate, she'd known she only had one chance to stay the course.

And so, she'd reached for the easiest defense at her disposal—*a handsome cowboy*—and the flimsiest of excuses—*they were in love*—and tried to sell the illusion—*by kissing him*.

CHAPTER ONE

RHETT DIAZ HAD a way with the ladies and a weakness for a dare.

He knew he had an attractive mug and that he managed to string together words that often brought a blush to a woman's cheeks. He knew fear rarely factored into his rationale. But when he'd dropped out of the rodeo circuit to help run the family ranch, his dating life and adventurous dares became pretty much non-existent. Second Chance, Idaho, offered little in the way of either.

He fingered the lips Olivia Monroe had just finished thoroughly kissing.

A warm mountain breeze tugged at the brim of his cowboy hat, as restless as Rhett was inside, wondering why Olivia would tell everyone standing in the parking lot of the Bent Nickel Diner that they were a couple, and then when it seemed like a half dozen of her family members were closing in with doubt, she'd kissed him.

Him, a cowboy she'd only talked to a handful of times. Rhett allowed himself a rueful smile.

That kiss was one that couldn't easily be forgotten. Half plea, half passion. It had left Rhett and the rest of the Monroes speechless.

Across the narrow two-lane highway, the wisp of a woman in question disappeared into the medical clinic where her friend Sonny was recuperating from an apparent heart attack. She shut the door firmly behind her. Word had come down that an ambulance would be arriving soon to take Sonny to the hospital in Ketchum.

"We need to talk." Shane Monroe took Rhett by the arm and headed toward the Bent Nickel. He was one of Olivia's many cousins in town.

Without a word, Holden Monroe took Rhett's other arm. He was cousin to both Shane and Olivia.

"Hey." Rhett shrugged them off and tipped his hat back, ready for a fight. "I…" Overcome by protective instincts, he cut himself short of explaining how he'd been caught off-guard and lip-bombed by Olivia.

Olivia was gaunt, the way folks got when they were recovering from a serious illness or a devastating heartbreak. But her caramel-colored eyes held a spark of intelligence and, sometimes, humor. If she was being bullied by her family and had reached for him as her savior, he wouldn't betray that trust.

Shane held up his hands. "We just want to talk." He wasn't as tall as Rhett, or as broad shouldered. But he dressed like a corporate man on one of those casual Fridays in the city—khakis, loafers, a crisp blue polo shirt— and he acted like he always knew what he was doing, even if Rhett sometimes suspected he didn't.

"Just talk," Holden reiterated. He was taller than Rhett, older than Rhett, and dressed like a cowboy, which was a bit mind-blowing since he was rumored to be a successful moneyman from Wall Street.

Rhett drew a long, slow breath, making it seem like he was thinking about walking away. In truth, he was thinking it might help Olivia if he knew what her family wanted, other than to send her away.

He gave a brisk nod and led them inside the diner, choosing a booth near the window where he could see the medical clinic.

Shane slid onto the seat across from Rhett, and Holden pulled up a chair at the end of the booth's table. They both wore serious expressions, borderline frowns.

Rhett crossed his arms over his chest and waited. If there was one thing he knew about this pair of Monroes, it was that they always had an agenda, a plan or an offer in mind. He'd let them play the first card.

"Forget everything that happened today," Holden said in a slow, deep voice.

"Well, almost everything," Shane said with just as much gravitas.

Rhett contained the urge to roll his eyes. The chance of him giving that kiss a memory wipe was slim-to-none.

Shane exchanged a glance with Holden, pressed his shoulders back and rearranged his all-business expression into a slight smile.

In a blink, Rhett went on full alert. He was more accustomed to seeing that kind of emotive flip Shane had just made from a cocky, young bull. Not a frown to a smile, per se. More like a little charge at Rhett, followed by a few moseying steps in the direction Rhett wanted the bull to go, and then a sharp pivot to charge Rhett again. Rhett knew what to do with young, ornery bulls—stand his ground. He kept his arms crossed and a sharp eye on the two men.

"We visited you at the Bar D a few days ago," Shane began.

Rhett nodded warily.

"We were there discussing the sale of your family's vintage carnival rides." Holden picked up where his cousin left off. "I recall you saying you wanted to start an adventure tour company."

"Is that so?" Rhett felt as twitchy as a steer waiting in the chute. He didn't like folks bringing up his dream, especially when it was so far out of reach. Talking about it felt like admitting he was a failure, since the odds of him making it happen were a longshot. His grandfather and sister couldn't run the Bar D alone.

"We were wondering if you could tell us more about the tour company you have in mind to open." Shane sounded friendly, but then again, the Bar D's ranch cat appreciated a good scratch behind her ears…until she didn't and nipped the scratcher.

"It's just that—an idea." Rhett wasn't about to spill all his beans on the table. He was just a cowboy with a skill throwing the rope. These guys were men of the world.

"Well, you see…" Shane continued with that reassuring smile. "Between Holden and me, we've got a lot of business expertise. I want to increase tourism in Second Chance. And Holden wants to mentor people, like you, to make their business dreams a reality."

Rhett's pulse picked up, hastened by a sliver of hope.

"It wouldn't be hard to get a small business loan," Holden began.

"Stop right there." Rhett shook his head, mentally trampling the vestiges of optimism to dust. "I won't take out a loan. My grandparents did that fifteen or twenty years back, and that gave *your* grandfather an opportunity to buy us out."

Harlan Monroe had come back to his hometown a decade ago and bought out its residents. He'd then turned around and charged them a lease of one dollar a year, hoping to keep the town afloat. Despite that, the Bar D continued to struggle to turn enough profit to support three people.

Shane and Holden exchanged glances.

Holden nodded slowly. "Okay. A business partnership, then. Something could be worked out."

"With who?" Rhett regarded the men with suspicion.

"That remains to be seen." Shane shrugged his shoulders.

"You two?" Rhett was beginning to catch on. "Why would you want to partner with the likes of me? A former roping champion and nearly broke cowboy."

"You're not broke. You have a decent amount of seed money," Holden said slyly. "We delivered a check to you, remember?" The one for several thousand dollars that Rhett had been given as a bonus for signing on as a roping consultant to a Western film that was going to be shot in Second Chance come spring.

Rhett shook his head. He hadn't planned on cashing that until he got the job for real in six months. He never counted his chickens before they hatched.

"You'd bring that check and your enthusiasm for the business to the deal." Holden tipped his hat back. Unlike Rhett, he didn't look like he was ready to pick a fight. He looked like he'd adjusted that hat so he could see Rhett better. "What kind of business did you have in mind?"

Rhett hesitated, faced with a fork in the road. He could either trust these men with his dream or cling to his pride and the same old, same old dead-end existence.

He heaved a sigh, choosing to expose his aspirations as well as his lack of business knowledge to the Monroes. "I don't know what kind of adventure tour company I want to run. I love a good adrenaline rush, but what do I do with that? The easy answer is a white water river rafting company. There used to be a river rafting company in town. The owner turned into a snow bird after your grandfather's buy-out. He only comes back for a few months every year, but he didn't return at all this summer."

"That sounds like an opportunity," Holden said.

Rhett didn't agree. "It would if lazy floats down the river excited me. Around here, the Salmon River meanders past. There's no white water rush."

Shane glanced from Holden to Rhett. "Seems like a hard way to make a living—being open just five or six months out of the year."

Rhett nodded. "I was also thinking about ziplines. We've got some steep slopes here in town. But again, it'd be seasonal. And ranching..." He gave a small laugh. "Ranching is seasonal, too. If I ran a touring company, I wouldn't be able to pull my weight at the ranch. Which is why I'll have to turn you down, I guess." He felt a strong measure of disappointment, and then a stab of anger. "Why me? Why now? If you were interested in helping me, why not discuss this business when you were out at the ranch recently?"

"Things have changed." Holden leaned forward, placing his elbows on the table and nodding toward the parking lot where Olivia had kissed him.

Rhett pressed his lips together and said nothing.

"You're dating Olivia," Shane stated matter-of-factly, as if he'd bought into Olivia's stunt. "You know what she's been through. The accident. The near-drowning. The loss of everything that was important to her."

"Are you trying to buy me out of the relationship?" Fake though it was.

Holden and Shane exchanged another glance.

"Okay, that look you two share is beginning to annoy me. Words, gents. Use your words and get to the point."

"There are conditions to us investing in you, of course," Shane said finally.

"Not interested." Rhett refused to sell Olivia out that way. She needed him. What else could that knock-your-socks-off kiss be but an SOS? He swung his feet around his seat, preparing to stand and leave.

"Hang on." Holden extended an arm in his

path. "We don't want you to break up with Olivia. We want you to take her on a trip."

"A fact-finding mission." Shane nodded briskly, continuing before Rhett could argue. "You don't know what type of business you want to open—am I correct? Perhaps you need to analyze the competition—ziplining, bungee jumping, river rafting and the like. Check out how businesses are run in other places, other states, and see what fits."

Again, Rhett's pulse picked up, both hopeful of dreams fulfilled and of adrenaline-filled adventures ahead.

"From here to the Catskills," Holden added.

"Come again? Idaho to the Catskills?" Rhett shook his head. "A trip that long exceeds my budget, not to mention I don't have a week or so to spare. I promised Tanner I'd help him run a rodeo school soon." They were currently working out the schedule and building more chutes and gates for events.

"We have you covered," Shane said with a smoothness that matched his slick smile. "We'll help Tanner prep if you can return to Second Chance in time for his event."

Rhett was pretty sure Tanner didn't want Shane's help. Tanner had come to town claiming to be a long-lost Monroe and Shane had been doubtful. But there was something else about their proposition that bothered him. "The Catskills are close to the East Coast and… Philadelphia." Where they wanted Olivia to go. "I get it now. You created this whole cockamamie investment idea as an excuse for me to drive Olivia home."

Shane's smile widened. "No, we're sincere about bringing business and tourism to town, including helping you get a business off the ground."

"But also yes, we think it's best if she returns home." At least Holden was honest about it. "That's where she belongs."

"Does Olivia know about this?" Rhett suspected she wouldn't approve of their plan.

The Monroe men shook their heads.

Rhett tipped his hat back, tone dipping into angry territory. "Does Sonny know about this?" The old therapist Olivia seemed to rely on.

Again, they shook their heads.

"She won't agree to go." Rhett might not know Olivia that well, but he knew that much. There was Sonny's health and her determination to be independent. He understood independence. He wanted his independence back, hence the dream to open his own business. But he wanted it without letting his family down.

"You leave Olivia to us." Holden nodded toward the door where his sister Kendall had just come in.

Kendall wore a fancy outfit and black high-heeled booties. Her long black hair fell in smooth waves over her shoulders. She nodded to the men and headed for the community coffee pot.

"Kendall does all our family public relations and social media," Holden said in a tone that indicated she was the secret weapon they planned to use to convince Olivia to go on the trip with Rhett.

"Plan out your itinerary, Rhett." Shane wore that pleasant smile again, the one that didn't inspire trust. "We'll reimburse your expenses."

"I have a bad feeling about this," Rhett muttered after agreeing to their terms, partly because he wasn't sure how Olivia would react if she found out about it, and partly because he suspected when she did find out about his part in this deception, that his odds of further kisses would be nil.

"OLIVIA?"

Olivia jolted awake with a crick in her neck

and a foot that was asleep. It took her a moment to get her bearings.

A dim hospital room. Sonny sleeping in bed, tubes and wires attaching him to monitors and IVs. His snow white hair and beard looked limp. He seemed less like a mischievous garden gnome and more like an old man who'd suffered a health scare.

"Olivia. *Liv*." Cousin Kendall stood in the doorway, looking rested and ready to go on a coffee date in a casual black jumpsuit and heels. The outfit reminded Olivia of the cowboy with the black hat she'd kissed and then left to clean up her mess yesterday.

As kisses went, that one was what her Grandpa Harlan would have called a *humdinger*. But that wasn't important right now.

Olivia stretched and unfurled her legs, flexing her foot to bring back much needed circulation. Light tried to peek through the window blinds. The big round clock on the wall read eight-fifteen. It had been a night filled with interruptions from nurses and she was tired. "What are you doing here, Kendall?"

"Checking on you and the old man." Kendall closed the door until all but a sliver of light from the bright hallway distinguished the entry. "How is he?"

"He had three stents put in last night." Olivia tucked Sonny's blanket more firmly around his shoulders. "If the surgery had been earlier, they would have released him yesterday. Can you believe they'd let him go so quickly? Thank heavens for overscheduling."

Sonny stirred. "I'm fine. Unhook me and I'll race you to the door." He cracked one eye open. "Did you sleep here last night, Olivia? That chair looks uncomfortable."

"It is." Olivia stood, working out the kinks in her stiff body. "Why are you really here, Kendall? I told you that I'm Team Sonny until I'm back to being me. The only way I go anywhere is if I can take him, too." Besides which, he needed someone to take care of him.

Sonny reached for Olivia's hand and gave it a weak squeeze. "It's nice to wake up and know some things haven't changed. You're still hardheaded, although you'd probably call yourself determined."

"And you're still too short-sighted to see anything but the sunny side." Olivia gave him a tender smile. "Endearingly so."

Kendall moved to stand at the foot of the bed. "I hate to break up this tender moment—"

"No, you don't." Olivia rolled her eyes in Kendall's direction.

"—but Shane and Holden have a favor to ask you, Olivia." Kendall paused, perhaps waiting to see if either Sonny or Olivia would shoot the favor down without listening. When no further interruptions arose, she continued. "They're thinking of investing in your boyfriend's adventure tour company."

Olivia could feel a frown coming on, inspired by a suspicious thought—that her cousins had found a way to meddle in Olivia's life. She should have known that kissing Rhett wouldn't buy her a get-out-of-jail-free card when it came to family interference. Monroes were notorious for circling the wagons when someone was in trouble, whether they wanted to be protected or not.

"What's the favor?" Olivia asked, at the same time Sonny said, "Who's the boyfriend?"

Yikes.

"She's talking about Rhett," Olivia hurried to say before fixing Kendall with a hard look. "Spell it out for me, Kendall, including what my cousin Shane and your brother Holden didn't want you to say."

Kendall gave Olivia an encompassing look while she gathered her thoughts and finger-combed her hair. "They've asked your cowboy to provide a proposal regarding what type of adventures this as yet unnamed tour company would offer in Second Chance."

"And they want me to help him write this plan up? I'm sure Rhett is capable of conveying what he wants to do." He was completely capable of kissing her. An expert, in fact. He had to have skills in other areas, especially if he wanted to run his own business.

Kendall shook her head, sending all that black hair cascading around her shoulders. "He's going to visit several different tour companies and test them out, then decide what to do."

Olivia rubbed her forehead. "I'm at a loss. Where do I fit into this?"

"Isn't it obvious?" Kendall tsked. "The guys want you to vouch for Rhett."

"Consider him vouched for. He's a decent guy. I'm sure he'll be a good investment." At least Olivia assumed he was since it was increasingly clear he hadn't told anyone their relationship wasn't real.

"No. You misunderstand me. Shane and Holden want *you* to go with Rhett on this research mission of adventure companies and make sure he has the guts to be an owner and guide."

The guts? Who am I to judge someone else's courage?

A feeling of trepidation gathered in Olivia's stomach. "Take a trip with Rhett?"

"It shouldn't be a hardship." Kendall loaded her words with sarcasm. "He's your boyfriend."

"But Sonny just had surgery and—"

"Sit me up and call the nurse." Sonny fumbled with the bed's remote. "I'm fit and ready to hit the road."

Olivia took possession of the bed controller. "Slow down. You've just had surgery."

"And you're at a place in your recovery where you need a change of scenery, Olivia," Sonny said in a gravelly voice, accented by a wink that was reminiscent of the optimistic man who wasn't shy about confronting her broken parts. "Even if you won't admit it. What better way to ease back into the world again than with a road trip filled with adventure and accompanied by your cowboy?"

Because of the unknowns—both the adventure part and the cowboy part.

"The old you would have jumped at the chance," Kendall said with something akin to suspicion in her voice.

And there it was, the impulse to put up a

shield to keep her family, including Kendall, at arm's length. Or perhaps make a run for it.

Olivia stayed put and poured Sonny a glass of water. "I'll do this favor for Rhett if you'll come with me, Sonny. We won't leave until you're ready." Olivia wasn't going anywhere alone with that kiss-worthy cowboy. She could barely stand up for herself with her family. How could she possibly resist the temptation to kiss him some more?

"Child…"

The hospital room door was pushed open, and a doctor entered. He turned on the overhead lights. "I'm Dr. Jenkins. Is this your family, Mr. Horn?"

"No," Sonny said at the same time that Olivia said, "Yes."

"I'm his only family," Olivia said staunchly, daring Sonny to deny it. He had no living siblings and no children.

Sonny sighed. "Some family you're born into and some you find along the way, Doc."

Dr. Jenkins surveyed the room, paying particular attention to his patient. And then he faced Olivia. "If you two could leave us alone for my exam…" He gestured toward the door.

Olivia shook her head. "No, I—"

"Go on, Olivia." Sonny made a shooing motion. "Get yourself some breakfast and see to your hair. It's as limp as your courage on one side."

"Like I care about my appearance." Olivia stared at Sonny, registering the features that had become so dear to her. His soft blue eyes. His overgrown white mustache and haystack whiskers. He was out of shape and in poor health. A year ago, she would have taken one dismissive look at him and invalidated anything he had to say. But somehow, over the course of the past few months, he'd become closer to being a father figure to her than her own dad. "I'll step out if you promise to tell me everything when I get back."

"I promise no such thing." Sonny chuckled. "Kendall, take her away."

Kendall obediently hooked her arm through Olivia's. "Come on. I've got a comb and some makeup in my purse. I can make you look presentable." Kendall was obsessed with appearances.

"I'll use the comb, but your idea of presentable using makeup is the polar opposite of mine. Who do I need to impress?"

"Yourself? Liv, you haven't looked like Captain Olivia Monroe since the accident." Kendall continued to tug Olivia along the corridor.

"Are you really considering doing this ride-along with the cowboy?"

In her concern for Sonny, she'd forgotten about Rhett.

"Yes. He's my boyfriend?" Olivia said, trying not to cringe over stating it as a question, because Rhett's loyalty deserved hers. "Plus Shane and Holden will help his business if he passes inspection. Why wouldn't I go?"

"Because he's a cowboy with no steady paycheck." Kendall sounded as if she'd judged Rhett on the slimmest of information. "Because while he was on the rodeo circuit eating county fair food, you were on the racing circuit eating five-star cuisine in yacht clubs. Admit it. This is just an after-accident fling. You two make no sense."

"I don't like your tone." Annoyance pinched Olivia's shoulder blades. If Rhett had been around, she'd have kissed him again.

And liked it.

How was that for being incompatible?

CHAPTER TWO

"I CAN'T BELIEVE you're leaving us." Cassie fixed her brother with a hard stare. She flung her black braid over her shoulder. "I'm just recovering from a rodeo injury. Grandpa and I need you at the ranch for all the heavy lifting."

"You have Bentley Monroe to help out." Cassie's boyfriend. Rhett leaned against the kitchen counter, drinking his afternoon coffee. His gaze slid to his grandfather, who sat at the table sorting his numerous medications for the week. "When Grandpa got sick over a year ago, I retired from the rodeo and came home to help you with the Bar D. Our roots are here, but you know I never wanted to be a rancher." He'd been footloose on the circuit and happy about it. Heck, the more he thought about the trip ahead, the more interested he was becoming in leaving and doing things he'd put off since his rodeo retirement.

My excitement has nothing to do with bringing Olivia along.

Rhett covered a smile with his coffee cup.

I should hate myself, given I'll be deceiving Olivia.

Rhett's smile faded. That part wasn't so exciting.

"Your daredevil streak won't earn you a living," Grandpa prophesied in a dry voice that managed to poke Rhett's temper to life.

"That daredevil streak made me a champion roper," Rhett said evenly, hanging on to patience by the thinnest of threads. "And the Monroes believe I can make money for both me and a business partner, which is more than the hard-scrabble living this place makes."

Ajax, their black-and-tan heeler, gave Rhett a soulful look and a wheezy squeak of his new bunny chew toy.

Cassie sagged into a kitchen chair and took Grandpa's hand. The look she gave Rhett filled him with guilt, her words more so. "Will you be like our parents and walk away from our heritage so easily?"

"Rhett don't think about his roots like we do, Cassie." Grandpa patted Cassie's hand. "He's always looking for the next thrill."

"I know where my roots are," Rhett said in a voice that sounded one note above a growl.

"This is home. But it makes no sense to stay if I'm just one more mouth to feed."

Rhett didn't like to face reality any more than Cassie or Grandpa did. But things had changed for him since Olivia had kissed him, unwittingly opening a door to opportunity. And since opportunity didn't often show itself, Rhett was barging right on in, thank you very much.

That is, if Olivia agreed to go along.

He didn't like his future hanging in the balance contingent on someone else's whim. In addition to this trip being an adventure test run, there were pitfalls and obligations—all of which hung on the balance of keeping Olivia cooperative. How was he supposed to do that?

"Why now, Rhett?" Cassie asked. "Things are looking up."

"Are they?" Rhett rinsed out his coffee cup. "The ranch will get a boost of income when the old carnival rides are fixed up and sold. And come spring, we'll be supplementing our earnings by working on a movie being filmed up here." If it happened. He refused to bank on it. "And after that, then what, Cassie?"

"I'll still have my horse training." His sister's voice was weaker than before, and Rhett was sorry to have burst her bubble.

"Plus, I'm teaching others how to train their horses. And you coach the next generation of ropers. Money comes in."

"And money goes out. You and I both know you can pay a ranch hand less than I draw from the accounts." Rhett shook his head ruefully. "I'm not abandoning the ranch. I'm easing your financial load."

His family was silent, even the dog.

Rhett pressed on, "There comes a time in a man's life when he's got to take a risk and branch out on his own. And maybe I'll get flung to the dirt like that rodeo bull did to you and your dreams, Cassie. But I have to try. It's time for me to reach for something different before I'm too old and set in my ways." His gaze drifted to his grandfather.

"Do we have that Monroe gal to blame for your restlessness?" Grandpa gave Rhett a narrow gaze. "Folks in town are talking about you two as an item. I don't see much of a future between a cowboy and a boat captain."

Although he agreed, Rhett kept his mouth shut. Much as he loved the old man, no good would come of telling his grandfather the truth of the situation. Grandpa held a secret the way a colander held water...which was not at all.

Ajax lifted his head, ears cocked. The sound

of tires flying over gravel came through the open window, a sound louder than the gentle purr of a civilized car engine. The car didn't stop at the ranch yard. It was headed toward the old Bar D homestead, which was where Olivia and Sonny had been staying all summer.

Ajax bolted for the mudroom and the doggy door.

Rhett wasn't far behind the dog, putting on his boots and cowboy hat before exiting via the human door. He needed to know if Olivia had come clean to her family about their relationship. More importantly, he needed to know if she was interested in going on his trip. If she wasn't, the deal Shane and Holden had offered was off.

And then what?

He didn't know.

The afternoon sun was high above the pines, the air heavy with the muggy heat of summer after last night's rain. Ajax ran ahead, pausing on the road at the rise as he waited for Rhett, as if they were a team.

At least the dog has my back.

Two sedans were parked at the end of the homestead's gravel driveway. The red one's engine pinged as it cooled. Dust was just beginning to settle on its shiny fenders.

Ajax ran up to the front door of the one-story house and barked.

The door flew open before Rhett reached the small stoop.

"Honey, I missed you! I'm so excited for our trip." Olivia barreled into Rhett. She wore a black tank top, tan cargo shorts and flip-flops. She wrapped her arms around him and turned her face up, the way women turned their faces up when they wanted a kiss.

Rhett was inclined to oblige, and yet, he hesitated. Olivia Monroe was a slip of a woman with a tousle of sun-kissed brown curls and a tumble of baggage to work through. She was in no place to start a relationship and he had no right to pursue one with her. But she had a way of looking at a man—like she was doing now—that made Rhett forget the good and bad of the tangle she'd gotten him into and focus on the way she felt in his arms.

So, he kissed her, just a quick buss of his lips against hers. It shouldn't have caused a jolt to his system. It shouldn't have made him tighten his arms around her. But it did.

Rhett smiled.

Ajax gave an excited bark and then raced back toward the Bar D, as if he had a secret to tell Cassie and Grandpa.

So much for the dog having my back.

Although her arms were still around Rhett, Olivia's eyes flared with warning as she looked up at him. "Are you here for an update on Sonny? He's fine. Isn't that great?" Her tone was sharp. Almost mocking. She wasn't selling the idea that they were a couple.

"I'm glad he's okay." The craving to kiss her properly was strong. She was beautiful and he was a man, after all. But he was dancing on a thin line. He needed her cooperation if he wanted Monroe financing.

Voices murmured from inside the house— an audience. Olivia's performance implied his trip and their fake relationship were both still on.

Smiling again, Rhett released her. "I'm packed up and ready to go. Just say the word and we can hit the road."

"Slow down, cowboy." Olivia turned, darting back inside. "We can't leave until Sonny's better."

He followed her into the house like a puppy expecting more treats.

"Were your ears burning?" Kendall, that willowy Monroe who dressed like Second Chance was a big city, gave him a calculating smile reminiscent of Shane's. "We were just talking about you."

"I'm sure it was all good." Rhett removed his hat but remained in the foyer.

This had once been his grandparents' home. The dated orange and brown furniture still filled the living room. A painting of the lake still hung above the mantel and the room still held a hint of his grandmother's perfume. Or that might have come from the bouquet of yellow and blue flowers on the coffee table.

"Nobody has anything bad to say about Rhett." Olivia went to sit in a chair near Sonny, who reclined on the couch, looking better than he had the day before when the ambulance had taken him to the hospital. "Come in and visit. Kendall was just leaving."

"Thanks for driving us back, Kendall," Sonny said. His T-shirt read: What Are You Thankful for Today? The bearded old man favored T-shirts with sayings the way Rhett favored plaid shirts and cowboy boots. "We're leaving as soon as I get a delivery. We'll talk again when we return from our trip."

"*Our* trip?" Rhett echoed. "I thought it was just Olivia and me."

"It's not a honeymoon," Kendall said sternly. "If Olivia hadn't insisted upon taking Sonny, I would have chaperoned." She marched out the door, high heels clicking. "You be careful with my cousin. You may be convenient, cowboy, but you're far from being Monroe-approved."

Convenient? Approved?

Stung, Rhett was unable to let the dig slide. "I'm always careful with the ladies."

Kendall laughed.

"No one's ever called me a lady before." Olivia looked as if she wasn't certain the label was a compliment. "I've never been one of those girly-girls, like Kendall."

"It's a term of respect and I give points to Rhett for it." Sonny regarded Rhett levelly. "Even if it was delivered more for sarcastic effect than deference. I suspect our Kendall rubs him the wrong way."

"His wouldn't be the first feathers Kendall's ruffled." The corners of Olivia's delicate mouth tilted upward, hinting that she could be as playful as her short brown curls.

Rhett's gaze roamed from those curls down to Olivia's small feet. He'd never seen her in anything other than flip-flops, which didn't bode well for their trip. "Do you have sneakers? You'll need them."

"I don't know. I haven't seen or worn a pair in months." Olivia stood and strode purposefully toward him, blue flip-flops snapping with each step. "Let's take a walk." She clasped his hand and gave him a tug toward the front porch, not that it took much to draw Rhett along. "Back in a few, Sonny." She closed the door firmly behind them and led the way to the little wooden rowboat pulled up on the lakeshore. "Come on. I haven't been on the water yet today."

"I thought you didn't like the water." And Rhett wasn't a fan of boats. "Why don't we take a walk around the lake?"

"According to Sonny, being on the lake is part of the recovery of my confidence." Wading in, Olivia pushed the boat into the water, holding the bow near the shoreline. "Get in."

Rhett dug in his boot heels. "If you aren't up for a walk, we can take a ride. Your feet look small enough to fit in my sister's boots." A horseback ride was romantic and private. They could stop at the overlook up the hill and—

"I wanted to talk, not…" Her hand fluttered between them.

It's like she can read my mind.

Rhett bit back a grin.

"As a cowboy, I'm sure you've heard the saying about getting back in the saddle. I'm a sailor who capsized." Olivia flinched, and when she continued, her words had bite. "If I don't get on the water regularly, the fear gets in my head. Come on, *honey*. Humor me."

There was a power struggle going on and Rhett feared he was losing because he took a step forward before he realized what he was doing. "No." He planted his boots again.

Olivia's gaze narrowed. "If you're afraid of getting your boots wet, take them off." Her voice rang with that command she was rumored to have lost. "Get in. We need to talk and then I need to make dinner."

He noticed she didn't invite him to the meal.

They stared at each other while a breeze ruffled pine branches above them.

They were at an impasse. Someone had to give. Or at the very least, move things along without admitting to being a total fool.

All Rhett had to do was prove he was as obstinate as she was. "I'm not afraid of getting my boots wet." He stomped into the water and climbed into the boat without any finesse. "There. Are you happy?"

"Yes." She vaulted into the boat, losing a flip-flop in the process. With an audible gasp, she quickly snatched it back, holding herself still for a moment before blowing out a breath. "I'm okay."

"Good." She'd rocked the boat enough to make Rhett's stomach lurch. As a teenager, he'd capsized a canoe in this lake. It was why he didn't like small boats.

Olivia took a step toward him, climbing over the middle seat toward the back of the boat where he was.

Is she going to sit in my lap?

He didn't dare move.

Thank heavens for fake relationships and appearances!

"This is unexpected, but…" Rhett held his arms out. "I'm ready."

Olivia threw her arms out as well, only not to encourage an embrace. She looked like she was searching for balance. "Sailors don't sit in laps during a sail." She stopped moving, except to cross her arms over her chest. "I can't get by you to the outboard." Which was currently in the horizontal position behind him, keeping the blades out of the water and shallow mud.

"It's a small lake. We can row." He gripped the wooden oars and turned the boat around. He rowed facing forward, having no choice but to do so since she was standing between him and the seat best suited for rowing efficiently.

Arms still out, Olivia wobbled. "I like to go fast."

"That outboard is five horsepower." It was his father's old fishing boat. It didn't go fast.

She plunked down on the seat across from him. "Fine. Get us to the other side of the lake. Sonny won't be able to hear us over there."

Rhett did as he was told but only because he valued his privacy as much as she seemingly valued hers.

The lake was calm. They didn't speak. For several minutes, the only sound was the dipping of his oars and a twittering blue jay swooping past. Olivia stared at his hat or something in the distance behind him. The homestead perhaps? Rhett stared unabashedly at her, trying to figure out why he liked her. She was far from easy-going. She was too unpredictable and seemingly not susceptible to his charm.

"I'm sorry about your boots," Olivia said when they reached the middle of the lake, which hadn't taken long.

"They'll dry." Rhett kept rowing.

"I get snappy when I get stressed," Olivia admitted. "I didn't used to."

"Get snappy or get stressed?" He rowed some more, deep, long strokes that sent the boat moving quickly across the small lake.

"I didn't used to get stressed. Not like this anyway." Her hands twisted in front of her as if the admission was costing her. "It's like a well that rises up inside me and I lose my... composure."

He stopped rowing. They drifted into the shallows, bottom bumping against shore. "Like you lost your composure when Sonny was having a heart attack?" Unlike Cassie, she'd been the opposite of cool in a crisis.

Olivia nodded, staring in the direction of his wet boots. "Since the accident, I either have a total meltdown or I want to steamroll everyone around me. I'm striving for the in-between. I...uh...." She lifted her gaze to his. "I thought I owed you an explanation for the...uh...what happened yesterday?" She touched her fingers to her lips before tucking those same fingers beneath her legs.

"An apology doesn't explain why you told everyone I'm your boyfriend." And why she kissed him like it was true.

"I'd rather talk about ground rules for this trip of yours," Olivia countered, regaining some of her composure.

"As in how many miles between stops and bathroom breaks?" Rhett quipped, storing the oars.

"As in guidelines for you entering my personal space while keeping up the charade my loss of composure forced upon us."

Oh, this was going to be good. "Guidelines we wouldn't need if you left Sonny at home." At thirty-three, Rhett was long past the need for a chaperone.

Some of the spark returned to her eyes. "I can't leave Sonny behind. He has no one but me."

"He can stay at the Lodgepole Inn. Someone can watch out for him there."

"But that someone wouldn't be me." By her tone, this point was non-negotiable.

The blue jay swooped again, scolding them.

Rhett scanned the nearby pines for a nest, regrouping. "Then you have three choices. You can admit you lied—"

"Which you supported, by the way."

"—or pretend we're still together without your silly guidelines—"

She pressed her lips into a thin line.

"—or be very adult about a break-up. Sonny seems like the type who'd appreciate a mature parting of the ways."

"But that makes me look…"

"Juvenile?"

She rolled her eyes. "Please. I'm twenty-eight."

"Flighty?"

"No one who knows me would believe that. I used to have nerves as steady as a rock."

He let the past tense slide. "Incapable of—"

"Careful, cowboy." Those expressive eyes of hers flashed a warning.

"It's one thing to suspect you're not perfect, but quite another to admit it, eh?" Rhett wasn't giving her an inch. It was his future at stake, not hers. He had to lay down the law. He hadn't answered to anyone in fifteen years. He wasn't going to cater to her whims. And yet, those kisses made him want a mutually agreed upon compromise. "The quicker you rip the bandage off this scam—"

"I vote we stay together," Olivia said matter-of-factly, staring at her hands. "I'm dealing with too much right now and pretending to be together—however wrong—gives me some breathing room with my family. What harm does a little hand-holding in public do to anyone?"

"Hand-holding? What are we, twelve? This has mistake written all over it." *In other words, nothing in it for me.* There seemed no room for kisses, which Rhett selfishly had been banking on. "No one will believe I'd draw the line at holding hands. What's on your list of acceptable PDA?" Best to ask now. "Show me."

Olivia looked nervous. "Show you?"

"Yep. That way we won't get our wires crossed." He reached out and took her hand. It was warm, small and delicate. "Hand-holding is good, right?"

"Yes, I already told you. But only when necessary." She gently slid her hand free, leaving him feeling oddly bereft.

"Arms around each other, yes or no?" Rhett moved to her side with a minimum of boat rocking and draped his arm over her shoulders. It was a shame she was refusing to acknowledge the chemistry between them, because she fit beside him. She fit as if she belonged with him.

Careful, cowboy.

"Arms only when necessary." Olivia held herself rigidly next to him.

"Hugs, yes or no?" Turning, he slowly wrapped his arms around her.

Olivia's hands came up between them, fast as lightning, preventing hugs and squeezes, although her fingers curled into Rhett's shirt as if she were trying to control the spark of attraction between them.

Good luck with that, honey.

"No hugs," she said in a breathless voice. "Not unless it's a substitute for a good night kiss."

Great lead in. He eyed her hopefully and with more than a hint of curiosity. "And kisses…"

She ducked her head. "Platonic or none."

A shaft of disappointment pierced the bachelor armor around Rhett's chest. "You're very bossy."

"I take that as a compliment." Olivia moved to the seat he'd just vacated. At the far end of the lake, a flash of black-and-tan raced through the trees, headed their way from the Bar D. "Now about other logistics… You'll room with Sonny and I'll room alone."

"Sure, but…" Rhett scowled. "As long as the old man keeps his psychology to himself. The last time we talked, he told me I needed a five-year plan. Cowboys don't have five-year plans."

"If you become a business owner, you'll need a five-year plan of some sort." She arched her slender brows, daring him to contradict her.

He hated that she was right. He had a lot to learn about running a business.

Ajax bounded toward the water's edge,

dancing along the shoreline and barking. He wasn't a water-loving dog. Herding was in his DNA and part of his herd was currently outside of his comfort zone.

"I've got to go." Rhett turned and stood in the bow. He gripped the edge of the boat and hopped over, landing in ankle-deep water.

"That dog didn't summon you."

Rhett rolled his eyes. This woman would challenge a fish's instinct to swim upriver.

Where was her vulnerability, that fragile state that made him want to protect her? Because this side of Olivia—commands and edicts—tested the boundaries of his independence.

"No summons." Rhett slogged out of the lake. "But he did remind me that I still have chores to do at the ranch." And he was in need of a ride, because not only was Olivia Monroe a beguiling contradiction, she was also a frustrating one. Rhett needed her out of his head. He turned to look at her, partly to make sure she wasn't going to have a panic attack at being left alone in the boat, and partly because he liked looking at her and all those wild brown curls. "You can run that outboard motor now."

Olivia swiveled around to face the engine. And just like that, her body language switched into vulnerable mode—shoulders sagging, eyes cast down. "Can you give me a shove into deeper water?"

"Apparently, I'm yours to command." Rhett splashed back into the lake and took hold of one side of the little boat. He waited until Olivia met his gaze. "Are you going to be a problem on this trip?"

Some of the hesitancy left her eyes. "In my experience, I'm only a problem for people who are a problem for me."

"Find someone else to steamroll, sweetheart." Raising his hands, Rhett backed out of the water without pushing her off. "You can get yourself out of trouble."

"But…" She growled like an angry bear.

"Use one of those oars." He turned away, and then thought better of it and faced her again. "If you aren't up to the challenge of the experiences on my trip, you should stay at home."

"Maybe I will." She grabbed an oar.

"Maybe it's for the best." Rhett stomped off, calling Ajax to his side.

He didn't turn around when she shouted, "Don't you leave on this trip without me!"

Traveling with a woman who called him her boyfriend was supposed to be a pleasurable experience. It was disconcerting to realize that he was disappointed his journey was going to be thorny and kissless.

On some level, his brain wanted to believe otherwise.

His brain…

He was certain it was his brain, and not his heart.

"Don't tell me Shane is sending you along with Rhett, too." Olivia stared at her brother Bentley, who'd shown up with a bag of groceries and his suitcase. It was after dinner and growing dark outside. "Did Rhett tell Shane that we argued?"

"You argued?" Sonny rested the book he was reading on his chest. "That explains your mood this afternoon."

"Kendall filled your grocery order." Bentley handed Olivia the bag of food. "And no, you couldn't pay me to go on that trip with Rhett. Remember me? Rollercoasters make me nauseous." He entered the house and deposited his suitcase on the floor. He wore a maroon T-shirt, blue jeans and work boots. His understated look and attitude didn't give the impression that he was an engineer and intellectual whiz, a brilliant man who was currently fixing carnival ride engines for Cassie and Rhett, readying them for sale. "I checked out of the Lodgepole Inn. I'm going to stay here while you're gone. That way, Sonny can hang with me."

Immediately, Olivia was suspicious of his motives. "Did Rhett suggest you do this?"

"No." Bentley knelt to unlace his boots.

"That's nice of you to offer, Bentley, but Olivia wants me along." Sonny picked up his book—*How to Raise Goats*. He'd announced during their meal of spaghetti that buying a goat farm was his retirement strategy.

Olivia had been speechless.

But she had plenty of words now. "Nice? Let's be honest, Bentley. Your stay here has less to do with Sonny and more to do with being close to Cassie. Not that I'd begrudge you a room." Olivia shut the front door and pointed toward the tiny bedroom near the kitchen. She might have injected her summation with too much sarcasm because Bentley glanced up at her with eyebrows raised. "I'm sorry. I'm a bit cranky. I'm still landlocked and working on myself." If her rocky interaction with Rhett was any indication, she had a long way to go.

"Everyone is a work in progress." Sonny shook a finger at her. "Everyone."

"Not Bentley. He's practically a certified hero in every way." Olivia faced her brother. Not that she expected him to reply. Bentley spent too much time in his head, mostly losing track of conversations while he solved some weighty mechanical issue that was only of interest to him.

Sonny angled his head to pin Bentley with a stare. "Is that true? Are you a certified hero?"

"Not a chance. I've got my flaws," Bentley admitted as he stood. "Grandpa Harlan used to say 'Leave nothing unfinished.' I say keep on improving. But Olivia's right. I'm not here to offer Sonny an alternative to the trip. Although he can stay if he wants to. It's convenient for me to bunk here, a stone's throw away from Cassie and the Bar D, because she's going to need help while you continue to chase a thrill with Rhett."

A thrill.

Cassie hadn't given much thought to the adventure part of the journey.

Bentley's expression softened. "You're excited about this trip, aren't you?"

Olivia nodded, thinking about cowboy kisses and rocking the boat, although she wasn't sure if it was Rhett's boat or hers that needed rocking. Surprisingly, the metaphor of an unsteady boat didn't make her cringe in fear.

Probably because slow boats don't rock much on small lakes.

Or perhaps because she'd truly sunken to an all-time low when Sonny collapsed and there was nowhere to go but up.

That made sense, since in some unfathomable way, taking care of Sonny gave her strength, strength enough to argue with a cowboy in a way she might not have before the accident. She'd commanded her crew decisively, but they ribbed her and each other almost mercilessly, the way Rhett did her.

"Olivia, I want to be available in case you need me when you get back. That's what brothers are for." Bentley gave her an earnest smile. "Now, don't worry. I'm not going to constantly ask you if you need anything. And I'm not going to hover over you as if you're fragile. You'll get your space. But if you need something, I'll be here."

Olivia's mouth dropped open. Just last week, she'd unleashed her anger and frustration over her rock bottom, dead-end situation, and she'd unleashed it on Bentley, accusing him of being responsible for her accident—he'd made the boat she'd sunk, after all. And because that wasn't cruel enough, she'd told him he hadn't helped her recovery with his hovering.

She'd apologized later, but she'd still felt like they were two siblings who'd never been close and never would be. They'd both been closer to Bentley's twin, Bryce, who'd died a few years ago, than to each other.

Until now. Today. In this moment.

Things around her were changing, like the turning of the tide. She should have been anxious or upset about the trip. Instead, she was looking forward to it, which made no sense since Rhett was as tenacious as she was. The quicker she verified "his guts"—as Shane put it—the quicker she could return to this place and the business of conquering her fears.

"I knew there was a reason I liked you, Bentley." Sonny beamed.

"What's not to love?" Olivia murmured.

"Don't worry. I won't make a big deal out of our sibling devotion," Bentley said gruffly, bear-hugging Olivia before disappearing into the small bedroom.

Olivia sat down near Sonny. "This could get weird."

"Only if you make it so." Sonny put a hand

on her knee. "Do you know what a true family does?" He didn't wait for her to answer. "They weather the big storms and enjoy the smooth waters. Together."

"A sailing metaphor. I like that." But was this just the calm before the storm? Or was she over the worst?

Sonny splayed his fingers through his beard. "Do you know what I like? I like the fact that the real Olivia is returning, bit by bit."

"And who might she be?" Because Olivia wasn't sure she knew anymore.

CHAPTER THREE

"YOU'RE UP EARLY." Yawning, Bentley entered the kitchen and poured a cup of coffee from the pot.

"I don't know what's come over me." Olivia flipped an omelet in the frying pan. "For the first time in months, I woke up eager to face the day." Without the undefinable sadness and very definable fear that had weighed her down for months. "By the way, that coffee is decaf. And the omelet is made with egg substitute." Items Kendall had sent with him last night. "But you're welcome to both."

"Pass." Bentley dumped his untouched coffee back into the pot. "I'll grab real coffee and breakfast at Cassie's. Will I see you at the ranch later?"

Olivia plated the omelet and then glanced toward Sonny's closed bedroom door. He had yet to make an appearance this morning. "Why would you see me at the Bar D?"

"Oh, I don't know. Maybe because Rhett's

there." Bentley shook his head as he sauntered for the door. "And here I thought I was the clueless one when it came to relationships."

"I'm not clueless," Olivia mumbled.

Nor am I in a real relationship.

Rhett didn't need her fawning over his muscles and rancher skills. The man probably knew how strong and competent he was.

And how good of a kisser he was.

She sighed, wishing she hadn't felt so cherished in his arms. Besides, there was only one man Olivia planned to fawn over today.

She crossed the living room and knocked on Sonny's bedroom door. "Good morning, Sonny. It's time for your pills."

Sonny grumbled something unintelligible.

Olivia knocked on the door again. "The nurse said you need to take your pills regularly every twelve hours these first few weeks." It was 7:00 a.m. He'd taken last night's pills at 7:00 p.m.

"Such badgering." Sonny opened the door. He was wearing the same blue shorts he'd had on the night before and a wrinkled gray shirt that said: Seize Your Moment. "You're worse than the nurses in the hospital."

"I'll take that as a compliment. You need to eat a little before you take your pills." Olivia returned to the kitchen and the small round table.

"What's this?" Instead of sitting, Sonny gripped the kitchen chairback, staring at the omelet suspiciously.

"A healthy start to your day."

He turned his apprehensive stare toward her. "You don't cook."

"I can cook. A little." She hated admitting to being less than skilled in any area. But the truth was that she was an awful cook.

"That's kale, isn't it?" Sonny turned up his nose. "I want pancakes."

"Pancakes aren't on your suggested diet." Olivia snatched up a stack of discharge instructions he'd been sent home with before plopping them back on the table. It was a thick stack and landed with a substantial thunk.

Sonny sank into the chair. "Where's the salt? Where's the cheese?"

Olivia chose not to reply, allowing him time to come to his own conclusions.

Sonny sighed. "My existence will now be divided into life with food I knew and loved, and life with food I now have to eat to live."

"Cry me a river. It's not so bad. I'm making one for myself." Olivia returned to the stove and poured more egg mixture into the cast iron pan. While it cooked, she glanced out the window over the sink, looking for a tall cowboy on a black horse galloping through the trees on the other side of the lake. Finding nothing, she pushed the rim of the omelet with the spatula, testing it for doneness.

Sonny made a gagging noise.

"What's wrong?" She rushed to his side.

"Kale and fake eggs. That's what's wrong." Sonny pushed his plate away and reached for his mug of coffee.

Olivia returned to the stove, bracing herself for his reaction.

He gagged once more. "Decaf? How can I achieve my optimal self every day without a rich cup of coffee and pancakes?"

"Pancakes are comfort food for the healthy and very young." She gently turned her omelet over, then sprinkled some sautéed kale on top.

"I have it on good authority that I'm young at heart."

"Whose authority?" Olivia folded the omelet over.

"Mine. I'm in charge of my spiritual well-being, as I'm in charge of your emotional well-being. And now, I don't feel very much like being perky, positive or…never mind my well-being."

Olivia plated her omelet and came to sit with him, not wanting to justify his complaints with arguments. "Look. We're doing this as a team. That should make you feel better." She took a bite of omelet. It was slightly rubbery, moderately tasteless, and the kale was stringy and quickly tangled around her back teeth.

"You see!" Sonny crowed, pointing at her with both hands. "You don't like it either. Tell me where you hid the salt and pepper."

"This can't be right." Olivia stared at the omelet. It was an appealing yellow color and lightly browned on both sides. "It looks delicious."

And Sonny looked desperate. "I'll eat a salad today if you tell me where the salt is and allow me to add cheese. Not a lot. Just enough that I can choke it down."

She shook her head. "I can't. This is the first day of the rest of your life." And if she couldn't captain this ship, what good was she? "We have to eat right."

"The first day of the rest of my life was yesterday." Sonny stood, a determined gleam in his blue eyes. "What good is living if all I can eat is cardboard food?"

Olivia pushed the omelet around with her fork, considering taking another bite. It was just so…so…tasteless. Stalling, she tried to free the kale from between her back teeth with her tongue. "We'll compromise with just a little sprinkle of cheese."

"If only we had something bursting with flavor like Gruyère or blue." Sonny dug out the small packet of shredded cheddar cheese. He sprinkled a little on both omelets.

Dutifully, they both took bites.

"It needs salt." Sonny glanced around the kitchen. "Where'd the salt shaker go?"

"In the dishwasher. I dumped the salt down the drain." First thing. She'd felt so efficient, so purposeful. She hadn't felt that way in months. The feeling drained away. Her shoulders sagged.

"No sad face. Not to worry." Sonny went to the cupboard, rummaging inside. "We have garlic salt. Somewhere."

"No, we don't. That went first. And I dumped the last of the fully caffeinated coffee in the trash, too." Olivia took another bite of her omelet, chewing unhappily. An image of Rhett's charming smile came to mind.

According to Bentley, her fake boyfriend had fully caffeinated coffee at the Bar D.

"Finish your breakfast and take your pills,

Sonny. We need energy because after breakfast, we're going for a walk."

"I hear Captain Monroe in your voice." Sonny eased back into his chair. "And suddenly, I don't know if I'm happy or sad about it."

"HEY, OLIVIA! We thought you'd show up here sooner or later," Shane called out from the tailgate of his Suburban where he sat with Holden and watched Rhett work with four young roping students.

Having not expected Olivia, Rhett jerked in surprise at Shane's announcement. Unfortunately, his flinch came just as he threw the demonstration lasso.

Rhett's throw missed the practice steer. Instead, he'd roped Tanner's five-year-old son Quinn, to the delight of the three other cowboys-in-training.

"Ow." Frowning, Quinn let the lariat fall to his scuffed brown cowboy boots. "I thought you said you'd rope the practice steer."

"Even I can rope the practice steer." Six-year-old Adam kicked up dust in the dry pasture turned makeshift arena. "Probably even Poppa Shane can rope a practice steer. Maybe even Uncle Holden."

"Don't bet on it, son." Shane hopped off the tailgate and went to greet Olivia and Sonny. He wore a white polo shirt and blue slacks.

Holden, who'd been sitting next to him, did the same, adjusting his straw cowboy hat.

The presence of Shane and Holden on the slightly run-down Bar D had already set Rhett's teeth on edge. He suspected it had been doing the same to Tanner, and now Olivia.

"Take over for me, would you?" Protective instincts rising, Rhett hurriedly looped his rope and handed it to Tanner. The two cowboys were practicing some of the sessions they planned to hold for the rodeo school Tanner was organizing in a few weeks. Rhett hurried over to the gate, taking big strides to reach Olivia. "Hey, hon."

As soon as the endearment left his lips, Olivia's gaze sharpened. For the life of him, Rhett couldn't recall if they'd covered how he should greet his fake girlfriend in front of an audience. What a pain.

On a whim, Rhett picked Olivia up and swung her around the way he did when Tanner's little daughter Mia came to visit. He set Olivia down gently, pleased to note that she was both speechless and breathless. They'd left things on an off-note yesterday and he'd lost sleep over it last night, wondering if she'd call off their trip and their pretend relationship today.

What was it about Olivia that made things so difficult?

But now, having Olivia in his arms, he couldn't risk teasing her. "Plant one right here, honey." Rhett tapped his cheek, angling it toward Olivia. "Start my day off right."

Her fingers flinched on his biceps and her eyes flashed that familiar warning. She wanted to plant something on him, all right, but it wasn't a kiss.

"Young love," Holden intoned dramatically.

Rhett slung his arm over Olivia's shoulder at the interruption and snuggled her tight against him, tighter than need be, if truth be told. Was it his fault he enjoyed pushing her buttons? He deserved a little something for keeping up this ruse.

"Santa! Santa!" The kids in the pasture caught sight of Sonny and called him over.

Sonny happily played along. With that white hair and beard, he bore a striking resemblance to Saint Nick. "Who's been naughty and who's been nice?"

The kids joyfully answered. Summer was

coming to a close, after all, and Christmas was now on the horizon.

"Olivia, I know this isn't the right time…" Holden settled his cowboy hat more firmly on his head after Sonny left them. "But the investment group that sponsored your racing team wants to meet. And I thought—"

"This is a bad idea," Olivia said, petite features pinching. "I can't bear the idea of stepping on a racing sailboat. I might never sail again and—"

"I thought," Holden continued firmly, "that you could touch base with each of your corporate sponsors individually while you accompany Rhett on this trip."

"Hang on. Where are these investors located?" Rhett's question earned him dark looks from Shane and Holden. "I only ask because the point of the trip is to explore different adventure businesses for me. And you don't see too many white water rafting excursions heading out of Wall Street."

"Fair," Shane said slowly.

"I was thinking more of having Olivia visit each of their headquarters." Holden stuck his hands on his hips. "There's No Glare Eyewear in Bismarck. Non-Slip Footwear in Chicago. And Fantastic Fish Sticks in Baltimore."

Olivia set her lips together and glared at Holden the way she'd glared at Rhett yesterday.

Rhett much preferred the intensity of that look aimed at someone else.

"If I were a more suspicious person, Holden, I'd think you were trying to get me to leave Second Chance." Olivia smiled up at Rhett. "With my boyfriend." She turned that hard stare back Holden's way. "And return to Philadelphia and sailing before I'm ready."

Rhett's breath caught.

Olivia's tone, her stance, her smile—everything about her said she was poised and assertive. She didn't need Rhett's protection. And yet, she held on to him as if he were part of her support system and had been for some time.

Like we belong together. For real.

"Olivia, your job…your life… It's all in Philly," Shane pointed out, as transparent as a trotting bull with a cowbell on giving away the direction he was going.

"You're the only Monroe who wasn't directly employed by Monroe Holding Corporation." Holden somehow managed to look less conniving than Shane and more relaxed while supporting the exact same goal.

Olivia smirked, not buying any argument her cousins were feeding her, no matter how true.

She's something, all right.

She glanced up at Rhett. "When my grandfather died, his four sons inherited everything *but* Second Chance. The one condition to their inheritance was that they fire and discontinue support for the third generation of Monroes." She gestured to Shane, Holden and herself. "Meaning my siblings and cousins. But the racing team was an entirely different animal, funded outside of the family business."

"She was saved the emotional turmoil of being fired by her father," Shane said with an easy shrug. "In the end, I landed in a better space. How about you, Holden?"

"Same." Holden nodded. "You know, I invested in you, too, Olivia. And the only way I'll get some of my investment back is if you sail again."

Olivia clung tighter to Rhett. "A new boat requires significant capital."

"None of your sponsors has bailed," Holden said quietly. "Not even me."

"Because you're all hoping I'll make that back, and more," she said in a small voice. "Or at the very least fill in the gap that insurance didn't cover."

It sounded like a lot to put on one woman's

shoulders, especially the weight of her having family lose money as a result of her actions.

"All right." Olivia cleared her throat. "I'll make those sponsor visits on two conditions. First, Rhett needs to be able to find suitable adventure experiences to explore along the way. And second, you let me chart my own course toward regaining what I lost."

"If lazing around a lake all day is how to do therapy, I should have found a therapist long ago," Shane said with a deceptively simple smile. "You've been here two months, Olivia. We only want what's best for you."

"Listen closely, Shane. You, too, Holden." Olivia's voice was as cold and hard as a metal fence post during a mid-winter blizzard. "I came here with a fear of the water, a fear that was breaking my heart because I love the ocean. But while I've been here, Sonny's helped me overcome my fear. And not just that, some of my selfishness, too. I'm learning to open up, which is why I'm with the big guy here." Olivia elbowed Rhett, none too gently.

Oof.

Rhett tried to look blissfully happy.

"I made a mistake that cost me *everything.*" Olivia's voice was thick with emotion as tears welled in her eyes. "But don't presume to know what or who I need around me to find some internal balance."

Holden nodded, clearing his throat. "So, it's yes to the investor visits?"

"They hinge on my sugar plum's itinerary, don't they?" Olivia wrapped her arms around Rhett and backed him up to a fence post. "Excuse me, gentlemen. I have a cowboy to say good morning to. And trip negotiations to make."

"I like it when you're bossy," Rhett murmured.

"Shut up and kiss me," she whispered. "Give them a good show."

And he did. No cowboy in their right mind would refuse Olivia Monroe's invitation, even if they had to endure a nickname like Sugar Plum.

But darn if a thought didn't intrude: *Olivia would never respect a man who allowed her to lead him around.*

Good thing Rhett wasn't a man who allowed himself to be led.

She deepened the kiss.

Except maybe this once.

Rhett turned his complete attention to kissing her thoroughly, but it was only a few moments later that Olivia drew back.

She glanced up at Rhett through a set of thick dark lashes and whispered, "Do you know what I want most in this world right now?"

Me? He didn't dare say it out loud.

"Coffee." She grinned. "And if you were my Prince Charming, you'd offer me a cup."

"As you wish, Buttercup." Rhett slung her over his shoulder and carried her to the ranch house, ignoring her protests and the ribbing of her cousins.

Because there was no way a convenient cowboy could win the heart of Captain Olivia Monroe by simply granting her wishes.

CHAPTER FOUR

"You make my head spin." Rhett glanced over at Olivia, who sat in the passenger seat of his truck. "You can't just ask a man to pretend to be your guy and then disrupt the kisses I'm owed with a step back and a request for coffee."

Rhett was ruffled.

Olivia tried not to smile. There was just something about bickering with this cowboy that made her feel more like her confident old self. Still, he deserved a little payback after lugging her like a sack of potatoes to the ranch house. "Lingering kisses weren't in the charter of this ship. Therefore, they need to be brief and to the point."

"Ship? We're not a ship. And if we were, you'd be off-course." He turned into the parking lot of Second Chance's general store, which bordered the parking lot of the Bent Nickel Diner, location of their first kiss two days ago. "Sonny seems like he's ready to travel. I can't believe you're dragging your feet about leaving. Or that you didn't pack a pair of sneakers. Or that you'd insist I drive you into town to get a pair. Unlike you, I have work to do."

"You heard Holden and Shane. *I* have work to do." In addition to vetting Rhett's courage, she was supposed to pay visits to her former sponsors, who expected everything to be on track for the next racing season.

The next racing season.

It was coming up quickly. Olivia tried to swallow but her mouth was too dry.

Rhett turned the truck off, shaking his head. "Meet and greets. I'll never understand you Monroes. Your boat is sunk and yet you've got to schmooze people whose money you lost. Are you considering sailing for them again?" The emotion in his brown eyes shifted from annoyance to concern.

She didn't want his compassion; that always seemed to undermine her self-assurance, no matter who was giving it to her.

Olivia scoffed. "No one in their right mind would finance my racing again."

"That isn't what I asked you." Rhett hopped out of the truck, closed the door and strode into the general store without waiting for Olivia.

She climbed down at a more deliberate pace,

clutching her cell phone wallet. Rhett's truck chassis rode high above the tires and her legs had never been long.

"How are you doing, Miss Olivia?" A skinny old man in a pair of worn blue coveralls set down a red metal toolbox in front of the general store's window display. He gave her a friendly smile.

"I'm well, thanks." Olivia paused to greet Roy. "We just came into town to pick up something for our trip."

"Ah, yes. I heard something about you two lovebirds trekking about. You'll find plenty of adventure with Rhett. He's like a magnet for thrills. Why one time…"

In the window behind Roy, Rhett held a pair of hot pink sneakers over the top of the display of rubber rafts and water guns.

Olivia shook her head, trying to focus on what Roy was saying.

"…and Rhett…hahaha…he just kept on driving through the trees, bear or no bear." Roy grinned at Olivia. "Which is why he's the solid kind of presence a woman like you needs."

"A woman like me," Olivia echoed, noting the pink pair of shoes had disappeared, along with Rhett.

"Yep, flighty, emotional, susceptible to bouts of panic." Roy paused, tilting his head, not realizing she resented every word. "Not that you aren't capable of doing great things ever again. It's just that we haven't seen a Monroe fall to pieces like you did the other day… ever."

Pick yourself up, Liv. You're tougher than those other sailors.

That was Grandpa Harlan's voice in her head. He'd always recognized her strengths.

She lifted her chin.

Rhett returned to the window. He held up a pair of yellow and black sneakers.

Olivia shook her head again.

He disappeared.

"It's refreshing to see a Monroe be so real, you know?" Roy picked up his toolbox. "So, you hang on to that sturdy cowboy of yours and you'll be just fine."

"Right. Good talk." Olivia charged into the general store, craning her neck to spot a tall cowboy wearing a black cowboy hat.

"Hey, Olivia?" The brunette behind the counter seemed overly welcoming, as if Olivia needed to be treated with kid gloves. "Feeling better today?"

Olivia pulled up short. *Feeling better?*

"You had quite a scare the other day." A kindly older woman slid her arm around Olivia's waist and gave her a gentle squeeze. "What are you looking for? Vitamins? Smelling salts? Sit down and rest. I'll shop for you."

The sales clerk brought around a chair. "We've got a good selection of whiskey if you need a boost of another sort."

The older woman's words... The sales clerk's words... Roy's words...

Olivia turned to look at the parking lot, the slim ribbon of rural highway and the medical clinic across the street. Two days ago, during Sonny's heart attack, Olivia had been a panicked, tearful mess out there while Dr. Carlisle stabilized Sonny in no time flat.

A panicked, tearful mess. That's what these people think of me.

It probably wasn't much different than what the boat racing world thought of her. She'd left her ill-fated race in an ambulance and hadn't been heard from since.

Somewhere, deep down inside of Olivia, a determined bit of backbone gave a sharp cry of denial.

"You ladies have the wrong impression about Olivia." Rhett rounded an aisle carrying a pair of tan orthopedic sneakers. He gave

Olivia a deliberate once-over that made her pulse pound. "Olivia may look like a gust of wind can blow her over, but she's got a stubborn streak. Don't count her out yet. Right, my little hay bale?"

"Hay bale?" Olivia pushed his choice of shoes away, trying not to smile. His teasing lifted her above doubt and insecurity, but now wasn't the time to let him know it. "You need a lesson in endearments and shoe selection." She marched past Rhett and down the aisle he'd appeared from, flip-flops snapping.

"Aren't we just made for each other?" Rhett said to the two women before following Olivia.

She stopped in front of the small section of shoes, pointing to an open box. "I'm a size six, not twelve." She rummaged around. It was slim pickings. Finally, she found a pair of black Converse sneakers. They were made for boys, but they fit.

"These appear to be the only socks they have left in stock." Rhett held up a pair of black crew socks. "We can ask Mackenzie if she's got anything else in back or you can make your own kind of fashion statement."

"My socks are on order," Mackenzie called from the front, which was literally only twenty feet away. "We had a group of scouts come through here last weekend. They fell in the river and bought nearly every pair of socks I had."

"I'll take these crew socks." Olivia brought her selections up to the counter. A bag of unsalted nuts caught her eye. She added the package to her pile, along with a bag of baked kale chips and a bag of unsalted popcorn. "Do you have any other healthy snacks?"

"I saw a bag of carrots near a crate of pears in the back," Rhett said testily. "Shouldn't Sonny eat less processed foods?"

"We've decided to ease into a healthy diet." Olivia forced herself to smile at Mackenzie. "You know what they say—one change at a time sticks."

"Nobody says that," Rhett quipped.

Mackenzie grinned without ringing anything up.

Olivia glanced to Rhett and then back to the sales clerk. "What? Is there something on my face?" There was nothing on his face.

"You two are just so cute together. That's all." Finally, Mackenzie rang up the items. "I'm so happy to see Rhett finally getting settled. He's a legendary bachelor in these parts, more interested in the next adventure than the next step in a relationship."

Olivia gave them both speculative looks. "Did you date him?"

"No," Mackenzie said quickly. "No-no-no-no-no."

"That's a lot of negatives." Olivia wasn't convinced. Rhett was attractive. Mackenzie was cute. Olivia paid in cash and refused a bag, stuffing her socks and snacks in the shoe box as she sorted through her feelings about the situation. She felt...*jealous*. "Me thinks you protest too much."

"Nope." Mackenzie's brown eyes sparkled. "Someone dared Rhett, you see, and—"

"Come along, petunia." Rhett hustled Olivia outside, his hands warm on either side of her waist. "Butt out of my business. Need I remind you that *I'm* doing *you* a favor?"

Olivia dragged her feet, slowing his escape down to a crawl. "There was a bet and...?"

"I'll tell you about it if you tell me about your accident."

"No." She didn't have to think twice.

"You don't want to share your past with me? Then you shouldn't spend a moment worrying about my business." He climbed into his tall truck.

Olivia tossed her purchases to the floorboard and then scaled her way into the passenger seat. "This truck is over-compensating for something."

Rhett sighed, the complete picture of a frazzled, handsome cowboy who didn't quite know how to deal with an accomplished boat captain. "This trip would be so much more pleasant if you just broke up with me."

"THERE'S THE COWBOY I'm looking for."

Rhett lowered Big Boy's hoof to the ground and straightened, facing Sonny.

Rhett had just returned from a ride and he was giving his horse a good grooming before putting him up and giving him some extra oats since he was leaving in two days. "You broke away from your jailer to talk to me?" Sonny's jailer being Olivia. "This must be serious. Were the kale chips disappointing? I told her to buy carrots for you."

"A man like me doesn't eat kale by choice." Sonny entered the barn's breezeway, his face a bit pink from too much sun. His shirt today was a military green and read: I Am. I Can. I Will. I Do. "And Olivia isn't my jailer. You should be careful how you frame your thoughts about your significant other. Our thoughts often drive the comments that come out of our mouths. And your comments make you sound insensitive."

Rhett scrubbed his forearm over his damp forehead, ruing the bargain he'd made with Holden and Shane, which made him have to put up with Olivia's demands and Sonny's observations. "That was a joke. I was joking."

The old man sat carefully on a bench near Big Boy's head. His cheeks were flushed, possibly not from the afternoon sun, because he was breathless. "We often joke to hide our vulnerabilities."

"*I* often joke because the world is filled with ironies." Rhett picked up a spiral curry comb and began running it over Big Boy's coat. "And it pleases me to point them out."

"Huh. A self-aware cowboy." Sonny blinked as if processing the surprise Rhett had given him. "This is unexpected given my previous observations of you."

Rhett didn't like being under Sonny's microscope. "Save your analysis for Olivia."

The big black gelding stretched his neck and nibbled Sonny's whiskers.

"Oh, hey. None of that." Chuckling, Sonny leaned sideways and would have toppled over if Rhett hadn't caught him.

"Apologies. Big Boy is hungry and clearly

he thought your beard looked like old straw."
Rhett gave his horse an affectionate pat before
continuing to brush him down.

Sonny fingered his nibbled beard. "The
older I get, the more I think I should shave this
off. Frankly, because the older I get, the more
children mistake me for Santa." He leaned
back against the wall of Big Boy's stall and
sighed. "But I do enjoy the attention and enthusiasm of the younger generation. There are
worse things than being mistaken for Old Saint
Nick."

Rhett agreed wholeheartedly. Delivering Olivia to Philadelphia wasn't going to be easy.
She seemed to revel in making his life difficult, and she came with the added baggage
of Santa in the guise of a sports psychologist.

"You said you were looking for me." Best
get on with it. Rhett moved to the gelding's
haunches, easing the strokes over the ticklish
spot at the base of Big Boy's spine. "Does Olivia know you're here?"

As soon as he asked the question, Rhett
wanted to take it back. It didn't matter what
Olivia knew or didn't know. He wasn't dating
her and he didn't want to get involved with
the dynamics of her relationship with Sonny.

The old man shook his head. "She's meditating for another thirty minutes."

"Meditating?" Rhett had a hard time buying that. Olivia didn't seem the type to slow down, breathe and occupy herself in her own thoughts. She seemed the type to sit down and collect her thoughts in a handful of minutes and then be on her way.

Rhett walked around to the other side of the horse and continued to brush him.

"As you know, Olivia's a work in progress." Sonny stared up at the barn's rafters, a slight smile on his round face. "That's why I came to talk to you. It's important we interact with Olivia carefully on this trip. She's overcome so much, but if we push her too hard…"

"We?" Rhett leaned his arms on top of Big Boy's back and studied Sonny—the frown, the T-shirt, the flush to his face, the serious look in his faded blue eyes. "I don't plan to push her at all. She's coming along, that's all. The pair of you can sit and relax while I have some fun."

The old man's features tensed. "Forgive me. I got ahead of myself."

Big Boy stomped a front hoof, impatient for the after-ride ritual to be done and the feeding to begin.

Dutifully, Rhett got back to brushing.

"I find it serendipitous that you want to open an adventure tour business and explore all the options available to you first." Sonny ran his fingers through his thin white hair. "The biggest challenge Olivia has faced since her accident is puttering around in a dinghy on a calm lake. For a woman who led a yacht racing team, that's small potatoes. She needs a nudge toward something more exhilarating." He clapped his hands gently a few times and then pointed at Rhett. "And I think you're just the one to do it. She likes you. She trusts you."

"Listen…" Rhett felt pressured to come clean about the dating scam. He swallowed back the urge. "Olivia is coming back from a scary place. She doesn't need to be pushed by a cowboy. That'd be like you trying to train Big Boy here how to rear up on two legs on command. You're not qualified to do that, and I'm not qualified to repair Olivia's confidence." He put the curry comb away and untied Big Boy's lead rope. "Don't get me wrong. I want to help her. I just wouldn't know where to start."

"And that's where I come in." Sonny had his arms crossed high over his chest. "I'm very good at prompting people."

"She'll see right through that." And be angrier than a wasp on a hot day. Rhett returned Big Boy to his stall and removed his halter.

"I can be subtle." Sonny wasn't giving up.

He must be part Monroe. They didn't get subtlety either.

Rhett closed Big Boy's stall and went to get him his oats.

The snap of fast feet in flip-flops made Rhett pause. There was only one person on the ranch who wore flip-flops.

"Sonny!" Olivia appeared in the doorway, panting, short curls limp from sweat. "There you are. I've been looking all over for you. I was worried sick when I discovered you were gone." Her gaze roamed over Rhett before she charged into the barn.

Rhett would have liked her gaze to roam across him a little longer. But then again, Rhett would have liked this ruse to involve more kissing since it was becoming increasingly clear that he'd gotten the short end of the stick on his dealings with the Monroes, Olivia included.

"Calm down. I'm not an escaped prisoner." Sonny winked at Rhett. "I was out for a walk and couldn't pass the barn and its shade."

"You've come a long way." Olivia stopped

in front of Sonny, studying him from head-to-toe. "Are you okay?"

"My heart's purring like a kitten." He smiled reassuringly at Olivia.

She didn't look a bit mollified. "Kittens don't stray so far from home. We need to get you fed before you take your pills and it's a long way back."

Sonny rose slowly to his feet. "Did I worry you? Do you need a hug?" The old man gestured toward Rhett. "Your hug machine is at the ready."

"I'm always available to Olivia for hugs." Playing along, Rhett held his arms wide, knowing full well he was going to get the look.

"No hugs required, cowboy," Olivia said tightly, taking Sonny's arm.

Rhett lowered his, smiling a little when he noticed Olivia sneaking glances at him.

Thinking about cowboy kisses, no doubt.

"I walked over here under my own power. I'll get back just the same." Sonny gently extricated himself, but his tone gave away his annoyance at Olivia's over-protectiveness. "See you in the morning, Rhett."

Olivia huffed, but gave Sonny his space, matching his slow cadence as they made their exit. There was a strength to her carriage, a set to her shoulders that told anyone who was watching that she was prepared to help Sonny if need be.

But it was clear that Sonny wanted his independence.

"So much for subtlety, old man," Rhett muttered after they'd left the barn.

He lifted his cowboy hat and rubbed his palm from his forehead to the nape of his neck. He was gritty and sweaty. His jeans were worn and dusty. He didn't look like the kind of man who could help a world class competitor like Olivia get her mojo back.

But then again, neither did Sonny.

CHAPTER FIVE

"You're punctual." Olivia greeted Rhett on Sunday morning with a kiss to his cheek for Sonny's benefit.

And maybe a little for her own. She hadn't spoken to Rhett for two days.

It was the agreed-upon time—early morning. Despite the hour, the day promised to be clear and warm.

Bentley had left for the Bar D an hour earlier. Olivia had been anxious all night and morning, excited for the trip with the ever-challenging Rhett, but anxious about the reception she'd be given from her former sponsors, including what she'd say to them.

Olivia and Sonny had eaten heart-healthy cereal—translation: *a boring breakfast*—on the side deck which afforded her a view of Rhett riding that big black horse of his through the trees on the other side of the lake. From a distance, her cowboy looked tall and proud in the saddle. On some level, he was mesmerizing. And on some level, she was open to being mesmerized.

Who'd have thought this sailor would find a cowboy attractive?

She'd smiled at the thought until she'd remembered how ornery he could be.

In the here and now, Rhett said, "I'm punctual and you're both ready. Let's roll." He didn't waste time on other displays of affection, which was surprisingly disappointing considering his dangerously sexy vibe in that black hat and sunglasses. He grabbed their bags and pivoted, heading for his truck without tossing down challenges about who was in charge or good-natured insults about her… her…anything!

"Olivia was born ready." Sonny walked out after Rhett in those deliberate steps he'd been taking since his release from the hospital. "That's why I gave her that shirt."

Olivia glanced down at her neon orange T-shirt, which read: Watch Out, World. I'm Ready. But she wasn't ready. Everything between herself and Rhett felt wrong. He was being too nice. Not to mention, practically ignoring her.

He hadn't even swung her around the way he had the other morning.

She frowned.

"Olivia?" Sonny paused at the corner of the house. "What's wrong?"

I hate when anyone asks me that.

Even if she answered "Nothing," Olivia would dwell on the something. She scrunched up her nose.

Rhett closed the door to the seat behind the driver, where he'd stowed their luggage. "She looks like she didn't get a full dose of caffeine this morning. I waited days for you two to be ready to travel and I refuse to stop for coffee and bathrooms every hour. Am I making myself clear?"

That's more like it.

Olivia drew a deep, calming breath, and then launched a counter-attack. "Oh, boo-hoo on having to stop for coffee every once in awhile." She shut the door and marched toward the truck in her black-and-white Converse sneakers. "You can blame Sonny for the delay. He had to have a new set of motivational T-shirts made."

"Not a new set. My assistant went through inventory and found these." Sonny's brown shirt proclaimed: No Mountain Was Conquered in a Day. "I have one for you, my boy."

He reached Rhett's truck and shook out a neon green T-shirt that read: Show No Fear.

"I appreciate the sentiment, but I'm not the statement-making type." Rhett's T-shirt was plain and navy blue. The scuffs on his black cowboy boots said he meant business. But the look in his eyes as he opened the passenger door for Olivia made a statement about wanting and kisses.

This… This is what I need to crack my way out of my protective cocoon—someone treating me like I can take whatever they dish out.

In Rhett's case, sultry glances, smoking hot kisses, and electric repartee.

Rhett opened the front passenger door.

Olivia felt her cheeks heating under all that scrutiny, along with a need to establish control. "Sonny requires the front seat and a step-stool." She brushed past Rhett toward the back passenger seat. He smelled of hay and horse, which should have been a turn off. But she knew the taste of his lips and somehow, she knew he would never turn her off.

"Luckily, I happen to keep a step in the truck bed because my grandpa has to use it." Rhett set a plastic step-stool on the ground and helped the old man into the truck. "Front passengers are in charge of the radio. I hope you like honky-tonk."

"I hope you like opera," Sonny countered as Rhett went around to the driver's side.

"Well played, old man. But good luck finding an opera station in Idaho." Rhett climbed behind the wheel and then they were off.

"Never underestimate the capabilities of a patient man." Sonny took out his phone. "I'll search online before scrambling your radio. It's a challenge, which fits the theme of our little trip, don't you think?"

Rhett pursed his lips but kept driving. When he reached the end of the driveway, Rhett stopped the truck. He glanced at Sonny, and then captured Olivia's gaze in the rearview mirror. "We're at a fork in the road."

"I love forks. Options define us, you know." Sonny had been reaching for the radio knob. He pulled his hand back. "What are our choices?"

"*My* choices, you mean. I started out the day with a plan, but…" Rhett glanced again at Sonny and then cleared his throat. "But I can be flexible. Extreme adventure tours are what I love. But Holden advised me to pursue the more mundane…more marketable activities to appeal to more people. That's the planned route and frankly one I thought Olivia, who's my yardstick, might enjoy because it's tame."

This was news to Olivia. She hadn't planned on doing more than tagging along and watching.

"Olivia doesn't do tame," Sonny said unexpectedly.

"Me either. And if there's a possibility that attractions that are beyond tame can be profitable..." Rhett continued, "I owe it to myself to check out the extreme options. That is, if my yardstick is willing."

I should be annoyed that Rhett is using me as his tame yardstick.

But something unsettling gripped the back of Olivia's throat. Unbidden, the frightening image of being tossed in the air and trapped under water returned. "Define extreme."

"Exciting. Pulse-pounding." Rhett tapped the wheel with his thumbs, beginning to smile. "Something that feels a little...dangerous."

I'm out.

"I always advise my clients to start with the little things." Sonny glanced at Olivia over his shoulder, taking stock in that encompassing manner of his. "What's the easiest activity on your list of possibles, Rhett?"

"Mountain biking." Rhett pursed his lips and set the blinker to signal a left turn. "Tame."

She'd seen videos of mountain biking online. It was far from tame. "What's the other choice?" Olivia choked out, because she had to know, despite her fears.

"Base jumping." Rhett grinned and set the blinker to signal a right turn.

"Base jumping?" Sonny was still staring at Olivia, gauging her reaction. "That sounds dangerous."

"Not with the right preparation. I mean, sure, you're jumping off a base, like a bridge, a building or a steep cliff. But I always take precautions." Rhett sighed wistfully.

He was wistful? About jumping off a building?

Olivia struggled to fill her lungs with air.

"I haven't been base jumping in over a year." Rhett still sounded wistful. "You're going to love it, Olivia."

She should be flattered that he thought of her as that courageous. Instead, the continuous click-clack of the blinker chipped away at what little courage she'd regained. "Executive decision by your yardstick. Turn left."

Instead of obeying her, Rhett silenced the blinker. "First, tell me…" Rhett's gaze was as dark as his hat. "Did Holden and Shane encourage you to come along just to evaluate *me*?"

Sonny stopped staring at Olivia and frowned at Rhett. "I believe I've spoken to you before about the proper framing of your thoughts."

Her cowboy shrugged. "She's a Monroe. We haven't talked about this yet. Let's try this frame—I'm asking Olivia where her loyalties lie."

With my family. Who wanted to know how adventurous Rhett really was.

She didn't need to go any further to know the answer. Rhett was *extremely* adventurous. But if she told them that now, Rhett would go on his quest without her.

"Still waiting, Captain Obvious." Rhett slid on a pair of cheap sunglasses.

"My loyalties lie with you, my liege." Oh, how easily the lie fell from her lips when she loaded it with irony and humor. "I've got your back."

"And I've got yours." Rhett gunned it out of the driveway, tires spitting gravel across the road as he turned left. "Tame is the name of the game."

Sonny clutched the dashboard. "Olivia, you'd tell me if you had any fears about the activities Rhett proposes, wouldn't you? No matter how tame he deems it. You know fears are deflated when we say them out loud."

Olivia had never believed that.

"She'll be fine," Rhett scoffed. "I'll wager she does at least three-of-the-five activities on our fact-finding tour."

"Three-of-five?" Sonny scoffed right back. "She'll do them all."

All? Olivia opened her mouth to protest, but nothing came out.

"What's in it for me if she can't do all five?" Rhett demanded.

Olivia regretted being a tame yardstick. If she'd shown some backbone, Rhett might not have tossed out this wager.

"If she bails on any activity…" Sonny glanced at Olivia briefly, before looking away. "If she doesn't do all five, I'll invest in your tour company. I'll match whatever Holden and Shane put in."

"Sonny…" Olivia couldn't believe this was happening. Sonny didn't seem like he had that kind of money lying around.

Rhett smiled one of those easy-money smiles.

"But if she does all five activities, you'll name the tour company in her honor." Sonny cackled. "You're in trouble now, Rhett. Nothing can stop this woman once she sets her mind to it. Has she told you about the time she sailed to Canada by herself?"

"She hasn't." Rhett glanced briefly at Olivia in the rearview mirror, no longer smiling.

"We'll be calling the tour company Captain Olivia Monroe's Base Jumping." Sonny put a pillow against the window and punched it into shape, oblivious to the fact that Olivia was having a meltdown behind him. "Smooth out the ride, Rhett, so I can get some shut-eye."

Olivia watched a hawk soar above the trees outside her window, making turns with power and grace just as she'd once turned a sailboat. She doubted she'd be as graceful riding down a mountain on a bike. "Rhett, what got you interested in opening an adventure business?"

"I love to get my heart racing. I think I got bitten by the adrenaline bug one March when my dad had me spring break the horses."

"Spring break?" Sonny laughed. "I suddenly had an image of horses running through the surf for a week in Florida."

"It's nothing like that." Rhett slowed for a sweeping curve in the road. "Sometimes it snows five, ten or fifteen feet at a time in the winter. That means we don't take the horses out to ride for three or four months out of the year. When it's time to ride the range again, most horses want to air out the laundry, so to speak."

"The laundry being a rider?" Sonny chuckled.

"Yep." Rhett's smile softened his strong profile.

"A little horsey rebellion every spring." Olivia took a moment to enjoy that image. She could relate to kicking up one's heels after confinement.

"Anyway, about me being an adrenaline junkie…" Rhett continued. "I think I was ten when my dad put me on spring breaking duty. My mom protested, but Dad insisted. He figured if I ate dirt that I was young enough to bounce back. So, Mom stood by with the first aid kit." Rhett's twinkling gaze caught Olivia's in the rearview mirror for a brief second. "We traveled a lot when I was a kid, supplementing the ranch income by operating kiddie carnival rides. That meant I hung around the fairs and carnivals and rode the 'big' rides without Mom knowing. And then when I got older, I was game for anything that made my heart pound and my stomach drop. There's nothing like a good rush to make you feel alive."

Olivia said nothing. A year ago, she would have been on the same page as Rhett. But now, she associated stomach drops with danger and death.

"I DON'T THINK I've ever been to Montana." Olivia took in her surroundings.

They were about an hour outside of Billings, Montana. There were tall pines, rolling hills and a big bright blue sky.

"Not even to Yellowstone?" Sonny asked, more interested in the coffee kiosk menu than the local terrain. His thin white hair blew in the warm breeze.

"Okay, I've been to Montana." Olivia turned back to the teenage boy with thick black hair and thick black glasses who was working the walk-up coffee kiosk next to the gas station. "Two decafs and a regular coffee, please. Oh, and mark the lids for me."

"Sure." The teen dutifully marked the lids with a felt tip pen while Olivia paid with her credit card.

"They have scones." Sonny tapped the listing on the outdoor menu with one finger. "Made from local ingredients. Does that mean fruit? And if so, what kinds?" He gave Olivia a hopeful look.

"Don't even go there." She shook her head, tucking her card back in her cell phone wallet.

"It means all ingredients," the teen answered without looking up. "Apricots and peaches are in season. But we're out of apricot and peach scones. All we've got left is cinnamon."

"I like cinnamon," Sonny began.

"No baked goods." Olivia turned to watch Rhett pumping gas. He'd been regaling them with tales of the rodeo on the drive. He'd made her forget about the silly wager Sonny had made.

"We have apples and bananas." The enterprising teen could both pour their coffee and go in for the upsell.

"Olivia packed apples and bananas." Sonny's shoulders fell a little. "I can't believe you packed so much food."

"And I can't believe you made that bet with Rhett." Olivia plucked two packets of natural sweetener from a cup of condiments. "Do you have that kind of money to invest in a business?"

"Am I going to need it? He's your guy. He let you choose the less adventurous activity of the two. We'll be fine." Sonny looked around.

"*We'll* be fine." We. There was irony. She

had to go along on these excursions to protect Sonny.

"Are those goats over there?" Sonny perked up, shading his eyes.

"It's a goat farm, not a petting zoo. No trespassing." The teen was suddenly testy. He glanced up at Olivia before sliding the coffees over. "Everybody wants to hop the fence and pet the goats. It's the *sheriff*'s goat farm. He gives me grief every time it happens. Like I should police strangers." His attention was caught on Sonny. He waved a hand in the air to catch his attention. "Hello, old dude. Did you hear me say the goats belong to the sheriff? Mister? No trespassing. No trouble. Okay?"

"We get it." Olivia handed Sonny a cup marked decaf. She removed the lids on the other two, adding a packet of sweetener to each.

"I sure would like to talk to the sheriff about goat farming." Sonny continued to stare.

Olivia spared the goats a glance. They weren't doing much more than grazing. "That would be nice as long as you weren't talking to him from behind bars." She put the lids back on the coffees. "No trespassing, remember?"

"You mixed up the lids," the teen told her, shoving back his glasses.

"No, I haven't." Had she?

"You did." He sounded as pessimistically certain as Eeyore.

"If I had a goat farm, I'd make it part petting zoo," Sonny said in a faraway voice.

Olivia stared at the coffees, wondering if she'd mixed them up. She couldn't try one. The cups were practically too hot to hold, much less drink.

"You're nervous." Sonny was looking at her. "Why? It's just a little bike ride."

Her nerves had nothing to do with bike rides and everything to do with being a competent person who didn't screw up a coffee order.

"Are you going to Montana Mountain Bikes?" The teen showed the first signs of enthusiasm. "Cool. I was there in March during the first snow melt. They opened up this new trail—the Tumble Trail. It was gnarly. I just got my brace off this week. Me and my friends are going again tomorrow."

"Wait." Olivia shook herself. "You were injured?"

"Yeah." He proudly displayed his forearm, revealing a jagged scar. "Multiple fracture in my wrist. Had to have surgery, pins, two casts and a brace." He chuckled. "So gnarly."

Olivia felt hollow. Forget coffee mix-ups.

Her worst fears about mountain biking were about to be realized.

"Now, Olivia. Don't think this boy's experience will be anything like yours." Sonny glanced over to the goat farm. "I wish we could hold a goat. There's nothing like cradling a loving animal to soothe your nerves."

"Hey, let's go!" Rhett called from the gas station.

Olivia sipped the coffee marked decaf. It burned her tongue so bad she couldn't tell if it was decaf or not, which seemed fitting for the day ahead. She was now anxious that Rhett wasn't just taking her mountain biking. He was taking her "extreme" mountain biking.

Which was why when the coffee cooled enough to drink, she didn't tell Rhett she'd mixed them up. She needed that caffeine to be on her toes for this.

And besides, he didn't seem to notice.

CHAPTER SIX

"RHETT! WE HAVEN'T seen you in over a year." Clark, the middle-aged man behind the counter and the owner of Montana Mountain Bikes, greeted Rhett the moment he stepped in the door. "I didn't know the rodeo was in town. You can park your rig out in back if you need to camp."

"No rig, Clark." Rhett held open the door for Olivia and Sonny. It had taken them hours to arrive at their destination, and he was ready to shake off the road kinks. He'd already changed out of his boots and into mud-stained sneakers and left his cowboy hat on the truck's dashboard. "Set me up with bikes and safety gear for two."

"Two? Things *have* changed." Clark placed two sheets of paper and pens on the counter. "You know the drill. Is your girlfriend an experienced rider?"

"First-timer." Olivia's voice was as tight as the arms locked around her chest.

She seemed wired, possibly because she'd mixed up their coffees at that last stop. He'd been convinced his was decaf instead of regular.

"My *girlfriend* doesn't have to go." Rhett glanced up from the paperwork. He didn't like to see anyone afraid, but he refused to let Olivia's hesitancy ruin his day on the slopes.

"I'm going," Olivia said with more determination than enthusiasm. She snatched up a waiver and a pen. "We made a bet."

"Technically, Sonny and I made a bet." Rhett scribbled his name on the paperwork. "Any new trails, Clark?"

"Oh, yeah." Clark rang up their tickets. "We opened the Tumble Trail. It's a keeper."

"The Tumble Trail?" Olivia's pen paused mid-signature.

Rhett chose to ignore her, handing Clark his credit card. "How often do you open new trails or reshape existing ones?"

"We've always got something in progress. Can't rest on your laurels if you want the regulars to be regulars." He made short work of processing their purchase and giving them safety gear. And then a few customers came in, followed by a few more. "Since you know what you're doing, Rhett, I'll let you pick out the bikes and make the adjustments. If your granddad wants to watch you come in, we opened a café out back last spring."

"Excellent." Sonny rubbed his hands together. "I'm ready for another coffee."

"Decaf." Olivia swept her safety gear into her arms. "And no sweets."

Sonny shook his head. "No sweets equals no fun." He struck up a conversation with someone in line while Rhett and Olivia moved outside.

No fun.

Rhett was afraid that's what the afternoon excursion was shaping up to be. He'd fallen into a trap with Sonny back in Second Chance. Sonny only made that bet to push Olivia. He was sure of it. And now, Rhett was paying the price.

He stared with longing at the pine-filled slopes and sighed, slightly consoled by the fact that the bet with Sonny would keep her on this trip until she backed out of an adventure.

At the bike rack, Rhett gave Olivia another out. "You don't have to do this. I'm going to make a few runs and then pick Clark's brain a little more about the business. Honestly, if you're afraid, this will be a challenge for both of us."

"I'm not afraid." But there was trepidation in her gaze. She needed bolstering and he needed her to be happy on this trip so she'd hang with him all the way to Philadelphia.

"Let's say you're not afraid and that the bet doesn't matter," he said slowly. "Let's say you're a little worried. Anyone would be their first time out." Rhett brushed a curl out of her eyes, a tender caress that he knew wasn't in her approved fake boyfriend guidelines. It'd be perfectly legit if they were dating for real. And this felt like a date. A first date. "Would a kiss give you courage?"

Olivia shoved the black helmet on her head. "Courage doesn't come from kisses. It comes from within. And I have plenty of courage. Just read my T-shirt."

Rhett did. "'Watch Out, World. I'm Ready.' Okay, I guess that means our first date will be mountain biking." He was joking, of course.

"Our first date?" Olivia sat on a bench and scoffed. "I've created a monster. We're not really dating, remember?"

She was good at putting up fences to keep him and others at a safe distance. But he was better at tearing them down and getting in her way.

"You just wait." Rhett kept up the dating

charade, strapping on his safety gear. "We'll tell our children about this ride one day."

"Let's hope the story doesn't include details about a hospital visit and a broken arm." Olivia leaned from one side to the other, trying to see around him. "But seriously, why are you keeping up the charade? Sonny's not around to hear."

"I like flirting with the ladies." He liked flirting with *her*.

"Ladies?" She scoffed again.

"Fine." He cast about for a term she'd be happier with. "I like flirting with boat captains."

She laughed, looking more at ease.

Mission accomplished.

A few minutes later, Rhett had their bikes out and adjusted to their leg size and arm reach.

Olivia studied her reflection in the rental office window. "I look like I'm ready to compete in the roller derby."

"Almost." Rhett tightened her helmet's chin strap, brushing his knuckles over the soft skin at her neck, noting the resulting pink bloom in her cheeks. "Now you're properly kitted. Helmet, gloves, elbow, knee and shin pads. None of which will fall off if you do."

Sonny came out the bike rental office door, arm raised and clutching a small box. "You won't believe the stories those riders tell. I bought bandages in case someone crashes."

"It's mountain biking." Rhett grinned. "Half the fun is in the crashes."

Olivia pressed her lips firmly together.

"Not that you're going to crash." Rhett tried to backpedal. "I was joking. We'll warm up on the pump track over there. It's got banked turns and rollers—little hills—and it's designed to help you get used to working with momentum. After a couple of laps, we'll catch the shuttle van to the top of the beginner trail."

"As opposed to the Tumble Trail," Olivia grumbled. "I guess I should count my blessings."

Rhett put his helmet on and then mounted up and headed over. He went around the pump track slowly the first time, glancing back to make sure Olivia was all right. She had a determined look on her face. On the second lap, Rhett sped up, achieving some real air off the well-groomed practice hills.

He pulled off at the exit and waited for Olivia.

She came to a stop, brakes squealing a few

feet away. "That wasn't terrible." She gave a little laugh, contradicting her words.

They exchanged smiles, as if they really were on a date and had found something in common. He liked that she had game. Maybe there was hope for the day and a business like this, after all.

Movement in the parking lot caught his attention. "There's the shuttle van. Let's get on it." And not get carried away by one almost-exhilarated smile.

They secured their bikes in a trailer and then they crammed into the van with the other riders, sitting next to each other.

The van, Rhett noticed for the first time, was old. There were no floor mats, the odometer wasn't digital, and the seats had cloth covers that were removable. The cushions squeaked and bounced over every pothole. The van's suspension did, too. It needed maintenance—shocks or something equally expensive. As a customer, Rhett didn't care that much about comfort. Later in the day, the van got really dirty, sometimes muddy, and the seats sometimes wet. It was all part of the rugged experience. But as a potential business owner, Rhett was seeing things from a different perspective.

"You used to stay here?" Olivia plucked at a loose thread on the seat cover in front of her.

Rhett nodded. "When I was on the rodeo circuit, I'd pull in here with my horse trailer, catch a ride or two, then camp out. Take Big Boy on a trail ride in the morning, then move on."

"I take it you did the same at the base jumping place."

He nodded again. "And my regular zipline site, the white water rafting tour, my favorite hang-gliding place."

Her smile was best classified as attempted. It was clear she was nervous again. "Given your preference for honky-tonk music, I would have thought you'd spend your spare time in bars."

The van lurched dramatically from side to side.

Olivia gasped, grabbing on to the seat in front of her.

"It's all right." Rhett didn't like seeing her this way—cautious and afraid. She needed a distraction. "Back to your favorite topic—*me*. Given the expenses involved in my hobbies, I couldn't afford the rodeo entry fees *and* the adventure tour tickets *and* a hefty bar tab. Something had to go." That wasn't quite true. He'd never been a big drinker. But he'd always been careful with his money.

The van slowed, lurching over a particularly pitted section of road.

Olivia's knuckles were white. "You're fiscally responsible. I like that."

"We're approaching the beginner trail," the driver announced. He was a teenager Rhett had never seen before.

Sourcing employees will be a problem in Second Chance.

Rhett shoved operational thoughts to the back of his head as the van slowed. There was fun ahead. He glanced at Olivia, wishing she felt the same way.

"LADIES FIRST," Rhett told Olivia at the trailhead.

"I suppose it was inevitable that this tomboy would someday be called a *lady*. Repeatedly. But I draw the line at ma'am." Olivia was joking, stalling if truth be told. Fear gripped her gut.

And Rhett wasn't helping. He was kind and patient about her balking. She needed him to bust her chops, toss her a dare, make her laugh.

They stood alone at the top. She clung to her bike's handlebars. They'd let the others go down first. Their laughter and enthusiastic shouts filled the air.

The narrow trail was pitted, channeled and steep. Not only that, it had muddy patches, wasn't straight, and looped sharply to the right just a few feet from the start. The pump track at the rental office had been well-groomed and gently curved. This was…

This was a mistake! Olivia should have taken the bandages from Sonny, because there was no doubt in her mind that she was going to need them.

There were flashes of color and movement below. Those riders that had gone before them were on a second leg, shrieking and laughing as if they were having the best time ever. A year ago, this would have been her kind of thrill.

I might even have called it tame.

"If you want, you can take the road back down," Rhett said considerately.

Where was the cowboy who didn't let her push him around?

"I'm not afraid." But Olivia's heart hadn't beat this fast in months, even when she'd relived the boating accident. This was different. She just couldn't identify why. "I think… I think…" The last thing she should be doing right now was thinking. She stared up into Rhett's dark eyes, taking in his gentle, understanding smile. "I think I used to be the woman who'd fly down this mountain like I used to when I rode my bike as a kid." Fast. No braking.

He nodded. "We all grow up. There's no shame in that."

But there was! And it angered Olivia that she stood here being wishy-washy about a bike ride.

A bike ride!

She'd sailed across stormy seas. She'd sailed through the pouring rain. She'd sailed when she'd been wet and freezing and…

Afraid.

"Olivia, maybe you should—"

"Stop." Olivia closed her eyes, trying to recapture those memories. "I was afraid."

To Rhett's credit, he didn't so much as sigh. "I can walk you back down. We'll forget the bet."

"No. I mean, I'm not afraid. I am… But… I *was*…" She opened her eyes and stared up at him and said the first thing that popped in her head. "You look so different without your cowboy hat." In her mind's eye, she always pictured him with his hat on. Without it, he could be anybody…anything… Even an adventure tour guide. She shook her head, forcing her thoughts back on track. "I was just recalling my past, those times when I got caught in a sudden squall or sailed when I should have stayed in the harbor and…" She swallowed, lowering her voice to a whisper. "I was scared but I did it anyway."

His smile remained gentle, not mocking. "They do say that you can't be brave if you aren't at least a little afraid."

"Trepidatious." Olivia felt a smile grow on her face. Her heart was still pounding, but now she knew what it was. It wasn't just fear. It was excitement, too. "All this time, I've told myself I had no fear when I was sailing. But that was a lie."

"We all tell ourselves lies." His gaze felt as warm as his smile. "I feel like Sonny should be hearing this."

"Right? But not Kendall. She likes to paint me in the media as this fearless woman." She stared deep into Rhett's eyes, his understanding eyes. "I'll take that kiss now."

He laughed, a deep, rich sound that filled her pounding heart with joy to go along with her fear and excitement. "And I'll be happy to give it." He leaned over, tilted his head sideways and pressed his lips all-too-briefly to hers. "Back brake only or you'll flip. Follow me."

And she did. As slowly as she could. Between trees. Around boulders. Down rutted gullies. Back and forth across switchbacks with steep drop-offs that scared her more than rogue waves.

Rhett had to stop and wait for her three times. Each time he did so without complaint. Instead of feeling like the weakest link, Olivia began to feel more confident.

Twenty minutes later, they emerged from the forest into the meadow behind the bike rental office. Olivia's knees felt spongey, and her wrists and elbows felt like overused shock absorbers, but she'd made it without crashing.

Sonny stood up and waved.

They rode over.

"I was afraid," Olivia blurted when she reached him, feeling like she was in the third grade and telling Santa what she really wanted for Christmas, not what she'd told her parents. "Afraid!"

"As smart people usually are." Sonny handed them each a bottle of water. "You should always follow your instincts."

Olivia glanced at Rhett, who stared at the slopes they'd just barreled down. He'd opened her eyes to something she hadn't experienced before. And in the process, she'd discovered something important about herself. She didn't want the day to end. "I think we need to do that again."

Rhett grinned.

"Only this time, I'll go first."

RHETT WAS IMPRESSED that Olivia had worked her way through her fear.

That didn't mean she was riding like a banshee. She was still careful. But the second time down the beginner trail, she wasn't as cautious as she'd been the first time. She was getting the hang of it. Soon she'd be getting air and loving it.

Ahead of him, Olivia slid off the trail. She tumbled one way and the bike slid sideways downhill.

"Or not," Rhett murmured to himself, before asking in a loud voice, "Are you okay?"

Olivia picked herself up, laughing a little. "I was looking too far ahead when I hit that rock. Lesson learned."

Rhett pulled over and dismounted, setting his bike far enough off the trail that anyone coming down could safely get past. He moved carefully down the steep slope to where she was trying to pick up her bike. She stumbled and nearly fell over backward.

"Careful," he cautioned.

"What are you doing? I've got this." There was that command in her voice.

If he'd been worried about her giving up, he shouldn't have been. She still had game.

"I'm watching my investment. Don't forget that I'm liable for your equipment." He righted her bike and pushed it uphill. "Like any good boyfriend, I'm also checking you out for a concussion. Look at me. How many fingers am I holding up?"

"None of them," she said rather breathlessly from behind him. "All your fingers are on my handlebars." She laughed again. "That sounds risqué."

"The fact that you made that joke indicates your head is still on straight." He set her bike on the trail and held it for her. "Are you good the rest of the way down?"

"Yep. And then I'm ready for the next trail, a harder one." She looked determined, as if she wouldn't be deterred.

Here was the racing boat captain who pushed onward when things got tough. Here was a woman who enjoyed a physical challenge just as much as he did. But still, he had to ask, "Are you sure you want to take on the next-level trail?"

"Are you being condescending? If this was our first date, I'd think twice before accepting a second one."

It was hard not to grin from ear-to-ear. It wasn't often he came across a woman who could take what he dished out and fling back some of her own sass. "I'm trying to be polite. Where's Sonny when I need him?" The old man would give Rhett points for being considerate, not view it as a put-down.

"I'm used to being treated as one of the guys, not coddled." A crease appeared in Olivia's forehead. "And look, I'm not ready for the Tumble Trail, but I want to know what the intermediate one feels like."

He considered telling her she'd had enough for one day, but he didn't dwell on the thought for long. Olivia was a force to be reckoned with when she made up her mind. "I'd love you to take on a bigger challenge, but you might regret pushing yourself so hard on your first time out here."

"I'm Captain Olivia Monroe, cowboy," she said, her voice ringing with pride. "I think I know what I'm doing."

CHAPTER SEVEN

"WHAT WAS I doing today?" Olivia moaned when they arrived at the hotel that night. "I should have stopped at the beginner trail. Then maybe Rhett would have been the one to tumble."

"I tumbled." Rhett turned off the truck and turned on the charm, smiling at Olivia.

"You didn't tumble as much as I did," she grumbled, meeting Rhett's grin with a sad face.

"We've been in this truck too long, traveling almost the rest of the way across Montana," Sonny said in a conciliatory voice, stuffing an apple core into his empty coffee cup. "Your muscles have probably all stiffened."

"Stiffened?" Olivia made no move to exit. She rolled her head across her shoulders. "They're stuck."

Rhett took pity on her and went around to her side of the truck to lift her down to the ground before getting the step-stool for Sonny.

Olivia must have been very sore, because she didn't even accuse him of abusing his fake boyfriend privileges with dagger-filled looks.

"Every bone in my body hurts." She shifted her neck, arms and shoulders, as if trying to move them back to their proper places. "How many times did I wipe out on the intermediate trail?"

"Five times." The last one had been a head-over-wheels splat that had stolen his breath.

But Olivia was plucky. She'd picked herself up and gotten right back on the bike. It had made him wonder why she hadn't gotten right back on a boat after her accident.

Rhett went around to the other side and unloaded their bags from the truck's back seat. He grabbed the remains of his weak coffee, the cup Olivia had gotten for him the last time they filled up with gas. She swore it wasn't decaf.

"Five times on one trail, Olivia. That might be a record." That was an exaggeration, but Rhett was coming to understand Olivia needed him to make light of most moments, most especially the ones where she felt she didn't live up to expectations.

Which was the majority of the time since she set a high bar for herself.

Olivia groaned again, leading them to the

hotel with awkward steps. "As far as business opportunities go, mountain biking is a no for me."

Operationally, Rhett tended to agree. There were trails to create and preserve. Bikes and safety gear to have on hand for those who didn't have their own. Transportation to buy and maintain. Employees to hire and manage, which meant payroll and tax filings. It didn't matter if Holden was offering to partner and help, Rhett was feeling overwhelmed.

"You were enthusiastic after your first two runs," Sonny pointed out. "It's important to know your limits."

"There were no posted speed limits on those courses." Olivia stepped onto a sidewalk, groaning.

"I meant your physical limits," Sonny told her.

If his comment was meant to be taken philosophically, it hadn't registered. Olivia kept moving slowly toward the hotel entrance.

"You were supposed to watch out for her," Sonny said softly to Rhett.

Rhett cast him a quick, disgruntled look. "You try to stop Olivia when she's made her mind up."

"At this rate, she'll want to head back to Second Chance." Sonny tsked. "And here I thought you were good for her."

Back to Second Chance?

So much of Rhett's future hinged on her arriving in Philadelphia in a few days. Not that Sonny or Olivia knew that. He decided a little defensive posturing was in order.

Rhett fixed Sonny with a hard look and raised his voice so Olivia could hear, "Are you trying to get out of the bet we made?"

"I can make it, Sonny." Olivia continued toward the hotel's portico with herky-jerky steps. "Ignore my complaints. I'll be fine for the meeting tomorrow." They were driving to Bismarck, North Dakota, in the morning and picking up Kendall at the airport. "Rhett, you should be celebrating. I survived Day One of the Rhett Diaz Adventure Tour. By your standards, it was tame. But by mine…"

"Admit it. It was a thrill to step out of your comfort zone," Rhett said too quickly and with too much gush, wanting her to complete the trip. "That takes courage. Right, Sonny?"

She stopped, circling around to face the two men. "Stop with the nicey-nice, the kid gloves and the tip-toeing."

"Uh. Okay?" Rhett felt like tip-toeing around her and kicking himself in the process for not treating her like a new recruit in boot camp.

"She needs a hug," Sonny whispered beside him.

No, she doesn't.

"You've been nice and supportive to me all day, Rhett." Olivia pointed at Sonny. "But that's his job."

"Hug her," Sonny whispered again.

Rhett frowned. Sonny was convinced she needed a hug. Olivia looked like she was ready to slug someone. Both waited for him to say something. "I stand by my behavior. My mother raised me to respect a woman and her feelings."

"Olivia, your beau is well-meaning and needs a hug!" Sonny raised his voice. "Hug him. Now. Quick." He clapped twice.

"All right. All right." Olivia dragged her feet until she reached Rhett. She put her arms around him, bundling his arms against his torso. And then she began to count, "One, two, three…"

"What's happening?" Rhett held himself rigidly.

"…seven, eight, nine…"

"Hugs are therapeutic, my boy." Sonny wrapped his arms around them both. "A thirty-second hug can release much of the stress and anxiety you've been feeling."

"…eighteen, nineteen, twenty…"

"*I* wasn't feeling stress and anxiety." Not like he was now. Geez, the few people who were outside were beginning to stare.

"…twenty-four, twenty-five…"

"Of course, you were." Sonny rocked back and forth, nearly toppling them all. "You were worried about Olivia's physical condition or you wouldn't have helped her out of the truck. And you were unclear about her distress just now, which gave you a tick in your cheek."

"There was no tick," Rhett protested, feeling none of the cleansing relaxation Sonny had promised.

"Thirty," Olivia said. She and Sonny released Rhett simultaneously. She returned to her wheeled bag. "And yes, there was a tick."

Sonny studied Rhett's face. "It's gone now." He moseyed after Olivia, leaving Rhett standing in the middle of the parking lot not knowing what to say. Fake dating wasn't supposed to be this hard.

His stomach growled. At least he knew what to do about that.

"We'll feel better after we have dinner." Rhett set his feet in motion, tossing his paper coffee cup in the trash. "Where do you want to go? There's a nice steakhouse in town."

Nearly to the door, Olivia gasped, and faced him. "You do realize that Sonny was in the hospital a few days ago? He's supposed to have more vegetables, fish and chicken."

"Hence the ice cream I saw him eating at the mountain bike snack bar after our last run." Rhett smirked.

Olivia gasped again, staring accusingly at the old man.

"In my defense, travel is like vacation," Sonny mumbled. "And vacations have ice cream, not pills and doctor's orders."

"Pills? Holy mackerel." Olivia whipped out her cell phone. "What time is it? Sonny, it's seven-thirty. We're thirty minutes late. And you still need to eat before you take your pills."

"There's a restaurant here." Rhett moved briskly past the huggers toward the check-in desk. "I'll get us checked in. You get us a table and order food."

"Good idea." Olivia took hold of Sonny's arm, although it was more likely that as sore as she was she needed his support, not the other way around. "I hope they have salad."

"I hope they have steak." Rhett wasn't giving up on the idea so easily.

"Me, too," Sonny said cheerfully.

"There will be no steak," Olivia said in that commanding tone. "And no ice cream for dessert. We can all do with a little healthier eating."

Rhett heartily, if silently, disagreed.

He fixed Olivia with a suggestive stare, one designed to put her off-balance. "If I can't have steak, I'm going to need another hug and…"

He let her fill in the blank.

"IT'S TIME YOU lovebirds enjoyed some time alone without your chaperone." Sonny got up from the restaurant table. They'd eaten dinner and he'd taken his pills. "Besides, Olivia isn't letting me have a glass of wine or dessert."

"Didn't mean you couldn't have had either." Rhett raised his beer glass and took a good long sip while staring at Olivia in a manner that got her heart fluttering.

Olivia averted her gaze from Rhett's, taking in the uninspired décor of the near-empty hotel restaurant. "Your doctor will thank me, Sonny."

"As will I." Sonny separated his suitcase from the other two. "Someday." That last sounded down.

"Are you okay?" Olivia got to her feet,

slowly and with achy joints. "I'll come with you." Gladly, since she was torn about being alone with Rhett.

"I'm fine. Don't get up." Sonny headed for the exit in that steady gait of his.

"Give him some space." Rhett put a hand on her shoulder, guiding her back down to her chair. "When my grandfather was diagnosed with diabetes, it took him a long time to get used to all the changes he had to make, health-wise. Sonny needs the same time."

Olivia sagged back in her seat, trying to find a comfortable position that didn't tax her sore back, sore shoulders or sore behind. "He had a heart attack. He doesn't have time to adjust to a new reality."

"That's rich coming from you." Rhett sipped his beer without taking his eyes off her. With those broad shoulders and his cowboy hat on, he seemed to take up more space than he'd been allotted. "You're the one taking her time and not-adjusting to a new reality. You're just in limbo."

It was true. And it hurt, that truth. Not even Sonny accused her of that.

Suddenly, Olivia didn't like how brash Rhett was. Some things were better left hidden under rocks.

"Which is interesting to me," Rhett continued in that confident way of his. "Because you were so determined to conquer those trails today. Why wouldn't you get back in the saddle?"

"And sail?" she said thickly.

"And sail." He let that comment simmer between them, as if expecting more of an answer from her.

Olivia kept her lips closed, taking a moment to openly admire his good looks rather than think about his words. That strong chin? It was too stubborn. Those high cheekbones? They accented his heaping helping of pride. His five-o'clock shadow? It was a hard contrast to her softness.

"Soft," she muttered. "That's what I've become."

"Hardly." He scoffed. "You were tough out there. It makes me think that when you were younger someone made you determined to overcome obstacles in your path."

"No, I…" An image of her father came to mind, features drawn in displeasure, telling her to—*Keep up with the boys*. She reached for her water glass.

"That explains a lot. Father, grandfather or…" Rhett intercepted her hand before it reached the glass. He cupped it between both of his, seemingly offering his support if she needed it.

She needed it. The woman she'd been a year ago resented needing it. But the woman she was today appreciated a bit of nurturing by someone who saw both strength and vulnerability in her.

"My father was determined to raise Monroes who could weather any storm. Of course, his idea of shaping us was to put us in the eye of the storm." Which was usually in the path of his anger, which was fed by the illusion that his children hadn't done well enough, especially Olivia. "Dad only signed me up for boys' soccer leagues. He had me crew his races at the local yacht club. He wanted me to succeed despite my size and my wayward curls. Nothing was ever good enough for him."

"Not even winning races of your own on the world stage?" Rhett's question was barely a whisper.

"Not even." She drew in a ragged breath, feeling more battered than she had all day. "Sonny was right." She'd needed a change to rise above the dark place she'd been in after the accident.

"Funny you should mention the old man."

Rhett lifted her hand and pressed a kiss to her knuckles. His lips were warm and gentle against her skin.

She was grateful for that warmth, that gentleness, too.

"Sonny's been lurking behind the hostess station, watching us." Rhett released her hand and sat back, reaching for his beer. "He's gone now."

Gone, too, was the considerate cowboy.

"Was this…" Olivia didn't complete the question. *Was all that tenderness he'd shown her for show?* She reached for her Monroe strength. "Sonny should have been upstairs already." Olivia twisted around, beginning to rise.

Again, Rhett encouraged her to sit back down with a strong hand on her shoulder. "He must have visited that little snack bar by the check-in desk."

"Did he get cookies?" She craned her neck to try and see him.

"I can't tell you."

Olivia placed her elbows on the table and arched her brows at her fake boyfriend. "Why not?"

"It would be a betrayal of the Bro-Code."

Olivia opened her mouth to toss back a sharp

retort and then thought better of it. "You have a connection to Sonny. That's so sweet."

Rhett finished his beer and signaled the waitress for the check.

Having confessed so much, Olivia had a feeling that she was at a disadvantage somehow. "Back in Second Chance, Mackenzie referenced some kind of a dare…"

Rhett rolled his eyes. "I told you what it would take to have me share that episode in my life."

"You can read about my boat accident anywhere online. You can't hear about my Monroe upbringing anywhere but from me."

He considered her, gaze roaming her face as if he was committing every nuance to memory.

Such malarkey. He was a man used to charming women. He'd charmed her just now. She arched her brows, challenging him to share in his own right.

Rhett stared at her for so long that she thought he wasn't going to answer. "All right. The short version. It happened ten or so years ago on a Memorial Day weekend. A bunch of us were out at the lake by the old homestead, including a rodeo friend of mine and locals, like Mackenzie." He paused, drawing out his wallet to give the waitress his credit card. "This rodeo friend of mine... He told my other friends that I had a different girl in every city I visited."

"Was that the truth?" Olivia believed it.

Rhett shifted in his seat, looking uncomfortable, confirming Olivia's suspicions. "It doesn't matter if it was the truth or not. As a result, Mackenzie dared me to go dateless for a year."

"I take it you did."

"Of course, I did." Rhett pulled the brim of his hat low, perhaps to hide the fact that his cheeks were ruddy.

"Are you blushing?" Olivia chuckled.

He lifted his chin and his hat brim. "Look. I took dares and bets seriously back then. I'm not proud of it but... But then something strange happened." He seemed to regain that cockiness that was all Rhett.

"Tell me." She leaned toward him.

"I started winning events. Big ones." He stared at Olivia as if this was something he'd never dreamed of.

She laughed again. "Of course, you did. You weren't dating. You were able to focus."

"Funny how good you can get when you practice your craft more." He warmed her with a smile. "Did your father encourage you to sail?"

"His attitude encouraged me to get out of the house. We had a home on the Delaware River and I had a skiff I could sail by myself."

The waitress returned with their check folio and Rhett's credit card.

He scribbled a tip and signed his name. "I'm sorry you didn't sail because you loved it."

"I learned to love it." She was reluctant to get to her feet and leave the restaurant and this moment, this…intimacy. "I'm sorry you took a dating sabbatical. That must have been lonely."

He shrugged, not getting up either. "I wouldn't change anything about my past. You can learn a lot about yourself by stepping back. It allows you time to mature and get smarter."

"If that's true, I'm going to come out of this a certified genius."

But would she be a genius who sailed again?

CHAPTER EIGHT

"WHAT DO YOU like about Olivia?"

Uh-oh.

Rhett had been digging around his suitcase for his shaving kit, which held his toothbrush. He stopped digging and turned to face Sonny in their hotel room. The old man wore lime green pajamas dotted with baby goats.

Rhett lost his train of thought.

Sonny repeated his question.

Oh, yeah. What do I like about Olivia?

Rhett liked that she gave him guff when he tried to rile her. He liked that she had buried her fear so far below bravado that she was just rediscovering the difference between fear and tempered excitement. He liked that she spoke her mind, even if she was admitting to a weakness.

He could say all that and so much more to the old man. If he trusted him.

Instead, he countered with, "Why do you ask?"

"You're an odd sort of couple." Sonny settled under the covers of his bed, fluffing pillows and shifting about, adjusting that beard as if it had to be just so. "Like two magnets repelling each other instead of two people who can't bear to be apart."

Rhett was good at quickly spotting challenges and obstacles ahead—whether it was a calf coming out of a chute and zig-zagging or being locked in a room with an old man fielding a direct line of questioning.

Tonight's obstacle? Sonny suspected there was no relationship between himself and Olivia. And why wouldn't he? There had been no kisses today and only one instance of handholding. Rhett wasn't counting the thirty-second hug in the hotel parking lot as an expression of interest and devotion.

Sonny finally stilled, lying on his side and staring at Rhett.

At Rhett, who didn't like to lie and didn't want to betray Olivia's trust or put her at a disadvantage with her family. But this was Sonny, the man in charge of helping her reclaim her competitive spirit.

Rhett cleared his throat, made a decision and told the truth. "It was Olivia's idea to pretend-date. She felt she needed the relationship as a buffer for her family."

Sonny continued to stare at Rhett without a change in his expression, which made Rhett squirm. He scratched a sudden itch behind his neck.

"You didn't answer my question," Sonny said levelly. "What do you like about Olivia?"

Rhett slowly sat on the edge of the bed. "Didn't you hear what I said?"

"I did." Sonny nodded. "I suspected you weren't truly dating, but I can tell that you like her and I'm curious to know why."

Rhett scratched the back of his neck again. "You want to know what I think of Olivia?" A flurry of impressions clouded his brain. "Why?" Was this a trap to get him to renege on his promise to deliver Olivia to Philadelphia?

"During our time in Second Chance, she's admitted she keeps people, including men she's dated, at arm's length because she devoted herself to her sport. But you seem to disarm her. All without making her uneasy and launching her guard."

Pride filled Rhett's chest, squaring his shoulders. But it was putting the cart before the horse. "She isn't sailing right now. You know as well as I do that as soon as she steps foot on a sailboat, I'll be out of the picture."

"Do I? I've seen you look at each other. I've seen you embrace. Even an old man can spot an attraction under the guise of…an attraction," Sonny said gruffly. "Just answer the question. Knowing what aspects of her personality she's shown to you will help me build upon her progress so she can achieve her goal."

"Of sailing again." Rhett nodded.

"Of regaining her confidence," Sonny gently corrected. He yawned, leaving the conversational ball in Rhett's court.

"Well, I… She's smart. Quick-witted. And humble." She didn't make him feel like he was less of a man for being a plain old cowboy compared to her worldly accomplishments. "She can surprise me and make me laugh. You know, these are all basic things that a man looks for in a woman."

Sonny's mouth pulled to one side. "I've never been in love, but I've always imagined it's more like finding a really good dessert, the one dessert that makes you feel happy and satisfied, like in that moment, and all the moments to come. It's the dessert for you, despite all the other desserts you've tried or might be tempted with in the future."

"You're saying it's what *I* want in a woman."

"Yes." Sonny yawned once more. "I'm a pineapple upside down cake when it comes to romance. You seem like a cinnamon roll man, heavy on the icing."

Rhett's mouth dropped open.

"It's all in the nuances, my boy. You'll figure it out one day, whether it's with Olivia or not." He snuggled deeper under the covers. "But at least now I know."

"Yep. We can drop the dating ruse right now." He'd be relieved to do it. "We'll tell Olivia in the morning." And weather the storm that resulted together.

"No. Don't tell her. I think Olivia needs to sail the course she's laid out and then face the consequences of the situation she's made. She might even discover the flavor of dessert she prefers. Either way, I'm certain she'll be better for it."

Rhett wasn't so sure. "But—"

"No buts." Sonny yawned. "I'm exhausted. Get a good night's sleep because tomorrow I want you to be a better pretend date than you were today."

Rhett fell back on his bed. This trip was turning into a fresh cowpie on a steep trail.

SONNY SNORED LOUDER than a revving engine at a tractor pull.

Rhett had his back to the old man and a pillow pressed over his ear. Didn't matter. He could still hear the raw *rev-rev-rev-rev* as the old man sucked in air and the *blubububub* of him blowing it back out.

He hoped Olivia, who was in the adjoining room, was able to get some sleep. To be fair, Rhett might not have been able to fall asleep after his conversation with Sonny. Why keep up the pretense of a relationship with the old man?

Because of kisses!

Rhett rolled over, trying again to plaster a pillow against his ear.

Olivia was going to be angry when she discovered Sonny had figured things out and Rhett hadn't told her. But then again, she was going to be angry when he dropped her off at a marina in Philadelphia. She'd be angry, but perhaps by then she'd return to the place she belonged—aboard a sailing ship.

After an hour of tossing and turning, Rhett grabbed his clothes, hat and boots and slipped into the bathroom to get dressed. So much for saving money by sharing a room. He'd go downstairs and get his own.

Except when he got to the front desk, the hotel was full.

Rhett's groan may or may not have triggered his stomach growling. He shouldn't have caved in to Olivia's demands that they all eat healthy at dinner. He hadn't even had dessert. "Please tell me the restaurant is still open." Exhaustion and a full stomach might help him fall asleep.

"They closed at eleven." Olivia emerged from the snack bar at the end of the check-in desk. She placed a bottle of pain reliever, a water and a bag of cookies on the counter.

The woman against steak and dessert is sneaking cookies?

"You guilted me into ordering a chef's salad for dinner." Rhett snatched the cookies and opened the package, pausing when a thought struck. "Don't think I'm not on to you now. You didn't *accidentally* mix up our coffee order at the gas station or drink my coffee this afternoon instead of your decaf." She'd put one over on him. He vowed then and there not to tell her about Sonny having caught on to their ruse.

"A good captain knows how to motivate her crew." Olivia paid for her purchases. She had a slight case of bedhead and a full-on case of sore muscles, if her slow movements were any indication. "Sonny can't do a complete life change alone."

"I tell you what Sonny needs to do alone." Rhett bit into a chocolate chip cookie. "Sleep. You could have warned me that he snores. I would have made separate room reservations. Or at the very least, brought noise canceling headphones."

"We have ear plugs." The desk clerk handed Rhett a small packet.

"See? Problem solved." Olivia took a cookie from the package without any outward trace of guilt. "I'm so achy, I can't sleep. I'm watching *The Hunger Games*. You can nap on my sofa while I watch the last hour."

Rhett perked up. *Things just got interesting.* "Is the sofa a pull-out?"

"No." She led him toward the elevators.

Rhett wasn't ready to give up on a chance to get horizontal somewhere besides his hotel room. "Do you have a king-size bed? I don't take up much room. We can put my hat between us." No matter how sizzling their kisses, no way was he crushing his hat to get some. It was his favorite.

"Nice try, cowboy." The elevator doors opened when she jabbed the call button. "But it's a queen bed and our fake relationship hasn't progressed to having a sleep-over."

The elevator door slid closed on any hope Rhett had for a good night's rest.

Olivia rolled her shoulders back and forth. "You can still come in and nap on the sofa until the movie's over."

He didn't warm to the thought of falling asleep only to have to get up again. "If you let me use your comforter, I could sleep on the floor all night."

"No." A bit of color bloomed in her cheeks. "How many times are you going to ask?"

Rhett gave her his most charming smile. "By my account, that's two tries. Don't begrudge me a third. Good things come in threes."

"Like strike outs in baseball," she dead-panned.

The elevator door slid open, and they walked down the hall. At Olivia's room, Rhett could hear Sonny's snores next door.

"That can't be good for him." Rhett kept his voice down. "I bet Sonny needs a sleep apnea machine. My grandfather has one. He wears a mask that makes him look like a pilot in a fighter jet, but his snoring is now more like deep breathing than a window-rattling tremor."

He'd traveled with him recently and had been grateful of the whole setup.

"Good idea." Olivia brightened as she opened the door. The light on the nightstand was on and the TV was playing but muted. "I'll talk to him about it."

"You like taking care of him." Rhett realized this, following her inside, closing the door softly behind him.

"Yeah, I do." She plopped on the bed and set about opening the pain reliever bottle. "It makes me feel like I have some control over something."

He eyed the big bed. She'd turned down the linens on the side where she sat on. In theory, Olivia was only using half the bed. There was room for one well-behaved cowboy. "Since when do you *not* have control over anything?"

Olivia made a buzzer noise as if he'd just given the wrong answer on a game show. She unmuted the television, and tossed the remote toward the foot of the mattress.

Rhett claimed the remote and turned the sound back off. "What does that sound mean?" Remote in-hand, he sat on the small sofa. It was rock hard and square. "There's no way I'm getting any shut-eye on this thing. Quit stalling and explain."

"Then you're out of luck, cowboy. Time to change the subject." She swallowed two pills and then reached for another cookie.

"This isn't a lightning round. We're having a discussion." One she clearly wanted to avoid—

Sonny's snores drifted through the wall.

—not that Rhett wanted to upset her by forcing the issue. There was a good night's sleep and a business trip to consider. "Fine. What do you want to talk about?"

Olivia glanced at the television, which was currently running a cell phone commercial. "Okay, um… I googled you." Grabbing her phone from the nightstand, she toggled through it and then flashed her screen at him. "You have an online encyclopedia page. Quite impressive."

He shrugged. It wasn't like he'd made the page. He wasn't entirely sure he'd known it existed.

Olivia looked deflated. "But… Didn't you search me?"

Rhett shook his head.

"Why not?" Her brow furrowed. "We're dating."

"We're *fake* dating. Real dating involves marking milestones, like first dates, and kissing, remember?" He liked that his teasing made her blush. "And even if we were dating for real, I wouldn't stalk you on the internet."

"It's not stalking. It's… It's curiosity."

Sonny sawed large logs in the other room.

"We agree to disagree." Rhett stretched out his legs and tried to get comfortable. "What can I possibly learn about you on the internet that I haven't discovered myself?"

"Well, for starters…" She scrolled and toggled, ignoring the movie when it came back on the screen. "…Olivia Monroe. Born…yada yada. The first woman to captain a college yacht racing crew. Considered a rising talent in the yacht racing world. Sank a prototype sailboat during a race where she was on pace to break a world record. And then…" She tossed aside her phone just as she'd tossed aside the remote. "Nothing."

"I don't think *nothing* is bad." He could think of worse things, like her date of death. "I take nothing to mean *to-be-continued*."

"Hardly. Rising talents don't sink ships." She took her time choosing a cookie from the package, but then she held it up for inspection the same way she seemed to think folks inspected her online encyclopedia page.

"You're over-thinking." Wasn't that just like some uppity city-folk? "People sink proverbial ships all the time. They have bad days. They get pulled from the line-up. They mess up and move on."

"I knew you wouldn't understand." She waved a hand, brushing aside his opinion.

It may have been sleep deprivation, but Olivia's harsh self-judgment was beginning to annoy him. "I understand that I'm not defined by what I did or what I do or who I fake date."

"You can say that." She swung her legs around until they hung off the side of the bed and she faced him squarely. "You'll always be a cowboy who was a champion roper."

"And you'll always be that captain who was on track to breaking a world record when she capsized a boat." He mirrored her body language, leaning forward, compelled by the passion in her eyes. "You might notice they didn't list all the rodeos I competed in. There were plenty of times I came in out-of-the-money. Not winning doesn't define you."

"It's not about the sinking boat." She gnawed on that lip he wanted to kiss before blurting, "It's about being the first woman to…" She flopped onto her back. "I feel pressure to pick myself up and race again. But not because I want to. I feel pressure to live up to the image

Kendall created of me as a role model for women and girls."

At this late hour, Rhett needed a minute to fully process her meaning.

Sonny's snore broke rhythm, as if he needed the same thing.

Olivia pressed the heels of her hands over her eyes. "I knew you wouldn't understand."

She needs a hug.

Dropping the remote, Rhett came to his feet, drew her to hers and into his arms. "One, two, three…"

She buried her face in his chest, taut as a brand-new lasso.

He kept on counting to thirty. And when he got there, he held her at arm's length. "What I don't understand is why you define greatness as only doing one thing. You aren't just a sailboat captain. You can become whatever or whoever you want to be, even if it includes becoming a private citizen whose accomplishments are no longer public consumption."

"Says the champion cowboy."

"Says the woman who's a rising talent."

"And… You didn't finish their sentence," she pointed out in a whisper.

"Because it was *their* sentence, not yours," he said just as quietly. "How many athletes go to a championship final and return empty-handed. Lots. They aren't failures either."

The snoring through the connecting door grew faint.

Olivia cocked her head. "I should have had you unlock the connecting door so I could check on him." She'd deftly avoided addressing his point.

"He's fine," Rhett reassured her. "If Sonny's anything like my grandfather, he just rolled over, and this is a brief intermission before the symphony begins again."

As if on cue, the snoring started back up.

Much as Rhett didn't want to, he released her and turned off the television. He held up his earplugs. "We both need to get some sleep. Big day tomorrow. We're driving to Bismarck to meet with your muckety-mucks."

She groaned, following him to the door. "I'd rather go mountain biking again."

He opened the door, looking at her one last time to make sure she was okay. She was still too solemn, so he tweaked her nose. "You've forgotten what you learned on the mountain today. It's okay to be afraid. Whether you're sailing, riding a mountain bike or trying to decide who you want to be for the next act of your life."

CHAPTER NINE

"I LIKE IT when people are punctual," Kendall told them when they picked her up at the Bismarck airport in North Dakota at noon the next day. She climbed in the back seat and glanced at Olivia. "What's wrong with you? You look like you're hungover or lovesick." She swatted Rhett's cowboy hat, which happened to still be on his head. "Did you break up with her?"

"Kendall!" Olivia was horrified. She deflected her cousin's hands from a second swing.

"My, my, how you Monroes do jump to conclusions." Leaning forward, Rhett straightened his hat. "I'm still very much the apple of Olivia's eye."

As far as anyone was concerned, that was true. He'd held her hand this morning as they walked out to the truck with Sonny.

"I fell yesterday when we were mountain biking," Olivia admitted, rolling her shoulders in an attempt to loosen them up. "I'm still sore today."

"As would any human who wiped out on a bike five times." Rhett snuck in a tease.

"Five times? Don't tell our sponsors about that statistic." Kendall dug through her purse. "I have some muscle relaxers in here somewhere, as well as a natural organic pain reliever. You should avoid sugar and caffeine today."

"I don't need muscle relaxers or a special diet." Olivia held her hand in the stop position.

Sonny scoffed. "Meanwhile, she's regimented when it comes to me taking my pills and eating like I'm still in the hospital."

"Life is so unfair," Rhett said. He smiled at Olivia in the rearview mirror. The cowboy could say all the right things when it suited him.

When I need to hear them.

It was easy to pretend to be Rhett's girlfriend.

"We have a one o'clock appointment at No Glare Eyewear." Kendall fixed Olivia with a hard look while Rhett drove them out of the airport. "I need Captain Olivia Monroe to show, not Olivia from the corner bar."

"I'm not hungover!" Olivia glared at her cousin.

"Is it too late to put Kendall back on the plane?" Rhett slowed the truck as if preparing to change direction.

Kendall scoffed. "You need me at these meetings, Liv. And you need your cowboy, too."

"What?" Rhett tipped his hat back. "Olivia doesn't need anyone."

"In the state Liv's in, you, cowboy, are going to be a good distraction." Kendall offered a water bottle to Olivia. "At least hydrate, Liv. And before we get there, you'll need to change into your official team racing gear."

Olivia obediently drank Kendall's water, shaking her head. "I didn't bring any team racing gear."

"Is there still a team?" Rhett gunned it when the light changed, darting around a bus and preparing for a right turn, following the GPS directions in the dashboard. "Can you have a team without a boat to race?"

"Good question." Sonny twisted in his seat to look at Olivia, who decided there had to be something interesting outside her window. There wasn't. But she didn't stop looking. "Is there a team? Can there be a team without a captain?"

Olivia declined to answer because to do so would be a commitment one way or the other. She was either soldiering on as a racing boat captain or giving up. She wasn't ready to decide.

"According to the sponsor contracts, there *is* still a team led by Captain Monroe, which is why I packed racing gear for everyone." Kendall nudged Olivia's shoulder. "Not to say they couldn't replace Olivia if they lost confidence in her."

"I could be replaced?" Olivia's pride sharpened her words as she imagined that on her encyclopedia page. "But I'm the one who put this team together. I'm the one who worked with Bentley to design the boat. Whether or not the team exists should be my decision."

Kendall nudged Olivia again. "There's the Olivia we need today."

"Good. You don't need me." Rhett drove on with a carefree smile.

"We still need our prop piece," Kendall said briskly. "And we need him to be tall, dark and silent."

"Absent will do." Rhett smirked, not that

it detracted from his handsomeness at all. "I didn't sign up to be part of the show."

"But you're more than happy to support your significant other," Sonny said as if he were coaching Rhett on the fine art of relationships. His T-shirt today was a lemony yellow and said: Shine On! "Let's not forget to reframe."

Rhett heaved a sigh that was as fake as his and Olivia's relationship. "Anything for my sugar bear."

Sugar bear? Olivia nearly choked on another sip of water. No one had ever dared call Olivia such a ridiculous moniker. She should have been offended. Instead, she wanted to laugh. It was so like Rhett.

"There will be no smarmy nicknames while we're at No Glare Eyewear." Kendall raised her finger toward the truck's ceiling. "None. Do you hear me?"

"What?" Rhett gasped dramatically. "I can't express my feelings to my chicken nugget?"

"Or me to my puddin'?" Olivia did laugh this time.

That earned her a mischievous smile from Rhett in the rearview. "She's my bucket of oats."

"And he's my sugar-snap-pea." Olivia grinned. Their nicknames were truly terrible.

"Blech." Kendall covered her ears. "Blechety-blech-blech."

Rhett and Olivia chuckled. After a moment, Sonny joined in.

"Is it safe to uncover my ears?" Kendall lifted her hands.

"My sunny sunflower?" Olivia said immediately.

"My little cowbell?" Rhett wasn't at a loss for smarmy nicknames.

"Why me?" Kendall moaned, placing her hands over her ears. "I'm only trying to help."

"You owe me for this," Rhett told Olivia as they approached the front doors of No Glare Eyewear headquarters.

Kendall had insisted they both wear blue Monroe Racing Team T-shirts. Olivia also wore a blue ball cap with the team's logo. Rhett had refused to wear a cap instead of his cowboy hat. When faced with gearing up and abandoning his T-shirt with positive sayings, Sonny had decided to stay in the truck, which they'd parked under a tree to provide him with some shade. Rhett suspected he had a bag of chocolate stashed somewhere and wanted to eat it in peace.

Wearing her blue racing team T-shirt and

black slacks, Kendall trotted ahead of them on her high heels and held the door for the group.

Olivia wore her black-and-white Converse sneakers with black socks. They gave attitude to her T-shirt and cargo shorts. But it was her short brown curls that completed the picture and told the world that Olivia Monroe was controlled chaos.

Not that Rhett would ever tell her that.

The lobby of No Glare Eyewear was bright white—the floor, the walls, the furniture. It reflected the sun and made Rhett squint.

Two men came through double doors and called out greetings to Olivia. Both wore Monroe Racing Team T-shirts and blue jeans. One had a crew cut. The other had gray-blond hair nearly as long as Kendall's.

"So good to see you, Matt. Sven." Olivia shook their hands. "You remember my cousin Kendall. And this is my…good friend Rhett."

The men were shorter than Rhett, much shorter. They glanced up at him, staring as if he had something unusual on his face.

"You need a pair of sunglasses." With a toss of his long hair, Sven went over to a display of sunglasses and brought back a pair with bright purple rims. "Try these on."

Purple? Not on my life!

"I have a pair." Rhett pointed to the sunglasses balanced on the brim of his hat.

"But these are No Glare Eyewear." Sven held them toward Rhett's face.

"How nice of you to offer Rhett a pair." Kendall gave Rhett a warning look.

"Thanks." Rhett relented, sliding the sunglasses in place. They made the lobby less blindingly white.

"Kendall mentioned you're taking a cross-country trip back to Philadelphia." Matt opened the double doors and led them deeper into the building, rubbing his crew cut self-consciously.

Eager to get this visit over with, Rhett strode after Matt.

"An extreme sport trip." Sven trotted along next to Olivia. "We're so envious. We'd love a picture of you on an adventure for our social media page. Wearing our sunglasses, of course."

"In addition to a picture of you visiting our headquarters," Matt amended, trotting backward. "With your good friend Rhett." He paused in front of a wall that had hundreds of sunglasses attached to it, facing every whichway. "This is our latest art installation. What do you think?"

"Art?" Rhett glanced at it over the top of his purple sunglasses. It was like no art he'd ever seen. "Did you guys put this together on a Saturday?"

Matt sucked in a breath.

Sven placed a hand over his collarbone, looking like he might faint. "We commissioned a well-known artist from Finland."

Rhett started to feel hot under the collar. He removed the purple sunglasses, ready to donate them to the so-called art on the wall.

"Pay no mind to my cowboy." Olivia caught up to Rhett and took his arm. "He's used to rectilinear, perspective-based art."

What did that mean?

Rhett felt his temperature rise. There was nothing he despised more than being made to feel less than. "Actually, my preference is black velvet paintings. Have you seen the one with dogs playing poker?" Rhett forced himself to smile and pretend to admire the wall, while in his mind, he was retracing his steps to the lobby.

"I prefer John Wayne in black velvet." Olivia squeezed Rhett's forearm. "Classic cowboy."

He captured her gaze, debating whether or not a kiss was in order to let her know who was boss. "The tall and silent type, my little rust bucket?"

"Photo op," Kendall interrupted, whipping out her cell phone. "Everybody get close." She snapped a few shots. "Now just Olivia with Matt and Sven." She snapped a few more. "Perfect. I'm sending you these, Matt."

"Awesome. Could we get you something while we sit down and chat? Water? Sports drink? Maybe herbal tea?" Sven led them to a conference room. It was filled with photos of skiers, volleyball players and Olivia—all wearing a pair of branded sunglasses, none of which were purple.

Rhett clutched his abominably purple eyewear so hard it made marks in his palm.

"We're dying to know what's next for the Monroe Racing Team." Matt put his elbows on the table and leaned forward.

"I…" Olivia faltered, her gaze seeking Rhett's.

Rhett's, not Kendall's.

"Fellas, my snuggle-bun is taking a hiatus to get our house in order." Rhett pulled Olivia's chair closer, draping his arm over her shoulders.

Snuggle-bun? Kendall mouthed, giving Rhett a dirty look.

"*Our* house?" Matt clapped his hands together joyfully. "I sensed something was different about you, Olivia."

"You sensed right, Matt," Rhett reassured him.

"Congratulations are in order." Sven had been about to hand out sports drinks. He set down the bottles. "Should we break out the champagne?"

"No," Olivia rushed in. "We haven't announced anything official yet. And I'm dying for something to drink. Thanks. We were mountain biking yesterday and tomorrow Rhett is promising another extreme adventure. I was so excited about this trip that I haven't been able to sleep. Every day that we don't meet with a sponsor, we're having some fun."

"This break ought to make Olivia's next racing gig more appealing to our audience, don't you think?" Kendall jumped in a little too quickly, making her sound desperate. "Our shared audiences, that is."

Despite that, Sven looked completely sold. "Agreed. When Olivia changes tack, it only makes her more interesting to both our franchises."

"Before I forget, we need to send you off with a care package." Matt tapped his phone furiously. "Make sure they take pictures with the new product line on this trip of theirs, Kendall. And we'd love to be a part of your wedding nuptials, Olivia. I'm thinking samples as wedding favors for each wedding guest. Kendall can give us a guest count."

Olivia nodded blankly, looking every inch the woman blindsided by her private romance being outed. Rhett pressed a gentle kiss to her crown.

"I'll bet you'll have a ceremony somewhere by the sea. Think how fun it will be to take pictures with everyone wearing a pair of No Glare Eyewear." Sven glowed, no doubt counting social media likes or whatever it was businesspeople did nowadays.

That'll be me when I own a business.

Rhett forced himself to smile to cover his shock. He'd be no different than Olivia, catering to customers and asking them to post photos and reviews.

Olivia glanced up at Rhett, an apology in her eyes. She kissed his jaw, so softly, so briefly, that if it hadn't been for the rising color in her cheeks afterward, he would have thought he'd imagined it.

An hour later, they left with a bag full of branded hats, T-shirts and sunglasses.

Gripping onto Olivia's hand, Rhett stepped out in the sunlight and was annoyed to realize the purple sunglasses were better at removing the glare than his cheap pair. "That's demoralizing."

"You got that right," Kendall fumed in a low voice. "Olivia's brand isn't that of a snugglebun. Do you have any idea how it looks to deflate her accomplishments into that of a blushing bride?"

"Deflate?" Rhett tipped his hat back with one hand, still holding on to Olivia with the other. "I saved her bacon in there. I didn't see you charging in to her rescue."

"I should have been prepared to be asked about the future," Olivia said in an apologetic voice that Rhett took an immediate dislike to. "You can't blame him, Kendall."

Kendall made a sound of disagreement deep in her throat.

Rhett took that to mean that she'd blame him for a month of Sundays for whatever the negative fall-out of their meeting was. "Well, one thing's for sure. This cowboy doesn't need to be in any more meetings." They were due in Chicago in two days and he'd gladly wait in the truck with Sonny.

"Finally, something we agree on." Kendall

stomped over to the truck. "Drop me at the airport."

"With pleasure." Rhett released Olivia and got behind the wheel. He sniffed and stared at a too-innocent looking Sonny. "What'd you do?" The next thing he noticed were the chocolate wrappers crumpled on the floorboard.

Sonny covered his mouth with one hand and shook his finger with the other, which Rhett interpreted as a demand for secrecy. "How did it go?"

Olivia climbed into her seat. "It was a disaster and then a cowboy rushed in to save the day."

Kendall made another guttural sound of annoyance and slammed her door.

"All in all, in my experience…" Rhett checked the time, calculating the hours to their next stop in Minneapolis. "…it's about what you'd expect of a Monroe endeavor."

"Look, Rhett. There's another billboard for the turkey capital of the world. I'm putting in a request to visit now." Sonny gave up on finding a radio station that played opera and sat back in his seat, leaving the radio playing static. "You didn't stop for any of the historic markers or the sign that said there was a covered bridge nearby."

"If I stopped for every curiosity along the way, we'd never keep to our schedule." Rhett punched a button on the radio, filling the cab with country music before turning the volume down.

Olivia crunched unhappily on an apple in the back seat.

They'd dropped Kendall off a few minutes ago and were driving on a highway headed toward Minnesota and the next adventure Rhett had planned for them. He hadn't told Olivia what it was, and she hadn't asked. She needed to get her own house in order. The house of Captain Olivia Monroe, which included the management of a competitive racing team. Instead of taking the wheel during her sponsor visit, she'd relied on Rhett and Kendall. The only spokesperson for Olivia should be Olivia.

"You're a rancher." Sonny splayed his fingers through his beard while looking at Rhett. "Where do you think is the best place for a goat farm?"

"You can raise goats wherever you'll be happy." Rhett seemed pleased for the change in subject. "Happy farmer. Happy goats."

Would Sonny be happy on a goat farm?

Olivia shook her head. "Is a goat farm really the right retirement strategy, Sonny?"

Rhett tsked. "You're just saying that because you don't have a retirement strategy of your own."

"And she doesn't like goats," Sonny added. "Not that I think she's ever met one."

Olivia wanted to deny the accusations but nodded because there was truth to what they were saying. "It's just that farms and ranches… They seem like money-pits to me."

"One man's money-pit is another man's treasure," Rhett quipped. "Don't cast stones at Sonny's dream."

To keep herself from doing just that, Olivia stared out the window at rolling hay fields. The trouble was that the more Sonny talked about retirement, the more pressured she felt to fix herself. And the more pressured she felt to fix herself, the more she realized that Sonny wasn't going to be by her side forever. Add that to her taking a back seat while at No Glare Eyewear, and she was in a funk. A crabby, cranky funk.

"How long have you had this dream, Sonny?" Rhett was charming and upbeat, a good travel companion.

Crossing her arms, Olivia sank lower in the seat.

"About two years ago, I was working with a race car driver after he cheated death in a fiery race crash." The details might have been grim, but Sonny recounted them fondly, stroking his beard. "My client had goats on his property in South Carolina. We used to sit in the goat enclosure and talk. It was a joyous time for me, despite the topic of our discussions. The goats were mischievous. They made me laugh. They didn't care what kind of day I had. They just wanted love and a challenging set of platforms to climb on."

"Goats require care and feeding. You don't even own a cat," Olivia pointed out, still sulking.

"I've cared for and fed clients most of my adult life." Sonny half-turned to see her, a soft rebuke in his tone. "If a man wants a goat farm, you should wish him well. It's better than wanting to retire in a seniors' complex in Florida where they have dress codes and visiting hours."

"He's got a point there." Rhett began to grin. "Of course, I hear there are nudist retirement communities in the Keys. They probably don't have dress codes there."

The two men chuckled.

Olivia could feel her crankiness peaking. She drew a deep breath and forced herself to smile. Smiling was supposed to have a positive impact on mood.

Sonny settled back in his seat. "How did you come by your dream of running an adventure tour company, Rhett?"

"Purely by observation." He didn't sound apologetic at all. "A friend of mine bought a unique hang-glider, mostly for his own enjoyment. And then because it was so unusual— taking off from behind a speedboat—people began asking him for rides and they were willing to pay to ride with him. Now, he gets to do what he loves every day and makes money, too."

Olivia tried to just ignore her crankiness, but that didn't really work either. "Is that where we're going next?"

Please say no. Please say no. Please say no.

Rhett shook his head. "No."

Olivia relaxed a little.

"I could do that, too," Sonny said, adding quickly, "Not the hang-gliding. But I could make goats pay for themselves. Their milk can be sold or made into all kinds of products, like cheese, soap or candles. Or I could open a petting zoo."

"Aren't you the man who advises his clients to take small steps?" Rhett grinned.

"That sounds more like work than retirement," Olivia grumbled, feeling guilty for grumbling but who didn't grumble when they had hit their crankiness limit?

"Everybody needs a purpose." Sonny sipped his carrot juice and winced. "If you wake up with one, it keeps you young. Goats are going to be my retirement purpose."

"When are you thinking of retiring?" Olivia hated that she heard desperation in her voice.

"That's for me to decide." Sonny glanced at her over his shoulder, a quick look that was full of quick assessments. "You sound wound up and you look disgruntled. What are you thinking?"

She knew better than to filter. He'd only keep at her until he sensed he'd gotten to the bottom of things. "That I have no retirement strategy. No second act. And no purpose."

"You should meditate," Sonny told her.

Rhett's amused gaze flickered her way in the rearview mirror. Even he knew that she was no good at meditation.

"And while you're meditating," Sonny continued. "You should reflect on the fact that your glass isn't half empty. You have me, you have Rhett and you have a trip that's an adventure of a lifetime."

Olivia rubbed her hands over her face. Everything Sonny mentioned was temporary. She needed to get her bearings.

Sonny gasped. "Rhett, there's another billboard for that space alien–themed restaurant. Surely, we can stop there since they serve food."

"We're not going to pass by there until tomorrow." Rhett's expression looked grim. He was probably worried about his precious schedule.

"Have you eaten there before?" Sonny demanded.

Rhett shook his head. "Do I look like the kind of man who'd stop to eat with aliens?"

"Not *with* aliens." Sonny was working himself up, gesturing madly with his hands. "Alien-themed! Alien-themed! How do you go through life with blinders on to the joyful absurdity around you?"

"For one, I've never been much for absurdity."

While Rhett and Sonny bantered about the importance of stopping to view roadside attractions, Olivia's attention drifted inward, which was no less perplexing than what the men were debating.

CHAPTER TEN

"TWO TICKETS FOR the longest moonlight zipline." At sundown, Rhett slid his credit card across the counter, noticing the man running the place was also featured in a framed newspaper article about the zipline attraction opening nighttime rides. "Can you spare me a few minutes after our ride? I'm from Idaho and considering opening a zipline."

"Sure." The man ran Rhett's credit card. "But I can sum it up for you now—moderate start-up costs, low job requirements with high staff turnover, and if you don't have a strong customer base to draw from, slim to no profit." He laughed, but it was a mirthless one.

Rhett contained his disappointment. There were plenty of mountain slopes in Second Chance on which to build ziplines, but this didn't sound promising.

"That's great insight, sir," Sonny deadpanned from behind Rhett. "Do you have a five-year plan?"

"Sure. It's called survival." The owner handed Rhett's card back, along with accident waivers for himself and Olivia. "Sorry to be touchy. My wife's pregnant, due any day. We opened night rides this year to increase income. I spent most of the spring installing LED lights in trees. And now I'm always here because someone in my night crew always calls in *sick*, because there's a football game or a new movie out." He drew a deep breath, looking like he was trying to compose himself. "It pays the bills, and I can ride just about any time for free, which I love, but it's my life and my lifeline. You get what I mean?"

"He's a slave to the business," Sonny explained unnecessarily.

"I get it." Rhett handed back his ride waiver, torn between disappointment and relief. He moved away from the counter.

"Jamie is around back. She'll fit you with all the necessary equipment." The owner rattled off instructions. "And take you up the hill. Spectators can walk up the stairs to the viewing platform. We have binoculars. They go live with a couple quarters. Or you can enjoy our small café."

Olivia handed her waiver to the stressed

out owner, and then followed Rhett down the stairs. "What's wrong?"

Rhett held on to her arm, drawing her farther away from the ticket counter. "A zipline would be convenient to build, allowing me to be on or near the Bar D in case Cassie or Grandpa had an emergency. But they can also be somewhat tame in terms of a daily adventure."

"Tame in terms of *your* definition of adventure, you mean." Olivia turned toward the twinkle lights and the dense tree-lined slopes above them, which had a fairy tale feel, even he had to admit it looked pretty. "I've never done this before and my heart's pounding a little already. I've seen pictures of people ziplining, but I can't imagine what it's going to be like in the dark."

"Have you done this at night before?" Sonny joined them. He wore a green hoodie that read: I Gotta Be Me.

Rhett shook his head. "But if I was running the place at night, I'd only offer the run down the slowest lines. For safety reasons."

"Safety at the expense of your thrills," Sonny surmised. "That's the decent thing."

Olivia rolled her eyes. "I'm sure your friend Mackenzie stocks items in her general store that she doesn't like but she knows will sell. And she does it because it makes a profit."

"It does seem like you're approaching this business venture with lofty ideals." Sonny ran his fingers over his beard as he studied Rhett. "And one might say that's a formula for failure."

Olivia nodded, softening her tone. "You want to appeal to as many customers as possible. Move on, Rhett."

"Stop. Both of you. Yes, all right. It's all about me and it shouldn't be." Rhett stomped his boot heel a little because it was hard to let go of his own desires influencing his choices. "I spent a lot of time with Holden before we left. He recommends more approachable businesses, like mountain biking and ziplining. But I've got to love it, too. Like Sonny and his goats."

Olivia nudged Sonny with her elbow. "Finally, I see an advantage your goat farm retirement strategy has over Rhett's loose business plans."

Sonny playfully nudged her back. "I knew you'd come around to my way of thinking."

Rhett sighed. "This isn't helpful." He reached up to lift the brim of his cowboy hat, but he'd left it in the truck. He zipped his dark blue sweatshirt instead.

"Do you know what is helpful?" Olivia linked her arm through Rhett's, erasing the sting of her previous opinions. "Getting on with this." She tugged him toward the back, where, presumably, Jamie awaited them.

"You've got your sea legs, Olivia." Sonny followed, chuckling. "You may be afraid, but you're facing this squarely."

"Don't count your chickens before they're hatched," Rhett mumbled. "The hardest part about ziplining is stepping off the platform into the open air." He might have doubts about what type of business he'd end up running, but there were still days before he had to decide.

The zipline assistant, Jamie, started assembling the equipment they'd need. Helmets, gloves and harnesses, handing them over to the couple to put on before they left base camp. Jamie briefed them on the operation of the seats they used for ziplining, including braking operation. Olivia requested a second review.

"Promise me one thing, cowboy." Sonny called Rhett over, shoving his hands in his hoodie pocket.

"Only one thing?" This trip had been loaded with requirements and make-goods.

"If Olivia loses her nerve at the top, give her a thirty-second hug." Sonny gave Rhett's arm a little shake.

"Why are we having this conversation? She'll be fine." She looked calm and collected with Jamie.

Sonny shook Rhett's arm again. "She's going to sit in a little chair and barrel down the mountain in the dark. This isn't a romantic sleigh ride through the snow. Promise me you'll give her an emotional support hug if needed."

Rhett took stock of Olivia's body language. She didn't fidget or otherwise give away she was nervous. "Is she afraid of the dark?"

Sonny frowned. "I don't think so."

"Sonny." Rhett took the old man by both arms. "Go sneak an ice cream and try not to worry. She'll be fine."

"Hold her hand on the ride up, just in case," Sonny whispered as Olivia headed toward them.

"All aboard for the top." Jamie beckoned Rhett and Olivia to a four-seater ATV. "I'll take you up to the top platform. From there, you'll need to listen to our platform staffer."

"Rhett," Sonny said, making the high sign from a few feet away.

"Got it." Rhett buckled his seat belt and then took Olivia's gloved hand in his. "Are you up to this?"

"You're not getting rid of me that easily." She gave him a strained smile.

The whine of the ATV's engine prohibited discussion on the winding road up to the highest platform. Jamie parked near the launch platform.

"Look at all the lights." Olivia stepped out first. "I bet during the day you can see the entire valley up here."

"You can." Jamie pointed toward the stairs. "Adam is expecting you. Enjoy the ride."

Rhett took Olivia's hand again as they walked toward the stairs.

She gently extricated herself. "I heard Sonny. You don't have to coddle me."

She was always so stubborn. Rhett smiled and captured her hand once more. "Maybe I'm nervous. It's my first nighttime ride." The tall pines, the sparkly lights. It was romantic.

"And you're just being nice because it's our second date." She gave him an impish grin. "You live a deep fantasy life, Rhett Diaz."

"One you bought into at No Glare Eyewear today. Hinting that we were getting married?"

She gasped. "That was you!"

He shrugged. "They bought into it. Sven will be crushed when we break up."

They reached the platform. Adam waved them closer.

Olivia's steps faltered as they walked along the railing. "It's a long way down."

"You'll be fine," Rhett reassured her. "This is a side-by-side experience. I'll be right there next to you." But not close enough to hold her hand. He lowered his voice so that Adam couldn't hear. "Do you need a hug?"

"No."

"Then come on. The queen of the ocean can't be afraid of a little zipline," Rhett teased.

Her caramel eyes lacked enthusiasm and her untamable curls were squashed under a helmet. "Land has never been my element. Just look at what happened yesterday while we were mountain biking. I'm still sore."

Rhett tsked. "Hey, hardheaded people like us try everything at least once."

"I've been called hardheaded, but..." she said slowly, looking toward base camp far below them.

This wasn't the woman who'd sailed solo to Canada. Nor was it the racing boat captain Rhett had heard about in town. And yet, she wasn't a timid mouse, either. He wanted to see the side of her Kendall kept talking about. And he could only think of one way to do it. Some people had liquid courage and some people needed a good kiss.

"You know what you need," Rhett said in a low voice, letting his gaze drift to her lips.

Oh, he knew she knew.

"A kiss is the last thing I need right now. Thank you very much." The corner of her mouth was tilting upward, but she quickly frowned instead.

"I was going to say that you need a dare," he improvised.

"You've already dared me to do this. I need a bargain." She turned to him. "If I do this, we have to eat at the alien-themed diner tomorrow."

"All right, but I draw the line at stopping to see the largest ball of twine." He drew her forward. "We'll take the first three legs together. But on the last leg, it's a race to the bottom platform."

She was dragging her heels in those black-and-white sneakers. "How can it be a race?"

"My additional weight will naturally carry me down faster and I won't brake until the last minute."

"This is where I remind you that we aren't

responsible for injuries involved with irresponsible behavior or lack of braking," Adam said irritably. "Are you going to be a problem, sir?"

"No." Rhett grinned, thinking that he'd always been a problem. And to prove it, he kissed Olivia.

BEST. KISS. EVER.

In the afterglow, Olivia let Adam clip her harness into the flimsy chair and its pulley, forgetting for a moment that she was about to put her life at risk, no matter the safeguards. "What was that kiss for?"

"To throw off the competition, of course." Rhett's grin seemed brighter than the lights in the canopy overhead. "It's a race. Are you rattled?"

"I don't think so." Rhett looked so different without his cowboy hat. He looked like a man who could fit into her world. He gave her confidence. She managed a smile as the attendant rattled off the same instructions Jamie had given her at base camp, not really paying attention. She was still thinking about that kiss.

"You're not rattled?" Rhett's dark brows had come down the way a man's did when his version of a kiss was different than hers.

Except in this case, their versions most

likely jived. It had been a magnificent kiss. When their lips touched, it was like the synchronicity of a classic sailboat on calm waters with a solid breeze.

"It wasn't the worst thing ever." Olivia forced herself to continue the charade of nonchalance. "But you broke one of our rules about public displays of affection."

"Nothing we talked about was set in stone," he said gruffly. "And besides, that was a fantasy second-date kiss. No harm, no foul."

"They aren't just guidelines." She stared at him from beneath her lashes, shy when she'd never been so before. Because he made her feel feminine and protected. "There should be no kissing. And if there is kissing…"

I hope there's more kissing.

"If this is how adults date, I'll stick with high school drama," Adam said, having strapped them both in. "Are you ready?"

No. There were too many shadows. The sparkling lights in the trees didn't look so sparkling at the moment.

"Yes," Rhett said with complete confidence, and a hot glance toward Olivia's lips.

Olivia gulped and tried for bravery. "Yes?"

The metal wire could snap. The trolley holding her chair could fall apart. Her harness rigging could fail. The more Olivia thought about the dangers, the shallower her breath.

What am I doing? I already died once.

"No guts. No glory." Rhett pushed himself off the platform, barreling ahead of her, but not far, because her latent competitive spirit didn't allow her not to follow. "Yee-haw!" He stretched his arms out to either side like wings. "Do you feel it?"

"Feel what?" Olivia shouted back, trying to be heard over the whistle of the metal trolley on its guidewire.

"The wind in your face. The rush of adrenaline. Your pulse pounding." He grinned, an expression barely visible in the darkness. "This is what it means to feel alive. Yee-haw!"

She hated him.

It didn't matter that he was a great kisser. He loved this and it was not her cup of tea! She felt so...so...afraid.

They were speeding over the tops of trees. The wind chafed her cheeks. Her stomach had dropped the moment she'd left the platform. She was hollow, a vacant shell of a woman.

And yet...

Rhett was crowing nearby, clearly enjoying every minute. The wind was crisp and clean, not with the salty tang of the ocean, but with the earthy evergreen of the deep forest. And she felt…

Unlike a rollercoaster, there weren't hills and valleys. They were traveling at a steady rate.

Olivia breathed in, filling her lungs with air, filling her heart with confidence. "I'm not going to fall," she muttered.

"What was that?" Rhett was grinning from ear-to-ear.

"I'm not going to fall!" she shouted at him, smiling just a little, because this strange feeling wasn't new but the germination of it was.

They neared the next stop, descent slowed by slack and her pulling the brake handle.

"You've got the hang of it," Rhett said to her when their feet were on the platform. "Admit it. That was fun."

"It was fun," Olivia agreed. "Not entirely tame."

"You should try it over a ravine or river in daylight." Rhett's eyes lit up.

Olivia supposed her eyes had once done the same when she talked about boat racing.

The attendant hooked them onto the next run. Olivia launched herself into the air this time with only slight trepidation.

"Hey." Rhett swung out at almost the same

time. "You didn't need a kiss to bolster your courage?"

Oh, this man.

Olivia shook her head, shouting, "The queen of the ocean has her own courage."

"I like that!"

She liked him, she realized. Perhaps too much.

CHAPTER ELEVEN

WHEN OLIVIA CAME down from her hotel room late that night for a sweet treat, she found Rhett asleep on a lobby couch in the corner. The hotel hadn't had any rooms to spare when they checked in. He'd probably sought the couch to escape Sonny's snores.

Something was changing inside Olivia. She could feel it, unfurling like a long unused mainsail as she headed into the wind. She'd managed her fears twice in two days. If she hadn't come on this trip, she'd still be testing herself on a small dinghy on a small lake in a small town in Idaho.

There was something about ziplining that was reminiscent of sailing. All that wind. All that speed.

Her desire to sail again was returning, like a seedling growing in a kitchen window, too weak to be put out in the elements yet.

And she owed it all to an aging sports psychologist and a handsome cowboy with a smart mouth and a scorching skill at kissing. She wouldn't have come out of her shell without both.

But…a cowboy?

She stared down at Rhett in wonder.

Her cowboy didn't sleep in a tight ball the way she did, as if he were shutting out the world. Nor was he lying there as if he'd stopped to take a break and succumbed to heavy lids. He slept spread-eagled across the cushions as if he was staking his claim—one arm over his head, one leg on the couch back. His black hat covered his face.

She rarely had a chance to study Rhett without receiving a heated glance or superior smirk in return. But she knew the expressions of his moods—the broad smile indicating all-out-joy, the knitting of dark brows over something that annoyed him, the slight tilt to one corner of his mouth when he was thinking about kissing her.

She was convinced Rhett thought about kissing her a lot.

And…*likewise*.

Which made her curious. Was Rhett dreaming about kissing her? His slumbering expression would tell-all.

Unable to quell her curiosity, Olivia knelt

beside him and gingerly lifted his hat brim to peek at his face in slumber.

Before she realized what was happening, big hands circled her arms and she was swung upward, landing sprawled across Rhett. His cowboy hat slid beneath the coffee table, along with her wallet, phone and room key.

"It's not nice to spy on folk," Rhett said slowly, arms slipping around her. "Unless you had something in mind." Those dark eyebrows rose and lowered provocatively.

He needs to know who's boss.

Olivia's breath caught. Rhett was a force she could never control. Unlike her racing crew, he wouldn't bend to her will or follow her command without question. She'd always been the alpha in her relationships, directing the pace and the terms of engagement. And Rhett…

He scares me.

Not because he might hurt her feelings, but because she couldn't just tell him she wanted to eat sushi for dinner and expect him to go along with it. She normally didn't allow people in her life who were difficult. But with Rhett… Maybe difficult was okay.

Olivia extricated herself from his hold as gracefully as possible. "I thought you had earplugs."

"Yep." He stretched those long arms before rolling onto his side and propping his head on his hand. "But my earplugs need earplugs. Why'd you wake me?" His mouth tilted up ever-so-slightly in one corner.

Part of Olivia regretted missing out on kisses. But part of Olivia—the part that had been broken in the accident—abhorred the thought of relinquishing control on any aspect of her life any more than she had to.

Olivia collected her things from under the coffee table, along with his hat. "I woke you because you were sleeping in the lobby." And because she was annoyed with the situation—him being too much for her to handle—she settled his hat on her head. "Do I need another reason?"

"Yep." His gaze dipped to her mouth. "My hat looks good on you."

"Right." *That's why you're staring at my mouth.*

The sensible thing to do would be to return his hat and move along.

Olivia couldn't move, not a muscle. She wasn't being sensible.

Sensible doesn't win races.

"Command wins races," she murmured. Command, action, forward progress. She had none.

"Command won't get you kisses, which is clearly the reason you woke me up, darlin'." Rhett reclaimed his hat, lay back down and placed it over his face. "Go sneak your sweets from the snack bar. Remember to bring me coffee at six. Full-strength, not decaf. We've got to hit the road by seven."

He'd allowed her to pawn off her decaf coffee to him a few times on this trip, all under the guise of a mix-up of their cups. She felt bad about that, but not bad enough not to give up on her messaging. Sonny needed her support. "We should all be drinking decaf."

Rhett snorted. Or perhaps snored.

Olivia reached for his hat, needing an angle where she came out of this encounter the boss, and reluctant to give up on the conversation until she had one.

Or a kiss.

Startled by the thought, Olivia snatched her hand back. "I have to helm my own ship."

"Plenty of time for that tomorrow," Rhett grumbled.

"Where are we going tomorrow? What adventures do you have planned?" Suddenly, she needed to know.

He slid his hat up so that he could see her.

"You don't want me to tell you. You'll lie awake all night worrying about it."

"I won't." She stuck her chin out.

He tsked, clearly not buying it. "When we started on this trip and I was debating whether to turn right or left, you chose the safe route."

She didn't like the business-like look in his eye. "Are you giving me a choice tomorrow?"

"I don't want to because I get the impression you'll over-think it, but Sonny thinks I should because you like to know what lies ahead."

It warmed her heart that both men knew her that well. "Tell me."

"My first choice is white water rafting."

Olivia's breath caught in her throat. *Water. Being tossed about. Being tossed under water.* "And the alternative?"

"Hang-gliding. My friend Tad has a ranch south of here on the way to Chicago. Fair warning though. He launches from the Mississippi River behind a tow boat, kind of like parasailing."

Water, water everywhere.

She shuddered, trying to recover quickly so he wouldn't notice. "Tad's the one you talked about? The friend who started a business doing something he loved." The friend who apparently hadn't compromised with anything tame, like slow ziplines. "Maybe even the friend who was there when you made that no-dating bet?"

"Yes." Rhett's gaze softened—oh, he'd noticed her shudder, all right—but that tender look couldn't calm the turmoil inside her. "I know water is your weakness, Olivia. You can sit tomorrow out. But if you've got the stomach to fly…" His gaze grew distant. "…hanggliding with eagles is really something."

He was turning out to be something. "Sonny bet you I'd do everything." She forced herself to smile. "I can't let him down. Whatever money he's saved needs to go toward his goat farm. But you knew that, didn't you? That's why you didn't tell me what you had planned."

His expression grew guarded. "I really did think you'd sleep better not knowing."

He had that right. She'd lost her appetite, too. "I need time to think about this. Can I let you know what I decide in the morning?"

"Sure. As long as you don't bring me a cup of decaf when you wake me at six a.m."

"Good morning," Sonny greeted Rhett when he emerged from the shower the morning after ziplining. The old man sat at the foot of his bed. "I have questions."

"Don't you always." Rhett stuffed his shaving kit into his suitcase and then zipped it up.

"Your bed wasn't slept in," Sonny pointed out.

Rhett sighed. He was tired of crashing on hotel couches, and just plain tired in general. He'd had an especially rough night last night, worrying about Olivia's decision—white water rafting or hang-gliding from a river launch. He hadn't made it easy on her, but both tour companies were premium experiences.

As promised, Olivia had woken him up early, handing him a cup of coffee and accompanying him back upstairs, drinking her own. He'd bet anything she wasn't drinking decaf. Regardless, she hadn't told him what she'd decided, and he hadn't asked.

"Why didn't you just stay the night in Olivia's room to begin with?" Sonny asked baldly. "Why the pretense of staying with me?"

"You've got that all wrong." Rhett sat on the still-made bed to put his boots on, explaining about Sonny's snoring and over-booked hotels.

"And here I thought your relationship was turning into something real." Sonny stroked his white beard. "We need to do something about this."

"I think you need a prescription to get a

sleep apnea machine." Rhett stood, settling his cowboy hat on his wet hair.

"I'm not talking about my snoring. I'm talking about you and Olivia." Sonny shook himself as if this should be clear to Rhett.

"Your focus should be on Olivia's well-being, not playing matchmaker when we're playing make-believe." Rhett set his suitcase on the floor, anxious to know which way he was headed today.

"They're intertwined. Don't you see?" Sonny stood in his path to the door. "Olivia's never let a man get close. She's been afraid she'd get distracted by love and everything that comes with it. Instead of using this experience to acknowledge there's more to her and to life than being a racing boat captain, she's trying to suppress all that emotion. Except when she's with you."

"You can't believe that a few clasped hands—" and a few rare kisses "—make any difference in her personal life."

"You're right. I can't. I long for the day when she doesn't suppress her emotions."

"She shows plenty of emotion toward you."

"Me, openly, yes. And you, covertly."

Maybe not so covertly if their late night discussions were any indication. Rhett could swear she'd wanted him to kiss her last night before he'd told her what he had in store for her today.

"She needs to start speaking about the accident."

Rhett shook his head. "She'd rather talk about anything but that."

"She won't be able to live a public life without questions following her about it. It doesn't matter if she races or not. She's a Monroe. They don't tend to lead quiet lives out of the spotlight."

Rhett agreed. But what could he do? He had things mapped out in his head. This trip had an ending in a few days. And then he'd go back to Second Chance without her.

There was a knock on the door.

Sonny didn't move. "I'm not asking you to do anything rash. I'm only asking you to reach out, as one human being to another, and make her see how wonderful relationships can be."

"Dead-end relationships can't be wonderful. They aren't real." He grabbed the old man's suitcase and headed for the door, unable to last another minute without knowing what activity Olivia had chosen for the day.

He flung open the door.

Olivia was already halfway to the elevators.

"Come on. If we hurry, we can have lunch at that alien-themed restaurant before we head over to Tad's."

Tad's. Hang-gliding.

Yee-haw!

CHAPTER TWELVE

"LOOK AT ALL those horses." Sonny rolled his window down, which sent hot, humid wind into the truck. "Your friend ranches, too?"

"Yep." Rhett checked on Olivia in the rear-view mirror.

The wind from Sonny's window blew Olivia's short curls up, down and around, but did nothing to loosen her taut expression. She'd been closed off since they'd eaten a lunch of alien-themed sandwiches and salads.

Hang-gliding. Rhett was ecstatic. And feeling guilty. He could completely understand Olivia's hesitation. Didn't mean he was going to back out of hang-gliding and choose something she and Holden would deem tamer.

He drove fast over the smooth gravel driveway toward the Flying T. His friend Tad must be doing well with his hang-glider tours because Rhett noticed a lot of improvements to the property since his last visit—new fencing, a new roof on the red barn ahead and more stock.

"Baby horses!" Sonny exclaimed, hanging his arms out the window like a little kid. "This is almost as good as baby goats. Can we pet them?"

"We'll see." Rhett glanced over his shoulder to smile at Olivia.

She loosened up enough to smile back. "In all the time we spent in Second Chance, Sonny, you didn't mention goats once."

"I brought my goat farming books to read every night. It's just that my most recent hospital stay made me realize retirement is closer than I thought." The old man gasped, pointing to the next pasture. "Goat sighting!"

A white goat with horns grazed in a pasture next to a set of wooden platforms of varying heights designed to keep mischievous goats occupied.

And then they were pulling into the ranch yard—a large area bounded by the barn, a white two-story house, and a lean-to that sheltered a speedboat and had room for more. Rhett parked next to a fancy rig hooked up to a long multi-horse trailer.

"Blackwell Ranch Horse Training. Eagle Springs, Wyoming," Olivia read the rig's branding from the door. "They're a long way from home, too."

"Looks like Tad's in the market for some fancy horse flesh." Rhett knew Nash Blackwell by reputation. His horses were highly regarded in the rodeo world and commanded a premium price.

Tad hobbled out from the barn to meet them, wearing a clunky white walking boot that came up nearly to his knee on one leg. He led a compact bay mare. "Perfect timing, Rhett. I need your opinion on a horse for my daughter Jazzy."

Not having seen Tad for over a year, Rhett hadn't known he was married, much less that he had a daughter old enough to ride. He covered his surprise with a hearty, "Sure!" They could talk specifics later.

Introductions were made.

Before anyone could ask what happened to Tad's leg, a spritely little girl of about ten or eleven with thick black puff ponytails ran out of the barn. "Dad, I did all my chores. Can you just tell Nash Blackwell that we're buying Beasley?" She hugged the small mare's neck.

"Jazzy, I'm deferring the decision to my friend Rhett." Tad pointed at Rhett. He may have been in a mobile cast, but he was able to tap dance the difficult decisions with finesse.

Jazzy clasped her hands in front of her chest and beamed at Rhett. "Pretty please, can Daddy buy me this horse?"

The horse in question held her head high, sniffing the air and swiveling her ears, interested in her new surroundings, but not skittish.

"Look at that face," Olivia whispered, moving closer to Rhett and pointing toward Jazzy. "Whatever you do, don't say no."

"And don't ask how much it costs," Sonny whispered, moving in from the other side. "You're not paying."

"Nice spread," Olivia said to Tad.

"Thanks." Tad tipped his hat. "If you like it, the ranch next door is for sale."

"Do they have goats?" Sonny perked up.

"Back to me and Beasley," Jazzy cut in, twirling around like a dancer in the middle of them all, even though she wore blue jeans and cowboy boots. "Pretty please with sugar on top. *Please-please-please.*"

"Hey, Tad. Uh…" Rhett assessed the little girl's sweet face against his friend's hopeful expression. He didn't want to disappoint her. But he didn't want to bankrupt his friend, either. "What's in it for me if I make this decision, Tad?"

"If it was up to me, I'd bargain for goat yoga." Sonny stroked his beard and grinned at Jazzy. "That is, if your goat knows how to do yoga."

"Goat yoga," Olivia murmured with a slight smile. "There's a business opportunity with low start-up costs."

Rhett nodded. They'd discussed the large investment required to start a mountain biking business on the trip this morning. But that didn't solve the decision hanging in the ranch yard.

"Mr. Nubbins only knows how to eat and climb on his jungle gym." Jazzy latched on to Tad's hand and squeezed. And then she stopped and stared at Sonny. "Are you Santa?"

"I'm *not* the man in red. Just look at my shirt." Sonny held out the front hem of his hot pink T-shirt, presumably so the girl could read: Be a Unicorn. "If I was Santa, my shirt would say: Are You Naughty or Nice?" He knelt down to her level. "But I have an in with the jolly man. Do you have a request?"

Jazzy's head bobbed up and down. "Yes, sir. I want a horse so I can be a breakaway champion. In truth, I want Beasley." She beamed at Sonny.

Sonny blinked. "She's got one powerful grin, doesn't she?"

"Yep," Tad said. "Kind of makes you want to reach for your wallet, don't it?"

Rhett nodded. Jazzy's grin made a person not want to disappoint her. Ever.

He felt a sudden burst of empathy for Tad.

"Thaddeus Timmons!" a pregnant woman called from the front porch. She had the same black hair as Jazzy, but instead of twirling, she stood with her hands on her hips, and instead of cowboy boots, she wore bright red sneakers. "It's hotter than blazes outside. Invite your guests in for a cool drink and then make your decision so Nash can be on his way."

Tad chuckled. "That's my Sharon. As straight-talking as an emergency room admitting nurse, something Rhett and I know a lot about." He extended an arm toward the house. "If anyone's in need of air conditioning or a glass of water, head on in. Not including you, Rhett. We've still got a decision to make."

"Sonny, that's our cue." Olivia dragged the old man inside, leaving Rhett with his friend, a little charmer and a decision to be made.

Not that Rhett had it in mind to say no. Any

Blackwell trained animal was worth the price. But he didn't want to agree before he had the okay from Tad. There had to be a reason his friend was reluctant to pull the trigger on the purchase.

Jazzy tugged on Tad's arm. "Say yes, Dad. Please…"

"We need to ride her first, Jazzy." Tad gave Rhett a rueful smile.

And there it was.

"He's right, Jazzy." Rhett took the lead rope from Tad. The mare moved along toward Rhett with barely a swish of her tail. She didn't nip or crowd him. She seemed to be a good-natured thing. "Jazzy, you never buy a truck without driving it and you never buy a horse without riding it." And it was never wise to put a child on a new horse without an adult testing it out first. "What happened to your leg, Tad? If this wasn't an animal from the Blackwell Ranch, I'd say you're pulling my leg about your injury and want me to ride a hellion for you."

"Always the man with a joke." Tad shook his head. "This boot here is no lie. I fell out of the hay loft." He tipped back the brim of his cowboy hat, grin widening as he held both arms out in front of him, parallel to the ground. "Stuck that landing like a gymnast, all my weight on my heels. Snapped my Achilles on the right side."

"I think it hurt." Jazzy drew Beasley's nose down to her level, stroking behind her ears. "But Dad swallowed all his bad words. Mom told the nurse in Minneapolis that he was a gentleman."

Rhett figured it was a good sign that the horse accepted the attention from Jazzy as if it were her due. "Geez, Tad. I thought all that dirt you ate from riding bulls taught you to drop and roll."

"I had a little girl to impress." Tad settled his hat more firmly on his head.

"Dad…"

"I'm getting to it, pumpkin." Tad put his hands on his hips. "I need someone experienced to put Beasley through her paces."

"I figured as much." Rhett ran his hand over Beasley's withers. "The reason for you being flexible with my last minute visit now becomes clear."

The mare blew a raspberry, turning her head slightly to see Rhett.

"Just checking out your lines, Beasley." Rhett ran his hand over her back and haunches.

"A girl north of St. Paul wants her, too." Jazzy kissed Beasley's velvety nose. "Dad says

Nash doesn't usually train horses that aren't cutters, so Beasley is special. And she's mine."

Rhett took a moment to study the mare's form. Her confirmation was excellent. And given her temperament, if she was as good with a rider as she was on the halter, she was worth a pretty penny. He extended a hand toward Tad. "I'll do it for a free hang-glider ride."

"Like you were going to pay me anyway." Despite his belief, Tad shook on the deal.

Rhett took the bay's lead rope and headed toward the barn. "Let's get her saddled up."

Jazzy whooped and ran ahead into the barn.

A few minutes later, Rhett took to the saddle with a lariat and rode into the ranch's small arena. Tad shut the gate behind him. The men had decided a rope was needed for this test ride since Jazzy's rodeo event required her to throw a rope while chasing a calf.

Holding a snug rein, Rhett swung the lasso to the right side, making it hum. Beasley trembled, prancing a little as if ready to bolt after a calf, although there were none in the arena. Still holding her back, Rhett twirled the lariat over his head. Beasley barely shifted her weight. "She seems to have nerves of steel." The rope hadn't fazed her.

"See, Dad? She's perfect." Jazzy sat on the

top rung of the arena, a safety helmet strapped on her head.

"Perfectly expensive," Tad grumbled, setting out two lawn chairs next to a small cooler he'd brought out first.

"You always tell Mom that buying the best is the best value." Jazzy laughed, clearly smitten with both her father and the horse.

Keeping firm control on the bay, Rhett backed her up and turned her in a tight circle, as if readying her for a starting gate. Again, she obeyed without trying to fight his commands. Again, she seemed primed and ready to go.

Rhett took her for a controlled gallop around the arena. She had a smooth gait. Although Rhett wasn't competing anymore and the mare was a little small for him, he had a bit of envy. He'd never had a Nash Blackwell horse. But then again, he hadn't had the need for a good cutting horse.

"Can I try?" Unable to contain herself anymore, Jazzy climbed down.

"Ask your dad." But Rhett dismounted, prepared to let her ride. "She meets my approval."

"Daddy?"

"Go ahead." Tad sat down and waved her

off. "But curb all that energy. Horses need a steady hand."

After Jazzy skillfully rode Beasley around the arena, Rhett joined Tad, sitting in the empty chair beside him. "She's good."

"She is that," Tad reluctantly agreed. "Sharon says it's because she's taken dance classes since she was four. Apparently, dancing teaches body control which translates to advantages in other sports." He dug two beers from the ice chest. "You couldn't do me a favor and find something wrong with that mare? Beasley costs as much as the new car Sharon wants."

There was nothing like a cold beer on a hot day. Rhett drank deeply. "What are you worried about? You said the hang-gliding business has taken off."

"It has, now that I've got a business partner and speedboat driver in Sharon." Tad gestured with his beer toward the tree line behind the house where the Mississippi River flowed. "It's been my busiest summer yet. But you know how rodeo is. You travel to compete, and you compete on the weekends."

"And that's when you have the most hang-gliding business." Rhett chewed on that for a bit. He'd known any adventure business he pursued would have its highs and lows during the week and be seasonal. But he was single. No big deal. Until he factored in a rig like Tad had required two people to operate—the boat driver and a certified hang-glider pilot.

His gaze drifted toward the house where Olivia had gone. He knew that wasn't the answer. But the more he got to know Olivia and the more they kept up the deception that they were a couple, the more he was getting used to her being part of his daily life.

"Sharon's willing to truck Jazzy to events, which I can work around. There's a kid nearby I hire to drive the boat." Tad interrupted Rhett's train of thought. "But Sharon's pregnant, so everything's gotta change anyway. It's just that Jazzy's good, Rhett. And when a kid's good, you need to travel so she can get better, because competing gives a kid confidence to reach for their dreams, you know."

"And maybe the confidence to buy expensive horses." Rhett sipped his beer, smiling a little.

"Just when I thought we had everything all figured out, it's all changing."

"But it's all good, right?"

Tad nodded. "Except that I feel like my father back when you and I started out. Worried that I'm pushing her. Worried that I'm not pushing her enough. Scared to death that she'll discover boys in a year, and we'll have invested all this time and money on what turns out to be a hobby when those resources might best be devoted toward increasing the hang-gliding business."

Rhett clapped a hand on Tad's shoulder. "And then there's the new baby."

"A boy." Tad grinned. "And the cycle will start all over again."

Rhett shouldn't have been envious. He liked his single life and where he was headed now.

But he was envious of Tad. And it wasn't just because of a Blackwell horse.

"You have a charming home, Sharon." Olivia had enjoyed the brief tour of the downstairs Sharon had given of the hundred-year-old farmhouse. "You've done a great job with the updates."

Sonny sat in a brown antique wingback chair in the living room, head tilted back, eyes closed, breathing deeply. Nash Blackwell, the horse trainer, was out on the back patio. He sat in a wicker chair facing the tree line and the river, talking on his phone. Rhett and Tad were outside with Jazzy and the horse.

"It's beginning to feel like my home now

that the remodel is mostly finished." Sharon led Olivia into the kitchen, where they sat at a round oak table. The kitchen cabinets were white Shaker. The backsplash white subway tile. The real color was Sharon. She wore a blue-flowered maternity blouse and loose navy trousers, and radiated an energy that was captivating. "I convinced Tad that we needed windows in here. There's no sense living within sight of the Mississippi if you don't take advantage of every view."

Olivia followed the direction of her gaze. "You have your own dock." A large wooden one with a speedboat tied up at the end.

"Tad runs his hang-gliding business from here. You can't quite spot it, but we have a little office next to the dock and a picnic area, too. Our goal was to designate areas for clients versus family."

Rhett should probably be hearing this. "Sounds like you guys are thinking ahead."

"And keeping busy." Sharon picked up a glass of water, gold and diamond wedding set sparkling on her finger. "It's a rush now to establish the business before the baby comes. And try to figure out this junior rodeo piece for Jazzy."

Marriage. Babies. Olivia felt envious. What

was happening to her? While she sorted out her feelings, she kept the conversation rolling. "How long have you been married?"

"Since last winter. I'm due this Christmas." Sharon glowed, dark eyes shining with happiness.

Olivia was reminded of Rhett and how sometimes, for the briefest of moments, she felt as if he was all she needed.

"Life is so different out here," Sharon continued. "And time passes quickly when you're in love."

"You aren't from around here?"

Sharon turned in her chair, extending one leg so that Olivia could see her bright red sneakers. "No. I'm not a cowgirl. Jazzy and I were driving to visit my uncle last winter. There was a huge, unexpected snowstorm that stranded us out on the highway. If Tad hadn't come along… Well, we might have run out of gas and…" She heaved a satisfied sigh. "I used to fly supply planes for the Air Force, most recently out of Texas. Moving here has been a huge adjustment."

"You gave up flying for love?" She'd given up a career, no less.

"Not exactly." Sharon's smile didn't dim.

"I'd already retired and had accepted a job flying for an airline out of Dallas."

"You must love hang-gliding." Olivia glanced toward the dock, taking in more details. The speedboat had what looked like a trailer on the back and on top of the trailer was a hang-glider.

"You want the truth?" Sharon chuckled, tucking wisps of black hair behind her ears. "I like to fly a powerful machine that responds to my commands. The first and only time Tad took me up, I screamed non-stop. We were dipping and banking and I had no control over any of it. I was strapped in and riding above Tad. Just a passenger. I had to trust him. It was awful." She ran a hand over her belly, and everything about her seemed to soften. "And then…we flew across the river above a patch of protected forest and suddenly there were eagles flying with us. It was like… It was like we were one of them, soaring above everything, as if we were meant to be there and meant to be together." Sharon drank some water. "Have you ever felt anything like that? The soaring, I mean."

"It sounds a little like sailing." Fear tried to scale Olivia's throat. But she took a deep breath and swallowed it back down. "I... I used to sail."

"As a passenger or..."

"I was at the helm. Like you. Always in control." Riding the thin line between excellence and danger. "I should have known my limits." She hated that Rhett was right. She'd let her crew down, not just herself. She was ashamed to think that she hadn't answered their attempts to contact her.

"No one is always in control." Sharon's gaze grew distant again. "I retired from service because..." She drew a deep breath, much as Olivia had earlier when she'd admitted to sailing. Sharon connected her gaze with Olivia's. "I've read all these books about conquering fear. I know I'm supposed to just say what happened out loud often until it becomes easier. But still, when I try to, the words get all tangled in my throat."

"No rush. I understand where you're coming from." And Olivia admired Sharon for her courage to admit even a hint of her internal struggle to a relative stranger. She couldn't do the same.

But I should.

"Thanks, I..." Sharon sat up taller. "The long and short of it is that one of my engines failed while I was on a combined forces exercise over the ocean. My crew and I… We made it back. But… But after that, when I flew, all I could think of was Jazzy and what would happen to her if I didn't return home from work one day." Sharon's body seemed to draw in on itself in a way Olivia was all too familiar with. "I retired, and before I started the new job, we drove up here. The rest is history." She fell back in her chair.

"You found your second act." That's what Rhett was encouraging Olivia to do. And it was what Rhett himself was trying to do. And Sonny.

"Enough deep talk." Sharon took their glasses to the sink and refilled them with water. "I haven't met Rhett before, but I know he and Tad were close for years on the rodeo circuit. They shared a love of extreme sports. Rhett's even certified to operate a hang-glider."

"Really."

Sharon nodded, bringing their full glasses back to the table. "He's going to take you up today."

Olivia nodded, swallowing thickly. He'd told her as much.

"And when he does, let me give you a word of advice."

Olivia leaned forward.

"It's okay to be afraid. And to scream. No one but Rhett will hear you above the speedboat's engine before you release and fly." Sharon's eyes sparkled. "It's really glorious, if you can get past the fact that you aren't in control of anything. Your faith is one hundred percent in your man."

"One hundred percent," Olivia murmured. Not sure if she could put that much trust in anyone.

Especially when Rhett wasn't really her man.

CHAPTER THIRTEEN

OLIVIA WADED INTO the Mississippi River up to her ankles, testing the cool waters.

"It isn't often that one is given the chance to soar with eagles." Sonny waded into the water next to her. "If you're experiencing any anxiety about getting on a speedboat or flying through the air, you need to take slow, deep breaths and think how good the sun feels on your skin."

Olivia did as he advised, closing her eyes and trying not to listen to the men farther up-river preparing the speedboat with the hang-glider mounted on a separate platform hitched to the back of the boat. Sharon and Jazzy had stayed back at the ranch proper to see the horse trainer off and get Beasley settled.

"It's a beautiful day to sit on the riverbank and watch the other boats pass us by." Sonny splashed his legs in the water. "Looks like there's a sailboat out there. We could watch Rhett fly in the shade of those trees over there. He won't think any less of you, his special someone, if you take a pass on this experience."

Am I his special someone?

In her mind's eye, she saw him glance her way, flashing her a smile.

Am I his special someone?

The affirmative answer, though she dared not say it out loud, made her feel cherished.

"I'm not sitting this out, Sonny. I want my life back." Olivia opened her eyes, thinking about Sharon's experience on the hang-glider.

I know what to expect.

"I've never been a spectator, at least… I wasn't until…" She had to say it, just as Sharon had done. "…not until my boat…capsized. Not until *I* risked my life and the lives of my crew." Tears stung her eyes. That had been a big admission. She blinked them back. "But knowing I won't back out and stepping up to it are two different things. I just… I just need a minute." An hour. Maybe even a day or two.

"Okay." Sonny nodded slowly. "We may be standing still but this is forward progress."

"Progress." Olivia placed a hand over her stomach, which was currently wheeling like the eagles far up in the sky. "Toward whatever. It might not be the same life you're helping me rebuild, Sonny, but it'll be mine."

It was the first time she'd admitted out loud that she might not be able to go back to piloting a racing yacht. Just thinking about the repercussions of choosing that path made her head spin. She'd have to legally cut ties with the team and her sponsors. She'd have to admit to the world and all her fans and followers that she couldn't race anymore.

That felt an awful lot like failure.

Captain Olivia Monroe would reject failure and get back to sea, swallowing her fears until they were buried so deep inside of her that no one could see. But plain Olivia Monroe…she'd barely progressed beyond fearing her own shadow on the water.

Rhett admitted his failures. He hadn't always won.

I didn't always win either.

But she'd strutted around as if she had.

"Tell me what you're thinking," Sonny prompted.

"I used to captain a racing boat. My sailboats flew across the ocean at pulse-pounding speed." Some of her sponsors, like Sven from No Glare Eyewear, had lost their lunch when she'd barely reached top speed. "I let it all go to my head."

"That happens sometimes." Being a sports

psychologist, Sonny would know. "Everyone needs someone to keep them humble."

"Someone…" Her gaze found Rhett on the speedboat. "When I was a kid, the quickest way to escape all that Monroe expectation was to hop in a sailboat, raise the mainsail and harness the wind. Somewhere along the way, it became less about freedom and more about power."

He slung an arm over her shoulders, giving her a side hug. "It isn't often people self-search and realize they need a reset."

She scoffed. "Those are the only people you know!"

Rhett glanced her way and said something to Tad.

Olivia's time in the air was drawing near. Her mouth felt dry.

"Looks like you're about to be harnessing the wind for optimal speed." Sonny squeezed her once more before releasing her. "There's something to be said about sticking to the strengths in your wheelhouse." His blue eyes sparkled. "Some might say that flying with eagles, screaming as if you're one of them, seems right up your alley."

"Screaming…" He'd heard her discussion

with Sharon in the kitchen? "I thought you were napping."

"I was meditating," he said solemnly. "Sometimes it's hard to tell the difference."

"Rhett knows how to tell the difference." *Snoring.*

"The point is that you took on the world," Sonny said in that reassuring tone of his. "There's no shame in sitting back and watching the world go by now. And there's no harm in saying you aren't done yet."

Rhett walked down the dock toward shore. *Soon...*

Olivia needed to control her fear.

She closed her eyes again, did the deep breathing exercises, tried to get in touch with her feelings—the ones that revolved around excitement over trying something new and in her wheelhouse of likes. The flying part appealed. But the river... Her thoughts were on a loop, repeating the slap of the water as she was thrown in the ocean. "Why do we have to take off from the water?"

"You'd rather jump off a building and parasail?" Rhett splashed into the water as easily barefoot as he had in his cowboy boots. "I can arrange that, too."

Besides being barefoot, he was wearing

a blue swimsuit and the neon green T-shirt
Sonny had given him that said: Show No Fear.
Her gaze lingered on his legs. "Nice tan." His
legs were white with a light dusting of dark
hair. She needed to joke about something. If
she didn't tease him, she was afraid she might
fall into his arms and ask for a thirty-second
hug.

"Fact. Cowboys usually only have tanned
arms and faces." Rhett pulled down his new
purple sunglasses and stared at her over the
top of the rims, his mouth tipping up in one
corner. "Cowgirls find it sexy."

As did boat captains, not that Olivia was
giving him that piece of information.

"I'd like to take Olivia's place today." Sonny
waded toward the dock. "She's not ready."

"What?" Olivia shook her head so vehe-
mently, her neck twinged. "No. No way. I'm
going." Ready or not.

Rhett sized up Sonny in a blink. "Let's do
this, old man."

"No. I'm going." But instead of making
her way toward the dock, she threw her arms
around Rhett's neck and held on tight. "Don't
argue with me, either one of you. One, two,
three…"

While she counted, Rhett told Sonny to go get in the speedboat.

Olivia finished the rest of the thirty count through gritted teeth. When she was done, she didn't let go of Rhett. She didn't pull back to look at him either. "I'm going."

"I'm good with that." They were so close that his deep voice reverberated past her skin, her flesh, her defenses until she felt his casual bravado like a steady hand on her heart. "You're not going to be alone up there, unlike your infamous sail to Canada or your mountain biking experience. This time, you're going to be my passenger. My guest. Which means I'm in charge of your safety. I promise not to let you down."

She might have clung to him tighter.

He set his chin on top of her head. "You okay?"

Olivia liked how casually Rhett was with her, both physically and emotionally. He wasn't demanding of her time or attention, like other men she'd dated had been, although she'd expected him to be after that discussion of boundaries before they'd left Second Chance. He was quick with a joke and thick-skinned enough to handle the jibes she dished out. But probably best of all—second best if you counted kissing him—she liked how Rhett felt when her arms were around him. Like he was a safe port in a storm when she needed one.

"Olivia?" he whispered as Tad started the speedboat's rumbly engine.

"I'm fine," she said, clearing the fear from her throat and feelings toward Rhett from her heart. "I was just thinking about that trip to Canada." Which was a complete and total fib.

"Reliving the glory days?"

"Glory days?" she scoffed, easing back a little to look up at him. His black hair ruffled in the breeze. "I was seventeen, stubborn and lucky. Dad grounded me for… I can't remember what he grounded me for. Anyway, I rebelled by storming out the door and heading to the marina. I took his boat and sailed for Canada, not believing I'd actually get that far. I was thinking in the back of my mind that someone was going to stop me long before I got there."

"When you're a teenager, everything is about looking cool." Rhett's tender smile was a bit lopsided, and his gaze brushed over her lips.

Please do. A kiss is just what I need right now.

She waited a beat, but no kisses seemed forthcoming, which was a shame.

Her feet sank deeper in the mud. She picked them up and put them down again. Without meaning to, she ended up standing on Rhett's bare feet.

"It's okay," he said softly. "I've got you."

And he did. They didn't topple over and fall into the water. And she trusted that they wouldn't.

I trust him.

Trust was what Sharon said Olivia would need if she was going to hang-glide with Rhett.

A smile found its way onto Olivia's face. She felt it warm her all the way down to the bottom of her feet. "Do you want to know why no one stopped me? I didn't bring my phone charger and my phone died, so no one could track me by its signal. Meanwhile, I'd turned the radio off because I was dreading the rants my father was certain to make over public airwaves. And so, I sailed into a Canadian harbor and was detained by the authorities for lack of proper identification." She hadn't thought to bring her passport when she'd stormed out the door.

"And the image of the brave Olivia Monroe was born." Rhett's hands clasped behind the small of her back.

Her eyes were level with the words on his T-shirt: Show No Fear. "I tried to live up to that image every day as the leader of my racing team."

"But you don't have to hold yourself to that high ideal today," he said gently. "The world isn't watching. You can just tell that judgy inner voice in your head that the little girls who idolize Captain Olivia Monroe aren't around to hear you scream on the ascent. When the boat gets up to speed and I release the hang-glider from the tow platform, the air is going to be bumpy."

"Okay." Her arms were still around his neck. She didn't let her inner voice encourage them to drop away. She listened to her instincts, the way Sonny always said she should. And her instincts were telling her to hold on tight to this man.

"Once we're at a certain height, I'll start to circle, looking for thermals to push us higher. There are a lot of pockets of hot wind being forced upward by some of the hills and bluffs around the river. Our goal is to harness one to take us as high as those eagles up there." He glanced upward and then down again to her lips.

Olivia nodded. She wanted a kiss, too.

"When we descend, our speed will increase." There was excitement in his voice.

She wanted him to transfer some of that bravado and excitement to her lips. She was getting desperate for a kiss.

"And when we come down, we're going to do a shallow water landing, just like a sea plane would do. Right here in this little inlet of Tad's." He nodded toward the water. "That's why the hang-glider has pontoons on either side."

The water. So much could go wrong there.

Olivia forgot about kisses and one handsome, strong man because her heart was pounding in her chest for all the wrong reasons. Knee-weakening reasons.

Fear and weak knees had her drawing Rhett closer and counting to thirty again. This time, when she was through, she moved out of his arms and off his feet. "Is there an emergency protocol in case…?" *Things go wrong.*

She couldn't bring herself to say it out loud.

"I'll show you how to click out. But it's not going to come to that." He set his chin on top of her head again. "Tad and I have discussed the conditions today. He's gone over emergency protocol with me, and he'll do the same for you."

She bobbed her head multiple times. She couldn't back out, not when Sonny wanted to take her place. What if he had a heart attack in the air?

"How about a kiss for courage?" Rhett tapped his cheek.

"How about…" She drew his mouth down to hers and kissed him deeply. He was warm and solid, confident and cocky. All the things she didn't feel inside.

"Wow," he whispered when she'd had her way with him.

"That's right—wow. Nobody ever drew courage from half-measures." And pecks on the cheek were definitely that.

"Okay. Let's do this thing." Rhett hooked his arm around Olivia's waist and walked with her toward the small dock. "We'll put on our sneakers and life vests before we buckle in."

Olivia kept her eyes on Sonny, who was sitting in a rear-facing seat on the boat. She felt safe with Rhett's arm around her, and she trusted him to make good decisions on their flight.

But she didn't trust the water if she couldn't touch bottom.

"BREATHE, OLIVIA." Rhett tightened a strap around her.

"You're making that very hard." Olivia

squirmed. She was wrapped like a chrysalis from her armpits to her shins, fitted into a tight body hammock swinging from beneath the hang-glider. She wore a helmet and goggles and held on to her composure by a thin thread.

I have to do this.

For Sonny and his goat farm. For me and my quest for courage.

Tad was steering the speedboat away from the dock, accelerating slightly. Rhett and Olivia were on the platform the boat towed, the one that the hang-glider was attached to.

"I'm going to strap in beneath you," Rhett said. And in a smooth series of motions, he did. His harness put him closer to the control bar. It was also less constrictive than hers. "When Tad gets us going fast enough that we're a drag to his speed, I'll release the glider from the platform, and we'll start flying like a kite."

"Still tethered like a kite?" Her tone was high-pitched, panicky.

Sonny noticed. He stood up.

Olivia waved at him to sit back down.

I have to do this.

"We'll be like one big kite until we reach a good height and I release the cable." Rhett sounded happy and excited.

She might have been more excited if she had

experience hang-gliding or if she wasn't dreading a water landing. "I'm trusting you, Rhett."

Rhett glanced at her over his shoulder. "When this is over, you're going to give me a big kiss, because you'll be thanking me for the experience."

"Get me back to earth safely and it's a deal." She tried to smile. She really did.

But based on Rhett's expression, she failed. "Or we can hug it out again."

"Have a great time, Olivia," Sonny called from the speedboat.

I'm going to do this.

Rhett gave Tad a thumbs-up and then Tad pushed the throttle up to the max position. The boat responded, hull rising out of the water as it quickly picked up speed. The hang-glider drag was immediately noticeable. The hang-glider lurched backward a little as the wind filled their wings.

They passed other boaters, who waved, and sunbathers, who waved. The couple on the sailboat waved.

People are envious. People think this is fun.

Sonny would tell her to find the fun, those feelings of old that happened when the wind brushed her cheeks and the water glistened with sunshine. And for a moment, Olivia felt reassured by the glimmers of familiarity, by the thrill of speed and wind and the flap of sail—because that's what the wings above her sounded like.

Tad signaled Rhett with a thumbs-up.

Rhett released the hang-glider from the platform.

They shot up into the air twenty feet before Olivia's stomach caught up to them. And they didn't stop at twenty feet. They rose up, higher and higher.

Rhett glanced back at her, grinning. There was so much joy on that handsome face of his that Olivia should have felt some. She was screaming too loud for joy to get a word in edgewise.

They bobbed and dove a little, exactly as a kite would have done before it reached smoother air.

Olivia kept on screaming, feeling foolish and unable to do a thing about it.

And then they caught an upward draft, because all of a sudden, they were rising, faster and faster.

Rhett released the cable that connected them to the speedboat. He was moving the crossbar, guiding their little airship toward rising currents. The ride smoothed and became less like an airplane enduring turbulence and more like a gentle sail on calm waters.

Olivia stopped screaming.

This time, when Rhett glanced back at her with that elated grin, she was able to return it in kind.

I've missed this.

That feeling of movement without engines or traffic.

"Extend your arms," Rhett told her. "Like wings."

No flippin' way.

He pointed to their left.

An eagle banked in a circle, catching air to fly above them.

"Extend your arms," Rhett said again.

This time, she did as instructed. The wind lifted them and pushed her arms back, but not far, not painfully. She felt strong and powerful and free. Oh, so free. Like she had no cares, no fears.

No fear.

Tears filled her eyes and stung her nose.

There was nothing up here. No expectations. No roles to play. No people to answer to. There was only the warm wind and the man flying with her.

I could love him.

She was already smitten. He was a good man who didn't shy away from her baggage. In fact, he helped her to carry it.

I should love him.

She could become his second in command at this adventure tour thing, the way Sharon had with Tad. Be Rhett's rock in the Idaho mountains. Raise their children far away from the ocean. Be near the Monroe family that had settled in Second Chance and be around when the rest of the family visited. She'd be safe. Rhett would make sure of it. And if she occasionally watched the Salmon River flow past with longing to see the broad horizon of a deep blue sea, she'd draw one of their children close and know that she'd made the right choice.

Olivia drew a deep unburdened breath, seeing the fantasy instead of the landscape that was far beneath her.

It was then that a tiny voice deep inside of her protested. Protested giving up the sea. Protested quitting the flurry of activity of a racing crew. Protested relinquishing her command.

Captain Olivia Monroe would never live a landlocked existence.

Olivia brought her hands back in. She had to let go of racing, the same way Sharon had given up flying. But even if she retired, she couldn't see herself living in the mountains.

The Mississippi River grew smaller and smaller as they rose higher and higher. There were farms and houses on either side of its banks. There was a dense forest leading up to a rocky bluff. There were eagles. And there was Rhett.

She wanted to kiss him. She wanted to kiss him and hold on tight to his indomitable courage, pretending it was her own.

But she couldn't, because she was cocooned above him, as separate as their two worlds.

A cowboy and a retired racing boat captain.

IF THERE WAS a score for a perfect landing, on a ten point scale, Rhett would have earned a nine-point-five.

Didn't mean Olivia didn't scream upon their approach to the water. But it wasn't the drawn out screams she'd had when they'd taken off.

Didn't mean when Olivia was free from her harness that she planted a big kiss on Rhett. But she did lay her palm on his cheek while she thanked him for the experience.

He'd wanted to hug her, to hold her, to tell her how proud he was of what she'd done. But she made for shore as soon as she was able and walked toward Tad's ranch.

Sonny lingered at the shore for a moment but then followed her. "Why the long face?" Tad asked after they'd secured the hang-glider on the tow ramp and the speedboat to the dock. He walked slowly on the path back to the house, hindered by his big boot. "I thought you couldn't wait to fly again."

"It was fantastic. The air up there was like glass. It's just…" Rhett paused to look up in the sky. "I thought Olivia would love it. I mean, it seemed like she did once we were with the eagles." He'd seen that look of wonder on her face and thought, *It can be like this all the time*. Meaning he'd finally found a woman who shared his interests or at least she was willing to try what interested him. "But she barely talked to me after we landed." And the hand she'd laid on his cheek… The look in her eyes…

It was a goodbye.

Goodbye? They had days to go before Philadelphia. And then…

And then it was happily-*never*-after. Olivia would realize she'd been betrayed. The fake relationship… The real kisses… It would all be over.

"Sharon was like that." Tad waited for Rhett to catch up to him. "She screamed all the way up and all the way down. Laughed about it afterward. Never expressed an interest in hanggliding again."

"She didn't hate you for taking her up?" Rhett knew Olivia wanted to prove to herself she still had guts, but he also recognized that the bet he and Sonny made was pressuring her to do these things, perhaps before she was ready.

"Hate me?" Tad pushed Rhett off the path and into the knee-high wheat field. "Sharon's having my baby. What do you think?"

"I know what I should be thinking." Rhett stepped back on the dirt path, sneakers squishing with water. "I should be thinking about what it would take to start a business like this. Going up every day, several times a day would be a dream."

Tad named a figure. "That's the cost of a speedboat, the tow platform, pontooned hangglider and a full set of life preservers." He named another figure. "That's your business license and insurance for the year." And then another figure. "That's my six-month gasoline bill."

Rhett whistled, long and slow.

"Sharon did the math. We need two hundred forty paying customers to break even." Tad stopped walking. He was out of breath. "If we sell two flights a day, that's one hundred twenty days to break even. And here in Minnesota, we have about five months of enjoyable weather on the river from May to September. That's about one hundred fifty probable days to fly. April and October can be chilly but some folks like a brisk adventure. I had a great business in April this year. We hit our breakeven figure in late July. Sharon's exploring other ways to generate income."

"I hate math," Rhett mumbled.

"You need to learn to like it if you want a business. You need to know what you can spend so you'll have money left over to pay for a barn roof and put food on the table."

Rhett rubbed his forehead. "I don't know how many fair weather days there are in Second Chance."

"You'd best learn and take that into account before you decide what kind of business to open. It's not all fun and games."

Rhett was beginning to realize that. And wonder if what he wanted to run was a business. Or a ranch.

CHAPTER FOURTEEN

"YOUR FEET ARE as wrinkled as your brow," Sonny pointed out after Olivia helped him into the front seat of Rhett's truck.

"Soaked sneakers will do that to a person." Olivia put Sonny's step-stool in the truck bed next to her wet shoes and socks. It was good to be back in her flip-flops.

"So will over-taxing yourself," Sonny retorted. "I'm talking about your wrinkled brow, by the way."

"I figured." She glanced back toward the barn where Rhett was making his goodbyes to Tad and Jazzy. She didn't know what to say to Rhett. Her emotions had been on a roller-coaster ride today.

Yay, she'd gone through with the ride.

Yay, she'd actually enjoyed herself for half of it.

Boo, she never wanted to do that again.

"Olivia, I have something for you." Sharon hurried across the ranch yard carrying a navy blue cloth bag. "Kudos to you for soaring with eagles at the Flying T Ranch."

"What's this?" Olivia hooked the cloth handles over one forearm and rummaged in the bag.

"It's our promotional gift pack. I just unpacked the order yesterday. You're the first to receive one."

"I'm honored." Olivia held up a sky blue T-shirt. "'I Soared with Eagles at the Flying T Ranch.'"

"There's one for each of you. I thought Sonny deserved one since he was your emotional support." Sharon hugged Olivia. "I know what it took to go up there. If you can put your life in someone else's hands, you can do anything."

Olivia fashioned a smile for Sharon. "My body feels like a limp noodle right now, but I'll take your word for it."

"There's also some pictures of you in there." Sharon drew them out. "We installed a camera on the boat, and I printed a few." She sounded almost apologetic. "We haven't quite figured out how to make them more of a keepsake. The boat moves. The glider moves. The sun is at the wrong angle."

The first picture was of Olivia in the harness

looking like she was going to be sick. Hanging below her was Rhett, grinning like he'd just won a rodeo event. The second was a silhouette of them up in the sky circling with eagles. And the third was of their water landing. Water cascaded to either side of the glider's pontoons and the camera had been far enough away that it hadn't caught Olivia's expression. She'd bet she'd been screaming.

"Can you mount a selfie-stick on the glider?" Sonny reached for the photos. "Or build a sign for the business and take riders' pictures in front of it. I had my photo taken on a cruise one time. It was on the dock, and I held a round life preserver with the boat's name."

"I just had my picture taken in front of a wall of sunglasses." Olivia hadn't even looked to see how they'd come out. "You can be creative with your backdrop."

"Great ideas, thanks." Sharon beamed. "Sometimes I think it takes a village to run a business."

Rhett crossed the ranch yard with a jaunty step and a big grin. He'd changed back into his traditional cowboy attire and his black hat was angled low over his eyes. "Thanks for everything, Sharon." He hugged her. "If you haven't decided on a baby name, might I suggest Rhett?"

Sharon's hand passed over her baby bump. "That's sweet—"

"But we've got better names on our short list than that of washed up rodeo stars." Tad put his arm around Sharon.

"Ouch." Rhett shook his finger at his friend. "You'll be sorry when this washed up cowboy rocks his second act."

"I set a high bar, my friend." Tad drew Jazzy close with his other arm. "That said, call me if you need any more business advice."

"You see that," Sonny said in a low voice as Rhett walked around to get in the truck. "At the end of the day, that's what's important. Good friends. Close family."

Love. He was talking about love. But Olivia was learning there was more than attraction that went into establishing a romance that would thrive long-term. There were life paths to be considered.

Moments later, they were barreling back the way they'd come.

"That was fun, wasn't it?" Rhett was shifting in his seat behind the wheel. "I saw the way you smiled up there."

"You also heard me scream."

"I screamed, too, my first time." Rhett navigated the main road that would eventually take them to the highway. They were headed to Chicago tonight and wouldn't arrive until late. "And maybe my second."

"That's big of you to say." Sonny patted Rhett's shoulder. "It takes a strong person to admit they were scared."

"I think I've admitted I was scared enough this trip." And in this life. Olivia crossed her arms and stared out the window.

"I didn't get a chance to pet the goat or the baby horses." Sonny craned his neck as they drove past the animals he'd wanted to bond with.

Soon he'd be moving on to another client. And Rhett would be returning to Second Chance. And Olivia would be…

She rubbed her temples, wishing someone would say something that didn't make her feel that things around her were changing too quickly and things inside of her weren't changing quickly enough. "Isn't this where we debrief and talk about the pros and cons of running a business like this? The Salmon River isn't big enough for a speedboat, which makes this idea impractical."

"There's a big lake north of town that's large

enough to get up to speed." Rhett sounded like hang-gliding was still in the running. "I'd just have to check the wind currents and tree clearance."

Olivia's breath caught. "And you'd check them by…"

"Taking a test run with a boat and a hang-glider." Rhett looked pleased with himself.

"Of course," she grumped, crossing her arms over her chest. "No risk of crashing there."

"I'd take the proper safety precautions. At least admit that you enjoyed yourself up there, Olivia." Rhett's gaze sought out hers in the rearview mirror. "Forget about the take-off and landing."

"That does seem a valid point." Sonny twisted in his seat so he could see her. "That is, if part of the ride was significant."

She wasn't about to admit that it had been just this short of heaven or that she'd lost herself in a vision of what life might be like if Rhett cared for her or if she could somehow see living a life with him in a landlocked small town.

"I'm sorry if you didn't like hang-gliding," Rhett said remorsefully, not even looking in the rearview mirror. "I'm sorry if I pushed you too far past your comfort zone. In fact, I can drop you off in Chicago, so you don't have to do any more extracurricular activities with me. We'll forget the bet and I'll wish you well."

"Now see here," Sonny blustered. "That's almost worse than breaking up with her via text message."

"I'm not… She's not…" Rhett floundered.

"You are and she is," Sonny said.

Olivia needed to say something. But the thought of letting Rhett go twisted Olivia up inside. She wasn't ready. She had to say something… Anything…

"It was glorious," she blurted. "And you didn't push me. You've always given me a choice."

"It was glorious!" Sonny crowed, slapping his thighs. "Nothing has been glorious the entire time I've been with you."

Rhett grinned. "There's my little hay bale."

Sonny was wrong. Rhett had been glorious from the moment she first kissed him. She just hadn't realized it.

"Tell me more about this glorious feeling," Sonny commanded.

"It was like looking out a window of a jetliner at its cruising altitude. Except there was nothing but the wind and the vastness and…" *Rhett.*

"That does sound significant." Sonny rubbed his palms together.

"As long as you don't have flashbacks about the take-off and landing." Rhett's gaze in the rearview mirror held no mirth. "You'll tell us if that's the case, won't you?"

Olivia shook her head. It was time she picked herself up by her own bootstraps and started relying on herself.

"Of course, she'll tell me." Sonny was still exuberant over *glorious*. "I think we should celebrate with dessert tonight."

"There will be no celebration," Olivia said firmly.

Not even with caffeine.

"This is beginning to become habit," Rhett said when he sensed Olivia at his side in the hotel lobby in the wee hours of the morning. He lifted his cowboy hat from over his face and looked up at her. "It's not against the law to sleep, you know."

Olivia clutched a quart of ice cream in one hand—strawberry ripple—and a package of chocolate chip cookies in the other. She handed him the cookies and sat on the couch he'd found at the rear entrance to the hotel, bumping his legs out of the way. "We need to talk."

"About the big kiss you owe me because of the *glorious* experience I took you on today?" He pushed himself into a sitting position. "Or about how you've been cheating on Sonny on this healthy diet you two are on."

She blushed as she opened the ice cream container. "The glorious experience." But then she didn't talk. She made a show of squeezing the container on all sides, repeatedly, before taking a small plastic spoon and running it around the edges of the container.

"What is the strategy behind what you're doing?" Rhett had already devoured three cookies. "Why don't you just dig in?"

"It's frozen solid and might break this little spoon." She might have been right. The spoon was small, no bigger than her pinkie finger. She gave the container another round of squeezing. "I've never screamed like that before, non-stop, not even on amusement park rides." Her blush returned, deepening.

Rhett dug into the cookie package, considering her observation and the need to talk. "I've experienced my fair share of terror, but it's usually quick. I've slammed on the brakes when someone's suddenly come to a stop in front of me. That'll get your heart racing. I used to be put in charge of my sister when we were kids and working the carnivals. She had the worst sense of direction and was easily distracted. I'd turn around and she'd be gone. I'd be terrified while I backtracked to find her."

"That's just normal stuff." Olivia scooped around the edges of the container again.

"It is," he agreed. "But to me, so is hang-gliding. My stomach dropped today when we were climbing. But only a little, kind of like when you drive over an unexpected speed bump too fast."

"Or get air while riding a mountain bike?"

Was she trying not to smile?

He thought she was. "That, too. Something unexpected, like crashing a sailboat, has to be terrifying."

"Well…" She finally got a good size bite of ice cream and paused to savor it before continuing. "The terrifying part wasn't so much the boat flipping over. That's happened to me before."

"Hmm." This was interesting.

"The terrifying part was waking up with someone performing C.P.R. on me. And then for hours afterward, I couldn't get rid of the taste of salt water." She made that pronouncement matter-of-factly, as if it wasn't horrifying.

"I wish I would have been there." He

decided he'd eaten enough cookies and tossed the package on the coffee table. "I would have given you a big kiss. I'm rather fond of salt. And of your kisses."

They both froze.

He because he'd admitted too much. She because...

Rhett didn't know. If she wasn't into him, this was where a woman backpedaled, made jokes, excused herself.

Olivia sighed and leaned back, which meant she leaned back onto his legs as well as the couch back. "We're not practical together, you and I. Everybody says so."

"Everybody?" He knew his sister and grandfather agreed with her. But who was everybody?

"Well, Kendall." Olivia jabbed her ice cream with her spoon, non-stop.

"Nobody gives a dime about what Kendall thinks." Rhett huffed like an affronted bull.

"And..." She dug around the ice cream some more. "I might think that. Sometimes."

What?

Rhett's stomach dropped nearly as hard as it had when they'd been hang-gliding.

Olivia didn't look at him. Olivia, who could posture and argue with the best of them. What did that mean? That she didn't like it when someone said they weren't suited for each other? He bet the answer was yes.

He decided then and there that she liked him, which meant that this was just an excuse, another one of her barriers that she put up to keep people from getting too close.

She should keep me from getting too close. I'm not planning to bring her back to Second Chance.

But a part of him didn't want to go through with it.

"On the surface, it's hard to argue that our differences make us an unlikely pair." He waved a hand like his sister did sometimes, brushing off an idea he had or an excuse he'd made. "We're oil and vinegar. Carrots and lima beans. All the things that people don't think to put together until they do and realize it works." He lowered his voice. "You and me. We could work."

What am I doing? She doesn't belong with me.

"I've been thinking about it, Rhett, and I don't see how we have a future. I love the ocean—"

"Looking at it, I assume." Since she didn't sail anymore.

"—and you're a mountain cowboy."

"There are cowboys in all the states, along with rodeos and horses and people who wear cowboy boots and hats." He had to stop himself from arguing with her. What she said made sense. He had no idea why he couldn't accept it.

Because I've never been able to turn down a dare.

"But you… Rhett, you like to push the limits and I… I can't." Olivia's features pinched, as if she was loath to admit it.

"You stepped out of your comfort zone today," he told her softly. "And you said it was *glorious*."

She dug at that ice cream with her spoon. Jab-jab-jab. "I'm not sure the glorious parts outweighed the terrifying parts."

"Lots of couples have different hobbies." This felt like a losing battle over ground he felt he hadn't begun to win.

"But few lasting couples have *nothing* in common."

He nudged her off his legs, swinging his booted feet to the floor, suddenly angry. "We have plenty in common." He thrust his finger toward the cookies. "Snacks, for one. A love of strong coffee, for another. A taste for adventure." He hurried to add, "Don't you deny it. You've enjoyed being on this trip and seeing new places. You and Sonny jabber for miles complaining about me not stopping to see the largest ball of twine in the world or the birthplace of some person who was a footnote in history."

Her caramel colored eyes were huge. "But—"

"And we like to debate. We've debated everything from the proper color of cauliflower—" he was firmly in the white camp; she was firmly in purple "—to the best color for a sports car." He was firmly in the black camp; she was firmly for candy apple red.

"That just means we have a difference of opinion." She was regrouping, protecting this idea the way she protected the idea that she wouldn't sail again.

It angered him further. "That just means we're ornery enough to handle a difference of opinion and respect someone for it." Rhett squashed his hat on top of his head. "I apologize for using you as my adventure tour yardstick. But don't go quitting on me without giving us an official go, the way you're going to quit sailing without ever trying to go back."

Olivia gasped.

He'd gone too far. But his pride wouldn't

take the words back. His pride and the fact that he believed it was the truth. "Your father isn't around to make you angry. And because you always sailed angry, now you're balking at sailing again. That said, I don't know how to motivate you to give us a legitimate shot."

"You're right." Olivia stood, grabbing the bag of cookies. "You don't know how to convince me to make this farcical relationship real." She hurried down the hall toward the elevators. "I should just stick to the people and places where I belong."

Where I belong...

Her statement sucker-punched Rhett, and not just because it was clear he'd hurt her feelings.

He had to get his head on straight. Olivia was a Monroe. Worse, she was a Monroe who lived on the world stage. It was foolhardy to believe she could ever be with him, reckless to allow attraction and kisses to bloom into something more meaningful in his heart.

CHAPTER FIFTEEN

"I CAN'T HELP but feel I've stepped in the middle of a lover's quarrel."

Sonny's comment the next morning earned him a glare from Rhett, a quick one since he was driving.

If Olivia had been Kendall, she'd have swatted the back of Sonny's head for bringing up a topic she wanted to avoid. Instead, she said, "I can't have a discussion right now. I'm meditating."

"How can you think with that opera playing?" Rhett kept both hands on the wheel and his eyes on the road. They were driving from their hotel to Non-Slip Footwear in downtown Chicago, where they were meeting Kendall and Olivia's sponsors.

Olivia hadn't gone down to the hotel lobby to wake up Rhett with a cup of coffee this morning. She'd waited until Sonny was ready to go to breakfast to leave her room.

Rhett's comments last night about her reason for sailing stung, possibly because they held an element of the truth. She'd spent long hours last night staring at the ceiling and coming to terms with one hard fact: She was tough to beat when she was angry. And she'd been angry for as long as she could remember. Angry that she couldn't please her father. Angry that there were obstacles to her competing in a man's world. Angry at the world when Bryce died. Angry at Bentley when the racing yacht he was building for her fell behind schedule.

Angry. So angry inside.

Anger had driven her to be daring and seemingly unbeatable.

She didn't want to be angry anymore. But that only complicated the choices she made next. Because she was a more cautious person now. And caution didn't describe the way Rhett lived his life.

"Sonny and I are taking a pass on your business meeting today," Rhett said when he'd parked in a garage downtown.

"I don't need a babysitter." Sonny had apparently caught a case of the crankies from Olivia. "In fact, I want to go see what this sponsorship thing is all about, what pressure it puts on Olivia's shoulders." He opened his door and would have climbed down if Olivia hadn't demanded he wait for the step-stool.

"I guess I'll be staying in the truck solo." Rhett leaned back in his seat, crossed his arms and pulled the brim of his hat down, as if preparing to nap.

"You'll do no such thing," Sonny snapped. "We're a team. And teams don't give up on each other because they had a disagreement, do they?" He hit Olivia with a stern look and demanded, "Do they?"

"No, sir," she felt compelled to say.

"All this talk about having each other's back and just days in you decide things are a little uncomfortable." Sonny slammed his door. "I'm uncomfortable and you don't see me complaining. You should always finish what you start. I have a cheerful attitude all day, every day. Not that any of you care." He marched down the exit ramp, continuing to rant about how cheerful he was.

Olivia watched him go, reminded of the many times she'd ranted and raved at her racing team for petty obstacles getting in the way of a unified performance. She glanced at Rhett in the rearview mirror.

He was staring at her, chin thrust out. "Do you need me to go?"

Do I need him?

Something inside of her answered in the affirmative. It was that same something that mourned her decision to retire from racing.

"You were right. Last night. Rhett." The words came out of her in fits and starts. "Anger was my engine for every success I achieved. That engine isn't there anymore… Or at least not with the vehemence of the past. But without that anger, I don't know who I am or what I'm capable of or where I belong. So I've been more open to hear the opinions of others. And this trip… And you… I'm struggling to find my footing."

He stared straight ahead at the concrete wall of the parking garage, body still closed off. "Best get on to your meeting before Kendall gets all huffy."

"I'm not finished." Olivia found her backbone and pressed on. "I was going to say that someday I might like to try hang-gliding again. Someday. When I'm ready, not when there's a bet to be won."

He gave a curt nod. "I hope you enjoy hang-gliding more the second time."

She wasn't getting her point across, and he was beginning to annoy her through no fault of his own. "What I meant was that I'd like to try hang-gliding again someday with you!"

His head whipped around her way.

"And also, that I don't give a flip what Sonny says or what Kendall says about you coming with me or staying put for this meeting or the meeting I have in Philadelphia in a few days." Her words came out loud and forceful. "I want you to come with me today, not as a distraction, not to imply that we're going to settle down and promote Non-Slip Footwear as part of our wedding." Although she bet the marketing team or Kendall would have no qualms about going there. "I want you to come with me..." She shrugged. "And I don't want to have to explain why I want you along because frankly I don't feel like I know yet. I like you but if that doesn't make sense to you or offends you somehow, then I'll see you in an hour or so."

She slammed the truck door, half hoping that he wouldn't come along because everything inside of her felt snarled and awkward.

When Olivia was two parking spaces away, Rhett opened his door and hopped down. She stopped and waited for him.

"Now listen, my little hay bale," Rhett said as he fell into step with her. "Just because I'm coming along doesn't mean I'm going to be yours to command. Or Kendall's. You Monroes are a bossy lot."

"That's because bosses get things done." Olivia was probably imagining it, but it seemed she walked with less weight on her shoulders now that he was next to her. "You have enough opinions to be a boss."

"I think what you meant to say is that I know what I'm doing." He strutted to the exit where Sonny waited on the busy sidewalk. "That is, *when* I know what I'm doing. I'm man enough to admit that the business world is new to me."

"You'll catch on." That earned her a grin, which in turn made her think that she'd prefer to stroll down the flower-lined Michigan Avenue than take this meeting with her sponsors.

"That's more like it. I'm happy to see you two listened to me," Sonny said when they joined him. "Which way do we go?"

"I knew it." Kendall exited a car that had pulled over nearby. She wore skinny jeans and a blue and white striped blouse, along with a pair of red sneakers. It was casual attire for Kendall. "I knew you'd forget to wear your Non-Slip Footwear, Olivia." Kendall dug into her large red shoulder bag. "Good thing I brought you a pair." She thrust a pair of blue jean colored sneakers with thick white soles.

Olivia dutifully kicked off her flip-flops and slipped into her sponsor's shoes. "You can't be upset. I wore my racing team gear today." But she'd just noticed that Rhett and Sonny hadn't.

"That doesn't matter." Kendall pointed down the block. "There's a coffee shop next door to their building where you guys can wait. No need for a distraction. I'll jump in if Amanda or Jeffrey try to turn the conversation to Olivia's future plans. Or the past, for that matter."

"The guys are coming with us." Knowing the way, Olivia marched on ahead of Kendall.

"You don't need a crutch." Kendall surged past Olivia and into the lead. "Especially the cowboy."

"He gives them something else to talk about." Olivia injected her tone with more resolve, stretching her short legs to extend beyond Kendall's. "I don't have anything else positive to say on this visit except that I'm trying out extreme sports with…with my guy." She fell back on the dating defense.

"That's me," Rhett said in a chipper voice similar to the one he'd first used when they set out on this trip.

"These people make shoes for boaters."

Kendall darted through the crowd toward the revolving door of an office building. "They aren't interested in news that isn't about ocean endeavors, including cowboy flings."

"Rhett is coming with us."

"Suddenly, I feel like chopped liver." Sonny was huffing and puffing, and his cheeks were flushed.

They'd walked too fast. Olivia gave his shoulder a compassionate squeeze. "You're the foundation of my team. Of course, you're an asset in this meeting."

"Aren't you supposed to tell Olivia when she's making a wrong decision?" Kendall demanded of Sonny. "Tell her that it's best if you two hang out in the coffee shop while we conduct business."

"I'm not sure it is a wrong choice." Sonny fluffed his beard. "I've been encouraging Olivia to go with her instincts."

"And my instincts are telling me to bring my entourage," Olivia said firmly.

Kendall faced the revolving door, and then turned back around. "Okay, let's say we all go in. How are you going to introduce Sonny? As your shrink?"

"He can be my uncle Sonny," Rhett offered.

"No. Absolutely not." Kendall's hands

crossed and uncrossed the air between them in the universal "no way" signal. "Olivia's brand is above reproach. We can't weave elaborate lies about her inner circle."

"Fine." Olivia shrugged. "I'll introduce Sonny as my life coach."

"I've got the shirt on for it." Sonny held out the hem of his red shirt that read: Life Requires Courage, Not Planning.

"This is a mistake." Kendall tossed her long black hair over her shoulder, and then strategically drew it back, twisting it for effect. It was a nervous move, one she'd had since childhood. "If you do this, Olivia, you do it without me."

Retired racing skippers don't need a social media or public relations person.

Olivia covered her cousin's hand with her own, clasping it lightly. "Maybe that's for the best."

"What?" Kendall squeaked.

"It'll protect your reputation in case I go in there and make a total fool of myself." Olivia entered the revolving door, pushing it around to get in.

"You aren't going in there without me!" Kendall was right behind her, voice muffled by glass.

Soon Sonny and Rhett joined them in the grand brown and white marble lobby. The building housed many businesses. They cleared security and headed to a bank of elevators.

Olivia pressed the button for the thirty-third floor. The elevator took off with enough speed to unsettle her stomach. She drew a deep breath and faced the group. "I'm taking charge of my life, starting now."

"Good to hear." Kendall stared at the display indicating the floors they were passing. "But don't forget I'm your point person, so follow my lead. Our sponsorship relationships have been tricky since what happened in the last race."

"No. I'm taking the lead." Olivia barked the words with the same command she used with her crew during a race.

Everyone drew back a little. Kendall eyed her warily.

And then Rhett nodded, and Sonny smiled.

"Everything's going to be okay," Olivia said.

And if it wasn't, her team had her back.

Olivia stepped out of the office building elevator in her khaki shorts, T-shirt and boat shoes, as if she owned the place. Only her unruly curls belied that impression.

Kendall and Sonny fell in line behind her.

This woman is afraid of nothing.

Rhett smiled as he brought up the rear, and then he paused, taking in the décor and half-wishing he'd stayed in the parking garage.

The lobby of Non-Slip Footwear was designed to feel like a classic Chris-Craft speedboat from the nineteen forties. The floors were teak. The walls mahogany. There were slim cream-colored racing strips outlining small display cases with individual pairs of non-slip boat shoes for men, women and children.

A pair of corporate types stepped forward to greet them.

"Amanda. Jeffrey. So nice to see you again." Olivia performed the introductions, not seemingly bothered by the fact that she looked ready to step out on a boat while Amanda and Jeffrey looked like they'd never set foot on a boat in their lives.

In a showplace like this, Rhett wouldn't have expected anyone to pay a moment's notice to him, especially when Olivia was the star of the show, but Amanda, Jeffrey and the receptionist kept looking at him, specifically at his cowboy boots.

Rhett shuffled his feet self-consciously.

"We're so happy to have you here today, Olivia." Amanda's gaze shifted to Sonny, and then Sonny's Birkenstock sandals. "Sasha, take Sonny's and Rhett's shoe sizes. Everyone needs to leave with a gift pack today."

While Sonny and Rhett gave shoe sizes to the receptionist, Olivia and Kendall admired a display case where the shoes all had bright geometric patterns on them.

Rhett leaned forward. "Miss Sasha, just so you know, I'm a plain color shoe man."

"Finally, I've found an area where I'm more adventurous than you are!" Sonny slapped Rhett on the back and told Sasha, "Give me the brightest, happiest shoes you've got."

"Let's get this meeting started." Amanda led them through a set of wooden double doors with port holes and into a conference room with a table shaped like a boat—pointed on one end, squared-off on the other.

Rhett thought they were taking the boat theme a bit too far, but Sonny was full of praise for their creativity.

"Olivia, I hear from Kendall that you've been enjoying time off." Jeffrey gestured to Rhett's shirt, which sported the Flying T

Hang-Gliding logo. "Mountain biking, hang-gliding and such."

"I'm enjoying doing new things." Olivia's smile reached Rhett. "And meeting new people."

"Who knows what we'll do next," Rhett said cryptically, not ready to reveal the surprise.

"Whatever it is, we'd like you to be wearing Non-Slip Footwear." Amanda got right to the point. "We saw a post featuring you on No Glare Eyewear's social media account. We have a photo wall, too. It looks like the deck of my father's beloved wooden speedboat on Lake Michigan. It makes a great backdrop. We can create a post where we give away your favorite shoes." She gestured toward a poster of Olivia sporting a pair of their shoes while securing a sailboat to a dock cleat.

"We also need to schedule time with you on your new racing yacht," Jeffrey said, pen at the ready, presumably to jot down dates Olivia was available. "When it takes its maiden voyage."

Olivia glanced toward Kendall. "My new…"

"Once it's ready, we'll definitely let you know," Kendall inserted smoothly. "No set dates. We're waiting on Captain Olivia to make her return to our headquarters in Philly."

Rhett's brain was spinning at top speed. Was

this why Shane and Holden had wanted Olivia to return to Philadelphia? They'd referenced it from the time of Sonny's heart attack, wanting her to go back where she belonged. Was there a boat waiting for her? Was she ready to sail it if there was?

The rest of the meeting went the way of No-Glare Eyewear. There were pictures taken and not so subtle hints dropped that they'd appreciate photos of Olivia wearing their product so they could post them on social media.

"People love Olivia," Jeffrey told Rhett as they were preparing to leave, laden with bulky bags filled with multiple pairs of shoes he'd probably never wear. "They look up to her. And when they see her wearing our product no matter what she's doing, they want to wear our product, too."

"You make it all sound so simple." Rhett knew it wasn't. For a cowboy like him, it felt like smoke and mirrors. That might have been because Rhett was beginning to suspect he'd been lied to about what awaited Olivia when they reached Philadelphia.

They said their goodbyes and got into the elevator.

As soon as they reached the sidewalk, Rhett

held Kendall back. "Is there a new racing sail-boat waiting for Olivia in Philadelphia?"

"Of course, there is. But don't you dare tell her." Kendall's tone was low and fierce. "Olivia's going to be ready to sail soon. You saw it in the way she took command today, didn't you? When you reach Philadelphia, be prepared to say your goodbyes. She's had a love affair with the ocean longer than she's had with you. And no one gets over their first love."

Rhett let go of Kendall's arm, hating that he feared she was right, hating that he needed to help Olivia get back on track even if she'd hate him for it, hating that he'd benefit from it.

It didn't help that Sonny took that moment to glance back at Rhett, frowning.

As if he feared all that, too.

CHAPTER SIXTEEN

"WHY ARE YOU pulling into this campground?" Olivia leaned forward, trying to get a better view from the back seat of Rhett's truck. It had been a long day and she was ready for a warm bed in a quiet hotel room.

"You like the out-of-doors, don't you?" Rhett had been reticent since they'd left Chicago, and cagey about their nighttime destination all day. It was confusing since they'd made a truce of sorts before the business meeting.

"I. Don't. Camp." Sonny wasn't pleased.

"Camping isn't so bad. It can be like living on a sailboat." Cramped quarters without a lot of luxuries. "But we didn't bring a tent."

"Or air mattresses. Or sleeping bags." Sonny had his arms crossed over his chest, not open to the idea. "A cooler. A stove."

"This is a different kind of campground." Rhett parked in front of a small office that boasted an outfitters' store. He turned in his seat to face the doubters. "They rent out trailers for the night, the same as you'd rent out a room at a hotel."

"What about towels?" Sonny peered at the trailers around them. "Soap? Black out curtains?"

"Sonny…" Rhett gave the older man a patient look. "Each unit has sheets, blankets and the same amenities you'd find in a hotel."

"That sounds great," Olivia said in a cheerful voice that had Sonny twisting around to look at her. "It does. Kind of like a little adventure from the ordinary."

"I like ordinary," Sonny complained.

"This from the man who wants to retire and open a goat farm." Rhett shook his head. "I canceled our hotel reservation for tonight and made one here instead because I just… I just wanted you to see that not all adventures I take are thrill-seeking." He captured Olivia's gaze with one so tender that her heart melted a little. "Who knows? Maybe I should open a glamping campground in Second Chance. Be right back." He went inside to register.

Sonny huffed.

"What's wrong with you?" Olivia unbuckled her seat belt and scooted forward, leaning over the center console. "You should be happy. Rhett took us to dinner at the biggest salad bar in the state." Or that had been their roadside claim.

"I'd rather not say what's bothering me." His arms were back to being crossed.

"That seems unfair. I have to tell you everything that bothers me." She reached over and tugged his beard gently. "I have it on good authority that it helps to get things off your chest."

Sonny brushed her hand away, and then made a show of brushing imaginary crumbs off his chest.

"You really are in a bad mood." Olivia moved back into her seat. "Go ahead and sulk. I'll use the quiet time to practice my meditation."

They sat in silence for several minutes as the sun sank lower in the sky.

The campground felt friendly. A couple walked their dog past the truck. She could smell wood burning and hear the faint sound of laughter from children playing on a swing set down the road.

Rhett returned with two keys for side by side units, a bundle of firewood and two bags of groceries. "Olivia, you're in a little Shasta trailer from the 1940s. Sonny and I are sharing a 1950s Airstream. You can't complain about an Airstream, Sonny. They're top-of-the-line and highly sought after. This is what city folk call *glamping*."

"Glamorous camping." Sonny snorted. "I'll believe it when I see it."

"Do the trailers come with goats?" Olivia teased. "I don't think he's going to be happy unless they come with goats."

"No goats. But there is a clawfoot bathtub in the Airstream." Rhett drove past four trailers and then parked in front of a big silver trailer.

"A bathtub…" Sonny sounded like he was waffling. "Hotels never have deep bathtubs."

Olivia gathered her trash and cell phone wallet. "Do you stay at places like this a lot?"

Rhett turned in his seat, in no hurry to get out of the truck. "When I was on the rodeo circuit, I looked for campgrounds that welcomed horses. Back then I had a camper on the back of my truck and pulled a horse trailer. Being able to bunk in a camper helped me out quite a lot." His gaze was earnest, as if he were trying to tell her something. "Campgrounds like this sometimes allowed me to set a picket for Big Boy and save money by being able to cook a few meals for myself. I've been counting pennies my whole life. There's one thing that won't change when I open a business."

"But it's smart," Olivia said. He knew more about managing finances than he let on.

"What are we waiting for? There's a bath in my future." Sonny opened his door. He looked down. "I always forget how high up we are."

"I'll get your step-stool." Olivia hurried to help him. "I want to see the inside of your trailer before you take your bath." She caught Rhett's eye, smiling. "This really is like a mini-adventure."

His returning smile seemed wan. She filed that under fatigue. They'd logged in a lot of miles today.

A few minutes later, the trio entered the Airstream. It had a retro 1950s vibe, although everything looked brand-new. There was a twin bed and a dinette that converted into a bed. And in the back, there was a bathroom with the added luxuries of a chandelier, a pair of fluffy terrycloth bathrobes and a clawfoot tub.

"Heaven," Sonny said when he saw it. "I approve of your choice, Rhett, even if there are no goats."

"There are also public restrooms and showers back at the office. The store closes at ten." Rhett handed Olivia a small grocery bag and a significant look, which she took to mean there would be no trips to the snack bar later since it was almost nine.

She glanced inside the bag. *Ice cream!* "Are we having a campfire tonight?"

"S'mores?" Sonny perked up a little more.

"I bought firewood and the fixings for s'mores. It wouldn't be camping without them." Rhett was still looking at Olivia. "But I'm in solidarity with Sonny. If he can't have s'mores, we can't have s'mores."

"We can bend the rules this one time." Olivia was enjoying the feeling of togetherness.

"All right. Out with you, Olivia. I need my suitcase and my bath." Sonny's mood had done a complete turnaround since they'd arrived.

"You don't want to see my trailer?" she teased.

"Nope."

"I'll get your suitcase and then I'll start the fire." Rhett hustled Olivia outside and gave her a key to her Shasta trailer. "Let me know if it works for you."

"I'm sure it's fine. My grandfather used to have this huge motor home he hauled twelve grandchildren around in. It was the size of a concert bus and I always dreamed of having my own space." Given her anger issues, her family probably wished that, too.

The Shasta was nice, but more modern than the Airstream. There was a full size bed in the back and a small bathroom with a compact shower. It was a pleasant change from the hotel rooms they'd been staying in. She found a place for her suitcase, dug out a pair of jeans and a sweatshirt, changed, and went to join Rhett at the firepit.

"You've got a nice fire going." She settled into an Adirondack chair close enough to the firepit that she could put her feet on the bricks around the edge. "I've got sponsorship on my mind. I should take a picture of my shoes in action." She pressed a few times on her phone screen and snapped a picture. She'd captured the fire and the top half of her feet, but the photo didn't seem like anything special. "I'm no good at this social media thing. My photos stink. Look." She angled the display for Rhett.

"I see what you mean. It's boring." Rhett snapped his fingers, walking backward from her. "I know what you need. Count to three and take that picture again."

"What are you up to?" Whatever it was, she liked that mischievous grin on his face.

"Set up your shot and count. Trust me."

She did as instructed, making sure her

feet and the fire were in the shot. "One. Two. Three."

Rhett photobombed her picture, which was perfect considering he had a triumphant look on his face and the purple sunglasses on.

"You've made two of my sponsors happy." She showed him their work. "I'll send this to Kendall so she can post it." Once that was sent, Olivia realized her notification bar was crowded—texts, emails, phone messages, social media tags. "Ugh."

Rhett was whittling a stick into a point in a chair next to hers. He paused. "What's wrong?"

"Nothing. Just an overload of messages on my phone." She turned it off and tucked it back in her pocket.

"People care about you."

She nodded. "I know. I just don't know what to say to them. That's why my phone stays off."

"How about *I appreciate your kind thoughts and support*?" He went back to whittling with his pocket knife. "My grandfather sent flowers to your grandfather's funeral. And then your father wrote something like that on a thank you card."

"That part I've got covered," she told him. Although she still hadn't sent out any replies.

"It's the question they ask about how I'm doing and what I'm up to that throws me into a panic."

"You'll know what to say in due time." He stuck the tip of the knife in the fire, blackening it before pulling it back out.

"Meaning I should stop stressing about it?"

"Exactly. Let's talk about something else while I make you a s'more." Rhett opened packages of graham crackers, chocolate and marshmallows, setting up his ingredients. He always seemed prepared and to have thought things through.

"What's on the schedule for tomorrow? Jumping out of an airplane?" She hoped not.

"Actually, there are two attractions that interest me in the area—base jumping and waterfall rappelling."

Olivia gave him a dirty look. "What happened to tame and appealing to the masses? Or…or thinking about what might actually work in Second Chance?"

He put a marshmallow on the stick and held it over the fire. "We have sheer cliffs and waterfalls in Second Chance. Remember the steep road we took out of the valley north of town? There are several cliffs that would be perfect for it."

The way his eyes lit up… He loved the idea.

Olivia was captivated by his passion. *Is that what I looked like when I talked about racing?*

But the fact remained that his interests didn't jive with a thriving business. "Earth to the enterprising cowboy. How many families of four are going to stop in Second Chance to jump off a cliff or dangle from a rope in a waterfall? At this rate, you'll never pass Holden's standards for a viable business plan." She knew her cousin too well.

His smile said he wasn't going to be deterred. "Can't you chalk this up to my doing my due diligence?"

"No. It feels more like *your* vacation." She sat on the edge of her seat, which felt like where she'd been with Rhett the past twenty-four hours. "I have to be honest with you. Shane and Holden asked me to come along to vouch for your adventurous spirit. I feel like I could have given them my stamp of approval before we ever left Second Chance."

Her marshmallow went up in flames. Rhett didn't seem to notice.

"I thought you said you had my best interests at heart, not Shane and Holden's." He sounded hurt.

"You know it's not like that." Not now. "If

you really believed that, then you're as naive as I am." Or what she'd pretended to be on this journey; lying to herself had become her stock in trade since the accident. "The moment Holden mentioned sponsor visits, I knew this trip was just a sham to get me back to Philadelphia—not that I blamed you. It's like no one in my family has ever heard of the saying that you can lead a horse to water but you can't make her drink. Even if there is a racing yacht waiting for me there, I'm not going to see it."

"Then why did you agree to go?"

"Because of you." She closed her eyes, hating to admit her excuse was that flimsy. "Because you made me feel close to normal again. You brought out the fire in me. And then I had the perfect excuse to stay on the trip— the bet."

"Forget excuses." His voice was gruff as if he was offended. "You were starting to regain your confidence with every successful adventure you took. You can do anything you set your mind to now."

"Maybe," Olivia allowed slowly. "Maybe as long as you're by my side." As soon as she said the words, she knew they were true. "You're the yin to my yang. The salt to my pepper."

Olivia warmed to the idea. "I don't want this trip to end."

Because despite Olivia's best efforts to the contrary, she'd fallen for her fake boyfriend. She loved the way he pursued what he believed in. She loved the way he gently pushed her outside of her comfort zone. She loved the way the corner of his mouth tilted slightly when he was thinking about kissing her. She loved the way she felt in his arms.

There was no dancing around it anymore. Olivia loved Rhett.

"Everybody needs a safety net." Rhett stared into the fire. "And I guess I'm flattered to be yours."

Heart pounding, Olivia bridged the distance between them, covering his hand with hers. "You're more than that. You must know… You must feel it…" She couldn't bring herself to say the words. "Just last night—"

"We talked about how hard a future between us would be." His voice was as flat as the look in his eyes.

"But today—"

"You found your mojo."

If Olivia didn't know any better, she'd think Rhett was letting her down gently. And she hadn't even confessed her feelings!

Rhett set aside the stick he'd been using and shifted in his chair to face her. "Why do you think Sonny's been cranky all day? He knows his time with you is coming to an end. Frankly, so do I."

"Coming to an end, but..." She swallowed back her fear just like he'd shown her how to do. "I love you. I love you both."

Rhett didn't smile. He didn't jump up and down with joy.

But he didn't run away either.

"I know it's quick," she said when he blurted, "I need to slow things down."

Olivia's heart dropped. She stared at the Airstream, at the fire, at the Shasta trailer behind her. "I'm sorry. I'm diving right into this relationship and I shouldn't."

"I'm attracted to you, Olivia. I won't deny it. And I have feelings for you. I won't deny those either. But you...you're in a tricky place and I... I have a lot going on right now," Rhett said carefully. "I can't afford to mess up this business opportunity and the commitment I made to Holden and Shane...not to mention the bet I made with Sonny."

She couldn't do much about his agreements with her cousins, but she could take one thing off the board. "We're at a point now where we know each other well enough to forget about the bet. We can head back to Second Chance. I'll video conference with the last of my sponsors."

"We're not forgetting about the bet." Rhett's hard tone and unyielding expression seemed to box her in.

"Why? Are the last remaining adventures something Sonny feels will help me?"

"I… He…" Rhett gave himself a little shake, loosening his shoulders, his expression, the look in his eyes. He was once more the cowboy that had stolen her heart. "Sonny mentioned always finishing what you start. Bet or no bet, you can do the last two challenges, Olivia. I know you can." He hung his head, as if ashamed of making the bargain with Sonny. "And after it's over, we can talk more about our relationship and if it has a future."

She felt as if her heart was that ashen marshmallow. Olivia stood, prepared to retire for the night to a trailer with her pint of ice cream. "If that's what you want, Rhett. I guess it's waterfall rappelling tomorrow and Philadelphia by sundown."

"I CAN'T BELIEVE YOU," Sonny told Rhett in a whisper when he returned to the Airstream. "You sold Olivia out to her cousins."

"I don't know what you're talking about." Rhett pushed past the old man to get a glass of water.

Sonny tugged the bathrobe sash tighter around his waist. "I'm talking about what Kendall told you today about the racing sailboat that's going to be waiting for Olivia when we arrive in Philadelphia tomorrow. I stewed about it all day—only taking a time out for a long, leisurely soak. And then I overheard you mishandle Olivia's declaration of love. And now I'm upset again."

"I... Geez. I didn't know it was a boat for her." The old man had to have heard that much on the street earlier. Rhett drank the full glass of water.

Olivia had confessed her love for him and all he'd been able to think about was that her future was on the line.

She's meant for more than me.

He silenced that voice by refilling his water glass.

Sonny was still upset, hands tangling in the robe's sash. "I've been shepherding your relationship along—helping you—and how do you repay that help? By stabbing both Olivia and me in the back!"

Rhett drained his glass and put it in the sink.

And then he faced Sonny, keeping his voice just as low as the old man's because he'd noticed how sound carried in the trailer park. "I care for Olivia. I really do. But before we became close, I gave my word that I'd deliver her to Philadelphia on Friday. Don't you see? This is her chance now that she's got her confidence back. She'll sail again. She'll race again. And she'll leave us—me—behind. That's the way it's got to be. I don't fit into her world."

"You love her." Sonny splayed his fingers through his beard, once, like he was tossing down a challenge.

"I don't know if what I feel is love." The words felt wrong coming out of his mouth. Rhett tossed his cowboy hat on the counter. "To be fair, it could be. But if it is love, she won't get on that boat in Philadelphia."

"How do you know? She's needed someone like you…someone like the man I thought you were." Sonny's hands had fallen to his sides, but his arms kept jerking about as if he wanted to reach out and shake some sense into Rhett. "You can be the man in her corner, the one who cheers her forward."

"Or the excuse she uses to hold herself back and stay on dry land."

That silenced him. "Great things can be

achieved when you focus on yourself and your dreams. Love will only get in her way." Rhett knew that and yet, more than anything, he wanted to rewind his life to the other night when he and Olivia had gone ziplining. He'd been happy. She'd been happy. "I don't want to be the person she looks back on five or ten years from now and thinks about with regret." He had to cling to that belief, that his love wasn't what Olivia needed right now. "She might be the right woman for me, but this is the wrong time for both of us."

Sonny glared at him. "I don't like you right now."

"But you know I'm making sense. Olivia needs to stand on that Monroe dock and look out on that new sailboat. She shouldn't look back, not to you or to me."

Sonny's glare wavered.

Rhett pressed on. "You've told Olivia to talk out her fears. I bet you planned for her to face them, as well. You would have brought her to a sailboat eventually." But Rhett was willing to bet it wouldn't have been until much later in the year.

Sonny stopped glaring and counted something out on his fingers. "Three. She's done three of your adventure challenges."

"Yes. And tomorrow we're rappelling from a waterfall." Rhett momentarily got caught up in the image. "It's more like rappelling on the edge of a waterfall, but the reviews are great and—"

"That's four." Sonny moved closer to Rhett, lowering his voice even further. "We made a bet for five."

"Yeah, I was thinking we'd—"

"Help her get her sea legs again." Sonny smiled, so pleased with himself and energetic he was bouncing on his toes.

"And, once the fifth challenge is done, we can be on our way, after we drop her off in Philadelphia and she meets up with Kendall. I suppose." Rhett ran a hand behind his neck, trying to figure out why Sonny was suddenly not angry with him.

"There's one way to guarantee she sails." Sonny held on to Rhett's shoulders. "You're going to choose it as your fifth adventure."

"That doesn't seem fair."

"Tough love never is." Sonny released Rhett and paced back toward the couch.

"Listen, I've been a good sport about helping her and taking your cues to bolster her self-confidence. But this... Deceiving her about the last challenge goes too far. Olivia's going to hate me. And you."

"Why do you care? You aren't ready for love. Maybe in a year or so she'll forgive you." Sonny rolled his shoulders back. "And as for me, my assignment with her will be over. I'll have helped her, as much as I was able to, reconcile herself with the accident." Despite his words, the old man still looked sad.

Rhett tried again. "How can you be so clinical about this? She treats you like family."

"Ha!" Sonny poked Rhett's chest. "And she sees you as more than a cowboy her family wanted vetted. We're even."

CHAPTER SEVENTEEN

"YOU'RE THROWING ME off-schedule," Rhett fumed. "This isn't on my itinerary."

"Well, it's on mine. Turn here." Sonny pointed toward the highway exit. "Don't make me angry, young man."

"For the record, I'm not on board with a visit to a goat farm." Olivia wasn't exactly thrilled with the detour, but she wasn't happy that she'd declared her love for Rhett and had him back-pedal either.

"Just you wait," Sonny promised. "These goats will melt your heart."

They parked and headed toward the visitor center and gift shop. It was filled with stuffed goats, goat-themed coffee mugs and T-shirts with goat sayings. And then there was a refrigerated case with goat milk and cheeses.

"We're here for the full experience." Sonny grinned at the counter clerk. "The tour and the meal afterward. My treat. I'm hoping my

friends gain some perspective about their feelings and their future."

"Toward goats?" Olivia frowned.

"*I'm* not going to open a goat farm. No need
for a change in perspective," Rhett grumbled,
briefly glancing at Olivia before looking away.

That glance may have been brief, but it only
reminded Olivia that he had a firm grip on
her heart.

Go slow, skipper. Go slow.

"You never know what the future holds."
Sonny chuckled. "While we're waiting for
the tour to start, I want to treat everyone to a
T-shirt. Look at this one. It says I'm the
G.O.A.T. That stands for Greatest of All Time."

"I know what it stands for." Rhett was still
grumbling.

"My friends are the greatest," Sonny con-
fided in the counter clerk, whose name was
Margaret. "Rhett here was a champion roper.
And Olivia was a boat racing champion." He
placed the T-shirts on the counter. "And they're
not done yet." He plopped a black-and-white
stuffed goat on the counter, followed by a coffee mug that said: Goats Make Me Happy.

"Just give him one of everything," Olivia
murmured, adding a magnet and a goat-themed
tin of mints to his pile.

"I think he's got a case of the too-longs," Rhett said from Olivia's side.

"The too-longs?" She glanced up at him, planning to look quickly away. But he wore that smile that tilted up on one side and he was staring at her mouth.

"We've been on this trip *too long*. We've been stuck in that truck *too long*. And he's been daydreaming about goat farming *too long*." His smile turned apologetic. "I'm sorry I didn't handle things better last night."

"Me, too." She wasn't going to let him off the hook.

Sonny paid for his purchases and their tour. "Hey, our tour guide is Katie. She's waiting for us through that door." He pointed to the rear exit. "Hold this for me, will you, Margaret?"

The clerk placed his bag underneath the counter. "You'll need these." She handed over three handkerchiefs with the goat farm logo in each corner.

"What are these for?" Rhett shook his out and held it up for inspection. "Do goats spit like llamas?"

"No, but people cry," Margaret said matter-of-factly. "So many people cry that we had these handkerchiefs made up."

"Oh, I can't wait." Sonny hurried toward the rear exit. "Tears are so cathartic."

Rhett and Olivia exchanged glances.

"I'm betting Sonny's the crier," Rhett deadpanned. "You and I… We're hardboiled."

"Right." Olivia headed for the exit, vowing not to cry.

She shouldn't have worried. The tour started with a yawn.

"These are our milkers." Katie, their tour guide, went on to explain how the goats were milked, how often and what they were fed. The goats were every shade of brown, and some were black. They stretched their noses toward the visitors, cute as cute could be. Katie led them through a side door. "And this is their play yard."

The fenced yard contained platforms of various heights, similar to what Tad had provided his goat at the Flying T. But there were also boulders for them to climb on and big pipes for them to wander through.

"Look at that one kick up its heels!" Sonny was smitten. "And look how fearless they are, climbing up so high. People should live more like goats."

Rhett leaned toward Olivia. "I see it now. Sonny's going to close down his sports psychology practice and open a goat farm where he can still preach about living the good life but make up lots of metaphors involving goats."

"I heard that," Sonny said without turning away from the goats at play. "And it's a darn good idea."

Although Olivia agreed with Sonny, she exchanged an eye roll with Rhett because…

"Back here, we have our baby goat experience." When Sonny had his fill of playful goat watching, Katie led them to a smaller barn. "This is your lucky day. We had several babies born this morning. If everyone could find a seat on a bench, we'll get you a baby goat."

"We're not taking any with us," Rhett groused.

"Speak for yourself." Sonny beamed.

They each found a place on a bench.

Katie and another farm worker plucked up baby goats and placed them into their arms.

"Babies make everything right with the world." Sonny nuzzled his chin against the baby goat's nose. "Babies see all the potential."

Olivia cradled a small brown goat in her arms. It was soft. It leaned into her body. And its heart beat strong beneath her hand.

Unexpectedly, longing welled into her throat. For love. For a child. She'd always put off the thought of romance and children, assuming they'd come after she was done racing. Now that her career was essentially over, she could fill all the empty, uncomfortable spaces with love and children. Or if things didn't work out with Rhett…goats.

She glanced at Rhett, who was crooning softly to the little black baby goat in his arms.

He was going to make a good father someday. He wouldn't demand his children be perfect. He'd encourage them to spread their wings.

Her cheeks felt wet. She hadn't realized she was crying.

"What's wrong?" Sonny demanded from the next bench over as a tear rolled down his cheek. "Tell me what you're feeling."

Olivia shook her head.

Katie came forward. "Do you want me to take the baby back?"

"No." Olivia rocked the little goat.

Rhett returned his goat and came over to sit next to Olivia, placing one arm over her shoulder and using his other hand to wipe away her tears. "Good thing we got a hankie."

His tease should have stopped the waterworks.

Olivia only cried harder.

"ADMIT IT, OLIVIA. Sonny's drawn you over to the dark side when it comes to goats." Rhett was joking, of course. He'd almost come undone holding Olivia while she cried at the goat farm.

Business deal? What business deal?

Sonny might be right. There was no right time to fall in love. When Rhett held Olivia, he didn't need anything else in the world.

"No comment on where I stand on goats." Olivia snapped her harness into place and stared up at the tower where they'd be practicing rappelling skills for an hour before actually doing it down a rocky cliff while being pummeled by a waterfall. "I bet Sonny's at the snack bar making friends with everyone. He'll have more stories about this experience than we will."

"There's one bet I won't take." Honestly, Rhett was feeling the need to swear off bets and dares.

If only, if only, if only...

He wished he and Olivia were on this trip for real—no agendas, no sacrifices, no betrayals.

"Have you done this before?" She peered up at him. "You look nervous."

"Of course, I'm nervous. I've never done this before." Rhett shaded his eyes as he looked to the platform, which was a good fifty feet in the air, glad for the distraction from thoughts of what was going to happen tomorrow when the sun came up in Philadelphia.

"If you get a case of excited giggles, I'm calling this off." Olivia fixed Rhett with a firm expression, but it quickly gave way to her impish smile. "I need my adventure tour buddy to be focused, not giddy."

Rhett raised his hands in mock surrender. "Hey, this is serious business. The fact that it's run by two former drill sergeants kind of tells you how regimented the experience is going to be. Awesome but safe."

"I'm going to hold you to that." Olivia put on her helmet without regard to the fragility of her curls.

Rhett had already clicked into all his safety gear. He tugged on a pair of gloves. "You're approaching this experience differently." More confidently.

She's going to be all right without me.

Rhett wanted to grab on to her and never let go.

Olivia gave a little laugh. "I'm exhausted—physically, mentally and emotionally. There's no more room for trepidation."

Rhett forced himself into the here-and-now.

He'd worry about tomorrow when it arrived. "What about fun?"

She pressed her lips together like fun was a bad word.

"Have you forgotten what fun is?" Come to think of it, Rhett hadn't seen her actively pursue anything he'd consider fun or entertaining. She never talked about a hobby. She didn't play games on her phone, probably because it was never on. She stared out the truck window and talked.

"Next up!" barked one of the former drill sergeants.

"That's us." Olivia took a step forward before Rhett took hold of her arm.

"What have you done for fun? Pre-accident, that is."

She scrunched her nose. "I'd sail."

"Really. That's it?"

"Watch television?"

"That's decompressing, not fun." There must have been something she enjoyed doing that wasn't involved with her career. "You do know the definition of fun."

"Is it spelled *g-o-a-t*?" she teased, grinning.

"I'm serious!" No wonder this woman had been broken by her boating accident. She had nothing in her life but her career.

Olivia sighed. "All right, I... I had this little container garden on the deck of my condo. I planted bulbs and looked forward to seeing them bloom every season."

Rhett drew back. "That was your idea of fun? I expected something more competitive, like ping-pong tournaments at the yacht club."

She gave his shoulder a playful push. "It's what I like. There are no right or wrong answers to that question. I gardened in my spare time."

"Next up! You two!" The former drill sergeant pointed at them. "Hustle, people!"

Rhett followed Olivia toward the instructor. When he considered how she'd cried over a baby goat, he supposed gardening made sense. But when he thought about her career on the water, gardening made no sense at all.

But then he had no more time to think other than to process the instructions he was given, climb the stairs to the top of the practice tower, and rappel down.

"You're better than me at this," he told Olivia after their third descent.

"I've worked with rope tension and balance my whole life." Olivia flashed him that smile he was going to miss. "Finally. I'm better than you at something."

"We'll see who gets drenched rappelling down the waterfall." Although Rhett issued the challenge, he bet he was going to be the one to get soaked.

"THAT WAS INTENSE."
Olivia lay on a warm, flat boulder next to the waterfall. She'd managed to avoid the direct fall of water on the way down, but the spray had soaked her nonetheless.

Rhett hadn't been so lucky. He'd had trouble controlling his horizontal momentum and had swung into the waterfall. Not once, but several times.

He lay next to her on the boulder, his hand enclosed over hers. "I feel like I've had a deep tissue massage performed by an overly-enthusiastic linebacker. And you did do better than me."

"I did." She grinned. "I guess that means you aren't interested in doing something like this again."

"Is that a dare?" Rhett rolled onto his side, propping his head on one hand and looking down on her as if committing this moment to memory. "Best two-out-of-three?"

"I'm not pushing my luck." She plucked at his wet T-shirt. "Regrets?"

"Naw. I like to try everything at least once."
Like love? she wanted to ask.

She brushed his thick wet hair away from his eyes. These moments seemed precious, and perhaps fleeting if he couldn't find it in his heart to love her. "Whatever you've got in store for us tomorrow, Rhett... Your muscles will be sore." The way she'd been sore after mountain biking.

"It'll be worth it." His gaze left her face, rising to look toward the waterfall behind them.

She shivered, partly because her clothes were wet and partly because she knew practically everything there was to know about sailing, but she didn't know how to make him love her. "This trip has been worth it." No matter if her heart was going to be broken when it was over. "I feel like I've learned and experienced things I wouldn't have without you."

"Knowing you has been worth it, my little hay bale." He leaned over and kissed her.

It wasn't until afterward that she pondered the meaning of his words, which sounded a whole lot like goodbye.

CHAPTER EIGHTEEN

"HERE'S SOMETHING I *didn't* miss about Philadelphia. The traffic." Olivia sat in the back seat of Rhett's truck. She sipped her smoothie as they inched forward on the highway early Friday morning and hoped that by day's end there might be a chance for a different outcome for her and Rhett. "You never told me what we're doing for our fifth challenge, Rhett. What are our choices?"

"There's a lake outside of Philadelphia where people sailboard." She figured that's where they were headed now.

"Do they hydrofoil?" Olivia allowed herself a small smile. Maybe Rhett was realizing she was up for any challenge, but she was experienced in hydrofoil, at least. "I'll sign on for anything high tech. Are you still pouting because I did better than you at the waterfall yesterday?"

"I didn't pout." Rhett tapped his thumbs on the steering wheel. "I had fun."

"You dragged your feet on the way to the parking lot afterward," Sonny pointed out. "It was unusual for you."

"Pouting," Olivia proclaimed.

Traffic began to move faster as they passed the last main exit for downtown Philly.

"What else were you considering doing today, Rhett? We have a dinner meeting with Fantastic Fish Sticks later in Baltimore." It was a two-hour drive and that was in good traffic.

"Kendall will be there, I presume." Rhett sounded annoyed. "She's not a fan of anyone in the front seat."

"I bet she'd be a kinder person if she had a goat." Sonny raised his hands as the power of an operatic aria swelled through the truck's speakers. "You're so upbeat today, Olivia. To what do we owe this positive outlook?"

"I realized last night just how much I've accomplished in the past week." She'd faced her fears head on and she'd fallen for a man she trusted. "There's so much to look forward to."

"It's about time." Sonny craned his neck to look at her. "I'm proud of you."

"Me, too," Rhett said in a clipped voice. "You can do anything now."

They'd been tap dancing around each other since she'd told him she loved him, sometimes moving close, sometimes keeping their distance. But today would be different. She had a good feeling about their fifth extreme adventure—the final one of the bet.

"We should talk about next steps." Sonny turned off the radio. "We'll be parting ways soon and—"

Olivia experienced a moment of panic. "Do you have a new client?"

"No, but you're capable of doing anything. You just said it yourself."

"Does that mean you're returning to Boston?" Where Sonny was based. She wanted him to return to Second Chance.

"Yes. All good things come to an end. Just know that I have the utmost confidence in you." Sonny's statement lacked his usual enthusiasm.

"We both do." Rhett slowed to exit the freeway.

"Do we need gas again so soon?" Olivia glanced around. "Hey, this is my old stomping ground. I cut my sailing teeth at the yacht club near here. It's where we take prototype racing yachts for test runs, the ones that are made at Monroe Marine Works." Trepidation tangoed with her egg white breakfast.

Kendall had mentioned a new racing yacht was coming out of production, but…

Olivia shook her head. Rhett and Sonny would never take her to see it. Not without asking first.

Conversation in the truck came to a standstill.

They hit every green light. Too many green lights. They'd be at the yacht club in a minute.

"Most days, I've given you options on activities." Rhett stared straight ahead. He sounded like he was reading a eulogy. "Today, my choices are sailboarding or…sailing."

Olivia couldn't breathe, not even to say sailboarding.

"Give me a sign and I'll turn around," Rhett said quietly, still focusing only on the road. "You're in charge, right or left." He was referencing the first turn they'd made upon leaving the Bar D. Left had been the tame choice she'd made.

Sonny poked Rhett's shoulder, earning a scowl.

Sailboarding! I choose sailboarding. Turn around.

Olivia drew in a ragged breath, but she couldn't bring herself to speak.

Had she been played?

"I think Kendall is in the car ahead of us." Sonny didn't sound happy. "We'll get out at the yacht club and take a gander at this new racing sailboat. And then you can choose between Rhett's options."

Tall sails became visible above buildings. Nostalgia tugged at Olivia, beckoning her forward. She rolled her window down, smelling the tang of salt air.

I don't have anything to fear here.

"There's nothing wrong with looking." Rhett sounded like there was everything wrong with looking. And being here.

"Nothing wrong at all," Sonny echoed.

"Except for the fact that I've been betrayed by…" *The two men I love.* Olivia refused to finish the sentence out loud. She refused to make this easy on them because they should have told her where they were going.

But it didn't matter if she'd been tricked into coming to the yacht club. She wanted to see. She wanted to look. She wanted to give herself one final goodbye to the life of a skipper before she moved on.

To sailboarding.

Olivia squashed the thought. She wasn't going anywhere with these two ever again.

Her extreme adventure days were over. Sailboarding had probably never been an option.

An especially tall mast towered over the yacht club, one that belonged to a racing craft.

Again, Olivia was filled with curiosity. She could be curious about the new racing yacht without fear. There was no way Olivia was sailing her.

Rhett parked and they all got out.

"I hate that you did this to me," Olivia told them all, including Kendall. "And don't say it was for my own good." Knowing what had to be done, Olivia threw her shoulders back and strode toward the yacht club entrance, stretching her short legs to stay ahead of them. This was the last time she'd enter these doors as the captain of a racing team.

Nathan, the head of security, nodded at her from behind the desk, buzzing them through.

Olivia marched down the hallway toward the dock, barely acknowledging yacht club staff who called to her from their offices as she passed. That was usual for the angry, cocky Olivia Monroe. This would be her command performance.

She burst through the last door and out onto the terrace stairs that led to the main dock, nearly stumbling when she saw the craft in the first slip and read the name emblazoned across the hull—Bryce's Pride II.

Grief pressed in on Olivia.

Bryce would tell her to take it easy and take a breath. Bentley would caution her to stop and think before she did anything rash.

Like sail again.

There were people swarming the dock in racing gear, faces she recognized.

My crew.

Men and women she'd cut from her life because she couldn't bear to admit she was as adrift as an unanchored buoy inside.

Shame combined with grief to crowd her lungs.

She did slow then. She slowed and drew in a ragged breath and tried to think of something intelligent to say as the crew greeted her.

"You're early, as usual." Peter, her crew chief, came forward, giving her a hearty hug. "Great to see you, skipper."

"Isn't she a beaut?" Nancy, one of her longest-tenured crew members, crowded next to Peter to wrap her arms around Olivia.

Carrigan, a burly redhead, shadow-boxed Olivia's arm. "The new engineer consulted with Bentley on her improved design."

That was her older brother, always improving. He hadn't told her what awaited her in Philadelphia either.

"Good to have you back, skip." Another in a stream of crew member hugs.

Olivia wanted to cry, not just because they'd named the high-speed racing yacht after Bryce again or that Bentley had helped refine the yacht's design, but because none of her crew asked her why she'd gone dark in terms of communication. It was as if she'd never sunk them.

"I meant to return everybody's calls," Olivia told them, tears threatening to spill. "But I had some soul-searching to do."

"We understand," Peter said with a forgiving smile. "But we've waited to take the maiden voyage until you could join us."

Olivia's gut clenched. She'd never been this frightened of anything, not even hang-gliding. She opened her mouth to admit she wasn't going to sail anymore when a familiar voice spoke.

"She's ready," Sonny said from behind her.

Olivia turned to face the man who'd picked her up when she was at her lowest and nurtured her back to…whatever this was.

"She's done some amazing things this past week," Sonny continued, giving Olivia a solemn look. It was similar to the way he'd looked at her when she'd spoken to him months ago about taking her on. Only back then, he wasn't wearing a deep brown T-shirt that said: I'm the G.O.A.T. "Mountain biking and ziplining. Hang-gliding. Rappelling down a waterfall."

"Don't forget cradling baby goats," she murmured, feeling love swell for this old man because she sensed that this was goodbye. It had to be. He hadn't told her they were coming here this morning. He'd known. It didn't matter how long he'd known. The unforgivable betrayal was in the secret.

Rhett stood behind Sonny, holding his black cowboy hat on his head as he craned his neck to look at the tall, tall mast. His surprised gaze dropped back down to Olivia's. "It's a hydrofoil?"

She nodded.

His expression switched to one of wonder. "All this time, I thought you were racing a regular sailboat."

Kendall tsked. "It's all high tech on the world stage, cowboy."

"This baby can go faster than fifty knots," Peter said with pride.

"I guess you really do like to go fast. I was

right. This is where you belong." Rhett took a step back.

Olivia knew what that step meant. And pride refused to let her stop him. She'd told him she loved him and been asked to slow down.

Her heart ached.

He doesn't go fast. I don't go slow.

She'd been a fool to fall in love with him.

"Are you ready, skipper?" someone asked from the back of the crowd.

"It's a beautiful day to sail." Kendall had her phone out and was snapping pictures as if Olivia had something to celebrate.

"Come on, skip," someone else urged.

Olivia's broken heart pounded painfully in her chest. She didn't want to, but it felt like she had no choice. She'd come full circle. She'd lost her nerve. She'd gotten it back. She'd fallen in love. And now, she had to move on past racing yachts and cowboys. She had to let her loves go. "Let's do this." One last time.

Leave nothing unfinished.

So then she could start her second act.

"SOMETHING ON YOUR MIND?" Sonny had just climbed into Rhett's truck using the step-stool.

Rhett was standing there, looking out toward the Delaware River where Olivia and her racing sailboat had disappeared, moving fast out toward open waters, rising up on the hydrofoils.

"Rhett." Sonny placed a hand on Rhett's shoulder. "It helps to say what's weighing on your mind."

"I let her down." Rhett felt numb, chilled by the ocean breeze and the choices he'd made. "*We* let her down."

"I was paid to help her regain the courage she needed to sail." Sonny withdrew his hand and buckled his seat belt. "I did exactly what I was paid to do."

"Nice try, old man." Rhett picked up the step-stool. "I saw you crying when her boat left harbor. We should have told her this morning where we were going."

I should have told her I loved her.

Rhett winced. Why did he have to pick now to acknowledge his true feelings? He loved Captain Olivia Monroe and chances were that he'd never see her again. "We couldn't have clued her in," Sonny argued, although he wouldn't look at Rhett when he did so. "She'd have given us all kinds of excuses and commands to stay away. You saw how much her crew adores her. You saw how much that boat means to her. She needed to do this. She'll thank us later."

"I doubt it." Rhett tossed the step-stool in the back. "And it's not thanks that anyone needs to exchange, it's forgiveness. You, of all people, should know that." He closed Sonny's door only to reveal Kendall standing at his front fender. "Kendall? You scared the life out of me."

"I'm sure you're like a cat. You have more than nine lives." She approached him slowly in her bright blue sundress, taking stock of the damage the Monroes had caused, no doubt. "I'm here for Olivia's luggage. Thankfully, she's come to her senses and giving you two the boot."

"We're not the enemy." Rhett rounded the rear of the truck and yanked open the back door of the cab. He dug out Olivia's suitcase from underneath Sonny's. "You heard Olivia. You're just as guilty in her eyes as we are."

"I know." For once, Kendall didn't look like a haughty Monroe princess. "It had to happen. She had to move forward. I appreciate all you've done for her. Both of you."

Her sentiment was no consolation for Rhett.

"She'll be fine." But Kendall didn't look as

if she believed it. "You did the right thing. We all did."

Rhett shook his head. "That's what everyone but Olivia seems to be saying."

"She'll see it, too…someday."

Rhett rubbed a spot over his chest where his heart should be. "I should have told Olivia how I felt when I had the chance. Now she's moving on with her life and I'm moving on with mine." He was certain no matter how many times he said that out loud, it would never hurt any less. "I hope she can find it in her heart to forgive me."

"Olivia's more the type to hold a grudge." The business-like Kendall was returning.

"Do you know what the problem is with you Monroes?" Rhett pushed Olivia's suitcase into Kendall's arms. "You don't recognize that a wounded heart doesn't have a set timeline to heal. You and yours shouldn't have interfered with her process. We shouldn't have either, but…" He drew a deep breath and didn't hold back. "Someday, you're going to be in the same boat, Kendall. You're going to be faced with a choice to walk away from all your Monroe expectations or hold on to something new and different. And you'll have that Monroe family of yours at your back, pushing you to make a choice before you're ready."

"I might have deserved that," Kendall allowed, turning toward her car.

"Might nothing." Rhett backed away. It was long past time to let Monroes sort things out on their own. "On your drive to that fish sticks place, you might want to pay closer attention to Olivia. She's not the woman you remember."

Rhett climbed behind the wheel. "Where can I drop you, old man?" Because Rhett wanted to be alone. "Olivia mentioned Boston."

Sonny shrugged. "Second Chance will do."

Rhett stifled a groan. "You're not from Second Chance."

"I know. But Olivia will head back to Second Chance someday, and I think I'd like to be there when she does."

"You're more optimistic than I am."

"Hugging baby goats will do that to you. Do you think we can stop at that goat farm on the way back?"

Rhett huffed. If Sonny was going to insist on stopping at all the places they'd visited on the way out, it'd take an extra day or two to get home. "Do you at least have a plan for what you're doing back in Second Chance while you wait for Olivia? By my reckoning, it could take years."

"I'm going to open a goat farm, of course."

"Of course." He should have known.

CHAPTER NINETEEN

OLIVIA FINISHED SAYING goodbye to her crew and headed toward the yacht club proper, leaving the rest of the group to discuss her retirement announcement amongst themselves.

She was wind-blown with salt-spray on her arms and face. Her nose felt sunburned. Her hair was undoubtedly a mess—mashed helmet-hair with tangled, curled ends. And inside...

Inside she was frayed.

She'd come home again, in a sense, taking the helm as they sailed on a maiden voyage. She hadn't blown out all the stops. She hadn't tested the boat the way it needed to be tested before the crew raced again. But she'd tested herself. And she'd passed.

Yet as she entered the yacht club, there were two men missing from her life. Two holes in her heart that hurt every time she thought about them.

"Hey," Kendall greeted her. "Do you want to

shower here and change for our dinner meeting? We need to head out to Baltimore."

Olivia suddenly felt drained. She wanted nothing more than to sink down somewhere and have a bleak moment to herself, shed a few tears, slough off the self-pity. "I'm no longer the captain of the racing team. Maybe you should let the folks at Fantastic Fish Sticks know. They might not want to spend their Friday night with me."

"Don't be silly. You may have abdicated your throne, but you're still Olivia Monroe." Kendall hooked her arm through Olivia's. "I got your suitcase from the cowboy. Maybe there's something in there that doesn't look like you've been hiding out at a lakeside cabin all summer."

"My suitcase…" Olivia's heart sank lower than she thought possible. She'd been holding out hope that Rhett and Sonny would greet her as if she'd made a triumphant return. "Rhett left?"

"Sonny, too." Kendall nodded. She steered Olivia toward the locker rooms. "I've got something in my bag you might wear." She whipped a soft green jersey dress from her big black bag.

"What are you? Mary Poppins?" Olivia resolved herself to a shower, a change of clothes and a dinner with the Fantastic Fish Sticks team.

"I've got cute sandals in my bag, too." Kendall had obviously planned ahead.

How many people had been involved in the planning of this event? Anger pooled in Olivia's belly. She resented them all. And yet, she knew on some deep, painful level, that they'd only had her best interests at heart, too. "You knew I didn't pack anything remotely resembling a dinner dress."

"That's what family's for, to watch your back."

They entered the women's locker room. Their footsteps echoed in the large space. It was empty. So empty.

Like Olivia's heart.

Olivia sank onto a wooden bench. "Someone should have told me. Rhett... Sonny... *You* should have told me, Kendall." She stared at her cousin, who wouldn't look her in the eye. "Today was a big deal for me and I needed someone on my side."

Kendall sat next to her, slipping her arm around Olivia's shoulder. "We were all on your side, Liv."

"But they didn't wait to see if I made it back okay." Olivia didn't name names.

Kendall didn't ask for any. "They thought you'd be mad."

"I'm not that person anymore." The angry, fearless boat captain. "I was never that person with Rhett." There. She'd said his name and the earth hadn't cracked open to swallow her up.

Kendall tried to smooth Olivia's curls on one side. "They thought it would take time for you to forgive them."

"It will." Olivia laid her head on Kendall's shoulder, not knowing how long it would take but not wanting to hurt like this inside. "Of course, I'm going to forgive them. You always forgive the ones you love." She blinked back tears. "It's just so hard when someone doesn't love you back."

The clock on the wall ticked. Someone shouted outside.

Kendall sighed. "That cowboy loves you, Liv. I wouldn't say that if it weren't true because I'm not his biggest fan. Not by a long shot."

Olivia shook her head. "Rhett cares for me but he doesn't love me. He wanted to slow things down."

"Maybe he wanted to get past the commitment he made to deliver you here today." Kendall stood, drawing Olivia to her feet. "I shouldn't tell you this but... Before Rhett left he said he should have told you how he really felt."

"He did?" Olivia let Kendall lead her toward the showers.

"He did." Kendall placed her bag on the counter and began removing items—a makeup bag, a pair of flat leather sandals, a slim jeweled headband. "But you're not going to go running back to him or Sonny. You need to spend some time on your own."

"Time to make sure I know what I really want," Olivia agreed. She was already beginning to feel better.

And she hadn't even hugged a baby goat.

RHETT AND SONNY arrived in Second Chance four days later.

They had two brown baby goats in carriers in the back of the truck.

Rhett couldn't believe he'd been swayed into transporting Sonny's new best friends back here.

He pulled up to the old homestead where Sonny and Olivia had been staying and helped the older man down. "My grandfather says you're welcome to stay here as long as you need to." Rhett had made the request in part because Sonny wanted to return and in part because he was happy to have him around.

"It's awfully quiet here." Sonny looked around. "Better leave me Hester and Ester." His twin baby goats.

"That's not happening." Rhett carried Sonny's suitcase into the house. There was a pair of women's flip-flops by the door and a pair of forgotten sunglasses on the coffee table. "You don't have a goat enclosure. I'll put them in a stall in our barn for now."

"And we'll build a goat habitat tomorrow?" Sonny asked hopefully. He was wearing his I'm the G.O.A.T. T-shirt and blinked his eyes coyly.

"Not tomorrow. Tanner's rodeo school is this weekend. The Bar D is going to be crawling with junior cowpokes and I promised I'd help him run things." Tanner probably had a list a mile long of tasks left to do. Rhett turned to leave, which put his gaze directly on the little rowboat beached outside. In his mind's eye, he saw Olivia wade into the water and hop into the boat, challenging him to do the same.

"I could probably build something for the

goats off the back deck, right?" Sonny wandered toward the corner of the house, peering around, probably hoping that Rhett would bite and take a look, too.

One of the goats bleated.

Rhett needed to get them situated, take Big Boy out for a ride and have a long hot shower. His steps turned purposeful as he headed for his truck. "Don't rush the goat play yard. When Olivia comes back to collect you, you'll be moving on."

Sonny caught up to Rhett, fluffing his beard the way he did when he was pondering something. "Olivia's not rushing back here anytime soon to collect me or you. In the meantime, Hester and Ester need a home."

Fair enough, but did the old man have to say that? Rhett scratched the back of his neck, pausing at the truck door. "Still, it makes the most sense to keep the goats on the ranch proper, near the feed and water supply."

"Okay. I might be lonely though." Sonny glanced back toward the homestead. "Will you come by tomorrow and float around the lake with me?"

The memory of Olivia returned, along with the deep sense of regret.

"I…uh…" Rhett was certain he was going

to be busy, but the old man was still down about Olivia.

Like I'm not?

"I'll find time for boating." Rhett couldn't believe he'd offered. "But you should plan on spending time at the ranch proper. We can always use an extra hand and your goats will need their hugs." He turned away, opened his truck door, and then turned back. "I'll tell Cassie to expect one more for dinner."

"I'd like that." Sonny smiled.

Rhett drove back to the newer part of the ranch and parked in the yard. His family greeted him—Grandpa, Cassie, Ajax and Millie, the barn cat.

Hugs were exchanged and explanations about goats demanded.

"We've never had goats at the Bar D," Grandpa said suspiciously, following Rhett into the barn. "What good are two female goats?"

"Sonny plans to use them in his anxiety recovery program." Rhett opened an empty stall and turned on the water trough to fill before he realized it was too tall for baby goats. He went into the tack room to get a mounting block, thinking it might be tall enough for the twins to stand on and drink.

Grandpa took a stand in the barn's breeze-way. "Is this la-dee-dah program supposed to benefit our stock? 'Cause we don't have any anxious horses."

Big Boy stuck his head over the stall door and nickered.

"It's a program for people." First and fore-most, Sonny. Rhett paused on his way back to the goat stall to give Big Boy a proper greet-ing. "Did you miss me, fella?"

The big gelding nudged Rhett's shoulder.

It felt good to be missed, even if his home-coming was a bit rocky.

"I'm sure there's no folk in Second Chance who need such a program." His grandfather was in prime form today, grumpy as all get-out.

Rhett placed the mounting block under the water trough, deciding it was high enough for them to reach. And then he faced his next problem—his grandfather. "I'll be needing your help getting the goats out." Frankly, he had an agenda. Having been a doubter of the heart-melting power of baby goats, Rhett wanted his grandfather to fall in love.

"I knew there'd be more work in it for me somewhere." His grandfather headed out the door.

Outside, Cassie held one of the baby goats in her arms. Rhett wasn't sure if it was Ester or Hester. He couldn't tell them apart. But the little thing was tucked into Cassie's arms like a docile kitten. She'd been bitten by the baby goat bug. Rhett could see it in the soft expression on her face.

It reminded him of the day Olivia had held a baby goat and cried in his arms.

"Cassie, can you give that goat to Grandpa? I need help getting out the other one." Rhett bit back a smile, waiting to release the second baby from its carrier until his grandfather held the first goat.

"Why... Look at you," Grandpa crooned. "Aren't you a soft, sweet little thing?" Instead of heading into the barn, he stood in place, as if his first goat conversation deserved his full attention. "You won't be any trouble, will you?"

Rhett and Cassie exchanged smiles.

"Did you have a good trip?" she asked.

"It was better in some ways than expected." Rhett pulled the other carrier toward the tailgate. "And in others..." He didn't know quite what to say.

"Someone heard the Monroes talking in town about Olivia." Cassie released the carrier latch. "They say she's gone to Florida. I can ask Bentley about her if you like."

Rhett drew the little goat into his arms. "I'd rather you didn't." Olivia needed her space and Rhett was finding that he needed his.

Although holding a baby goat was definitely a welcome respite after so much heartache.

"I invited Sonny over for dinner." He held the baby goat tenderly, thinking of Olivia and goat hankies. "We're going to be saddled with him for a while."

"There's always room at the Bar D table for one more," Grandpa said. "Let's get these little scamps in a safe space. I bet they need to run around a bit." He led Rhett and Cassie into the barn.

"It'll be good for Grandpa to have someone from his generation around." Cassie separated a hay flake from a stack of hay bales in the corner and put it in the goat stall.

My little hay bale.

Rhett swallowed back regret.

Soon the baby goats were settled in the stall with a bit of food and water. Several horses peered over their stall doors, trying to get a good look at the new residents.

"How long is this Sonny character going to be staying?" Grandpa asked.

Rhett thought about Olivia's harsh words in the parking lot of the yacht club. It was going to take a long time for her to forgive him. "A long time, Grandpa. A long time."

CHAPTER TWENTY

"Why did we tell the family we went to Florida?" Kendall got out of her car and took stock of her surroundings with a jaundiced eye. "This is Michigan."

"You're the one who told me to take some time for myself." Olivia looked toward the nearby lake where a man was hovering over the water while wearing a jetpack. "And also, you're the one who didn't want me to go off on my own."

Kendall had agreed to take a two-week vacation from her fledgling social media business, which mainly consisted of Olivia's social media, as well as a few postings for some of their other Monroe cousins.

It had been a week since Olivia had sailed on Bryce's Pride II. Since then, she'd spent a few days hiking the Catskills with Kendall before they headed west. Their journey was slow since Olivia stopped at everything that interested her. But ultimately, Olivia was making the journey because she was intent upon discovering her limits without a handsome, protective cowboy at her side.

Today's adventure? Water jetpacks.

The man on the water face-planted.

"Ooh." Kendall cringed. "That looked like it hurt. I didn't promise you I'd do this, did I?"

"You told me you'd ride shotgun." Olivia walked toward the rental office, while keeping an eye on the man gasping for air in the water. "I assumed that meant you'd do everything by my side."

"Uh-huh." Kendall followed at a slower pace. She wore shorts and a flouncy flowered blouse. "Activities like this aren't in my wheelhouse."

"Grandpa Harlan would argue that you always need to expand your wheelhouse." Tension built inside Olivia with each step. Good tension, she decided. A bit of nerves and a bit of excitement. "You aren't scared, are you?"

"I'm not scared. I'm repulsed." Kendall leaned forward, peering at the price sheet posted in the rental office window. "Do you see how much that activity costs? For fifteen minutes?"

The man using the jetpack rose out of the

water once more. He propelled himself forward, then hovered.

"He's doing better this time," Olivia noted. "That's a positive, right?"

The man rose up sharply and then reversed course, diving into the water head first.

"Ooh," Kendall said again. "He can't have meant to do that on purpose."

He bobbed out of the water, laughing, so Olivia wasn't sure.

"Ladies." A young man wearing purple No Glare Eyewear sunglasses and a bathing suit appeared in the rental office's window. "I bet you can do better than that guy."

"We can try," Olivia muttered.

"I think we're just here to watch," Kendall countered, giving the guy a smile designed to distract.

"Actually, we're going to give it a go." Olivia stepped up with her cell phone wallet.

"What? No." Kendall moved quickly to Olivia's side. "I'd rather do some of those other things you talked about, like ziplining or mountain biking."

"Ziplining is for kids," the dude behind the counter said. He peered at Olivia. "Don't I know you?"

"Nope." Olivia pushed her sunglasses higher

up her nose. "We're from Philly. Just passing through. We're both doing this."

Kendall made noises of dissent.

Olivia took her by the arms and backed her away from the sales counter, wanting a little privacy. "What brand sunglasses am I wearing?"

"No Glare Eyewear," Kendall said in a sullen voice.

"And what brand of sunglasses is he wearing?" Olivia nodded toward the guy running the rental office.

Kendall tilted her head to get a good look. "No Glare Eyewear."

"If you try this, I'll let you take some pictures for social media." Olivia upped the ante by pointing her toe. "And look. I'm wearing Non-Slip Footwear and we're near a dock where people without these sneakers might slip."

The man with the jetpack crashed into the water again, creating a huge ripple, more like a concentric wave. He wasn't helping Olivia's case.

"Ooh," Kendall said a third time, looking unsure.

"I'm sure that guy has two left feet." Olivia inched back toward the rental counter. "My cousin is chickening out. Can you tell us more about this?"

"Sure." The young man lifted a laminated card with diagrams of the jetpack system. "Our jetpack uses water propulsion to make you fly. Every minute, one thousand gallons flow through the hose to create lift. The controls work best with gradual movements of your head and hands." He tilted his head around and squeezed one hand into a fist. "But the great thing is that you can ride double with our instructor to really get a feel for flying. Or you can be like that dude and just go solo."

Kendall and Olivia exchanged glances and then said at the same time, "We'll ride double."

Which turned out to be the best way to experience their first jetpack ride. They didn't face-plant or belly flop.

"That was fun," Kendall said afterward as they sat at a picnic bench near the water eating ice cream. She'd taken several pictures with her phone and was in the process of editing them.

On the lake, the instructor was taking out a young boy of about thirteen, who looked equal parts terrified and joyous.

"I had a blast," Olivia agreed, although it

would have been perfect if she'd been flying with Rhett.

She hadn't been able to keep Rhett off her mind.

"I'm going to post these photos and tag everybody…" Kendall lowered her phone. Her hair was in a braid that was utterly un-Kendall-like with frizzies and locks hanging where they shouldn't. "Except, if I tag this place, the family will know we aren't in Florida."

"Do we have to tag the rental place?"

"I told them we would."

And the guys had been happy to hear it.

"I wanted a little time to myself." Olivia took a bite of her ice cream sandwich.

"Time to make Rhett and Sonny suffer?" Kendall removed her sunglasses. "Or just Rhett?"

"Or maybe Shane and Holden, too?" Olivia finished the rest of her ice cream. "I don't want anyone to suffer. I just… I just want to do things at my own pace."

"Yeah, you keep saying that. But I get the feeling that's not the real reason we're out here doing things Rhett would be doing."

Olivia felt her secret building inside of her, pressing for release. "Okay, I… I can't go back to Rhett without knowing what I want to do with the rest of my life. That just seems unfair."

Kendall nodded slowly. "Did he present Holden with a business plan?"

"Who knows?" Olivia shrugged. "No one told me."

"Or me. But then again, I did text Holden and told him you needed space. I can ask."

Olivia drew back. "Don't ask." She wasn't ready to re-establish contact with the world yet.

"Okay, but… Give me some direction here." Kendall tucked a wayward strand of hair behind her ear.

"Well…" Olivia leaned forward. "First off, you're going to reach into your Mary Poppins bag and get out a comb and some hair product." She made a gesture toward Kendall's head. "And then I guess you just have to do the right thing and post our pictures to social media, tags and all."

"What's this?" Rhett came into the kitchen and peeked at an unfamiliar white casserole dish on the counter. "Is that enchiladas?"

"Yep." Cassie was doing the accounting at the kitchen table. Ajax was at her feet, gently chewing on his rabbit squeaker toy. "Gertie Clark brought it by for you."

"For me?" Rhett spotted a cookie tin near the casserole dish. He reached for it.

"Not so fast." His grandfather entered the kitchen and swatted Rhett's hand away. "Those are my cookies. Chocolate chip."

"I don't get it." Rhett moved a safe distance away from the tin. "I get enchiladas and you get cookies."

"Gertie is sweet on Grandpa." Cassie didn't look up from her stack of bills. "Although I think she's also sweet on Sonny."

"I like a good fight." Grandpa took a cookie. "I think I'm the better catch."

"You're playing the field," Cassie told him. "And you're going to get burned." She glanced up. "Hey, you already had a cookie this afternoon. Mind your diabetes."

Grandpa mournfully handed Rhett his cookie.

The doorbell rang, which was unusual given they lived so far outside of town.

Rhett went to answer it. "Odette. What are you doing here?"

The petite old woman had a yellow knit cap pulled low on top of her coarse gray hair. Her dress looked like a patchwork quilt with an apron sewed on the front. "Heard you were low." Odette handed him a casserole dish. "Get well soon."

"But…" He had no time to question her gift.

"And…" Standing behind Odette was Flip, who wore a bright orange hunting vest and cap. She handed him a plastic container. "Chicken soup is good for what ails you."

The two ladies turned around without further explanation or comment.

"Thanks?" Rhett carried the dishes to the kitchen.

His grandfather was sitting at the table with Cassie, sorting his medication. Next to him, Sonny did the same thing. They all glanced up at Rhett.

"Is one of you sick?" Rhett placed the dishes on the counter. When he turned back around, the rest of the kitchen's occupants had their heads bent over their business, which struck him as highly suspicious. "Hey, if one of you is sick, you need to let me know."

The dog stopped squeaking his toy, possibly because Rhett had a snappy tone. Could anyone blame him? He was lonely and on edge because he wasn't sleeping well.

Bentley came in the front door. "I'm back from town."

"We can see that," Rhett said peevishly, wondering why no one had brewed coffee this afternoon. And there was no iced tea in the fridge.

"Here." Bentley handed Rhett a jar. "I was at the Bent Nickel. And Sarah, who runs that bakery part-time with Cam? She sent me home with this jalapeño jelly for you. She said it cures everything from corns to the common cold."

Rhett set it down on the counter, hard. "What is going on? Somebody better tell me or I'm leaving and taking all this food with me."

Bentley moved to Cassie's side. The crew at the table still avoided eye contact.

The doorbell rang again.

Rhett crossed his arms over his chest.

The doorbell rang a second time.

"Aren't you gonna get that?" Grandpa asked. "It could be important."

Rhett waited.

No one said a word to him.

Whoever was at the door knocked this time.

The dog didn't move to see who was there.

"All right. I'll get it."

A skinny, old cowgirl stood on the front porch. She tipped her hat back. "Howdy. I'm Myrna from the Standing Bear Silver Mine.

I live up the road a piece. We're buying those carnival rides from you. Are you Rhett Diaz?"

"Yes, ma'am." Rhett caught a whiff of something. "Do you want to come inside?"

"No. Oh, no. My granddaughter is waiting for me in the ranch yard." Myrna held up a bag that had what looked like a grease stain on the bottom. "I made you hot pepper and black bean spare ribs. It's good to clear out the pipes on the up and down side, if you know what I mean." Her smile was as sharp as her steel-tipped cowboy boots.

"I... I'm not sure I do know, Myrna."

"Sinuses." She waved her petite fingers in front of her nose before gesturing to her stomach. "And what you young-uns call gut health, I think."

"Thank you." Rhett hoped he looked sincere, because that's what he was, albeit confused.

She turned to go, a careful pivot in the direction her boots were facing.

"But Myrna. Why did you make me this?" He barely knew her, after all.

She halted that turnabout. "Word gets out, my boy. And people pull together. We're rooting for you."

"Thanks?" Rhett closed the door.

There wasn't a peep from the kitchen, not so much as a squeak of a dog toy.

Rhett entered the kitchen, set down the ribs on the counter, took a kitchen chair, turned it around and sat in it, resting his forearms on the chair back. "Somebody better start talking."

"Hey, sorry." Bentley shrugged. "Myrna texted me earlier and asked if you were doing okay."

"To which you replied…" Rhett let the sentence dangle.

"Um…no?" Bentley looked apologetic, at least.

"Well…" Cassie didn't quite meet Rhett's gaze. "I might have mentioned to Sarah when I was in town this morning that you were feeling down. And because we were in the Bent Nickel and it was noisy, she might have gotten the wrong impression about what had gotten you down."

Meaning Olivia.

Rhett set his teeth, which didn't stop him from grinding out, "And…" Because there was a reason no one was looking at him and that reason was guilt!

"And I might have mentioned to Odette that you seemed to have low blood sugar," Grandpa admitted gruffly. "You have been sleeping in a lot since you got back."

Rhett washed a hand over his face.

"Are those cookies on the counter?" Sonny got to his feet and tried to sneak past Rhett.

He caught the old man's arm. "Not so fast. Spill."

"Um…" Sonny used his free hand to tug on his beard. "I may have mentioned to Gertie that you may not recover from an ailment I wasn't at liberty to talk about."

"Sonny!" Rhett couldn't believe it. "She probably thinks I am really sick. I've got a broken heart, not a broken…foot!"

"In which case, she'll be happy at your recovery." Sonny slid his arm free. "I think those are my cookies."

"From Gertie," Grandpa growled. "I think not, old timer."

"Old timer?" Sonny took a cookie from the tin and took a big bite.

"Oh, if Olivia were here…" Rhett let the threat hang in the air.

Sonny stuffed the rest of the cookie in his mouth.

"If Olivia were here," Bentley said in that deadpan voice of his. "She'd be laughing her head off."

He was probably right. And if Olivia were here, Rhett might have the heart to laugh along with her.

"Look at the bright side," Grandpa said. "We aren't going to have to cook all week."

"The bright side?" Rhett got to his feet and repeated, "The bright side?"

Rhett knew there wasn't a bright side as long as Olivia wasn't by his side.

"I'll be in the barn if anyone needs me."

"HAVE I TOLD YOU that I'm afraid of heights?"

"Never." Olivia adjusted her harness before turning her attention to Kendall, who looked pale. "You can't be serious."

"I think I am." Kendall stared at the indoor rock climbing wall, which must have been three stories tall. "Maybe I never told you before because I never realized it until just now."

Olivia put her helmet on. "You know there's a fine line between fear and a healthy adrenaline rush." A rush of longing filled her chest. It did so any time Olivia talked about the feelings resulting from going on these adventures. And it was all due to her missing Rhett.

"Fine line..." Kendall grumbled. "Who told you that? Adventure cowboy?"

"Everybody knows that." That might have been a fib. But Olivia didn't retract it.

The noise in the climbing gym receded as the current set of climbers came down to earth and unclipped their safety ropes.

Kendall didn't take her eyes off the climbing wall. "Are you ready to forgive him? Your cowboy?"

"No. Yes." Olivia shook her head. "I told you it was complicated. Don't back out on me. You started this. You and Shane and Holden. You wanted me back on the corporate train. That means you've got to tag along until I figure this out."

"Figure what out?"

"Who I am now. Where I belong." *Who I belong with*. Olivia took Kendall's helmet from her hands and placed it on her head. "Are you chickening out, because we tipped that guy over there twenty bucks to video us climbing."

"Twenty bucks to film me screaming." Kendall frowned as she snapped her chin strap in place. "You know, the last video we took was at that mountain biking place and my lipstick was smeared on my teeth."

"You posted it online, didn't you?"

"Only because the rest of it was awesome." Kendall rolled back her shoulders. "Mostly, you were awesome. I screamed the entire time."

She had. Olivia chuckled. "If you're worried about appearances, wipe off your lipstick now." Olivia took eager strides to reach the bottom of the climbing wall. Above her, numerous colorful plastic hand- and footholds were spaced up the wall. A rope with a steel snap hook dangled in front of her. The only thing that would have made this experience better was if Rhett was with her.

She cancelled that thought but not before a pang of longing put tears in her eyes. She sniffed and blinked them back.

"You should go to Second Chance." Kendall made a show of warming up, jogging in place a few feet away and swinging her arms. "You know you want to."

"I need to feel whole before I see either of them again." Rhett or Sonny, although she missed them both terribly.

The tears returned.

Olivia knocked them away. "You know, I have no purpose."

"Other than to do every adventure experience we come across?" Kendall handed the teenager who'd agreed to film them her cell phone. "I wouldn't be averse to our next experience being a knitting circle."

"That won't get my heart pounding." Olivia scoped out her path to the top. There was a tricky patch about halfway up where handholds were farther apart. "Knitting is a sleepy sport."

"Exactly." Kendall clipped on her rope with a heavy sigh. "Maybe if we do something sleepy, you'll realize that this search of yours to find yourself will only end up at the door where you started."

"Would that be so bad?" Olivia grabbed on to the first set of handholds, and then found her footing.

"Do you even listen to yourself?" Kendall banged her helmeted head against the climbing wall. "Go back to Idaho. Please. Because I've got to go back to Philadelphia, and you worry me."

"Look at me." Olivia was already twenty feet up. She glanced down. "You don't need to worry." But she'd gotten cocky. She lost her footing and dropped back to the floor, aided and kept safe by the rope and harness.

"Great. If you're falling, I'm going to fall. I'm telling you, Olivia, I liked you better when you were the haughty Captain Olivia Monroe,"

Kendall groused, finding some low handholds. "At least then, you only asked me along when you were sailing a luxury yacht and you offered me mimosas."

"Kendall, I've just realized something important."

Kendall stood two feet off the ground. "What?"

"I need to go on this journey alone."

"HAPPY BIRTHDAY, GERTIE!" Rhett entered the Bucking Bull Ranch farmhouse and waded through the sea of children gathered around Gertie Clark in the living room. He kissed Shane's soon-to-be grandmother-in-law and handed her a small, wrapped gift. "Thanks for the enchiladas. This is from all of us over at the Bar D."

"That includes me." Sonny edged Rhett over with his elbow. He introduced himself. "Raymond told me you were beautiful, but his praise didn't do you justice."

Gertie giggled like a school girl.

"Don't you go poaching on my turf." Rhett's grandfather elbowed Sonny aside. "I've always had a spot on my dance card for Gertie."

"Along with a handful of other eligible wid-

ows in town." The gray-haired woman har-
umphed.

"Now, Gertie." Grandpa tipped his hat to
her. "You know you're my best gal."

Sonny hip-checked Grandpa out of his way.
"Whereas I only have eyes for you, my dear."

"I have got to get a life." Rhett left the fuss-
ing men and went in search of a beer, refusing to think about a smart-mouthed woman
with a tumble of short brown curls or to wonder where she was or what she was doing or if
she missed him.

"Because I got what I deserved," he muttered, happy to discover a cooler full of beer
in the backyard, along with several adults, one
of which was Shane, who he didn't want to
talk to.

"Lookin' good, Rhett," Ivy from the Bent
Nickel called to him.

"He does, doesn't he?" MacKenzie from the
general store grinned.

"I'm one hundred percent," Rhett reassured
them. He grabbed a beer and turned to go, only
to have a little cherub slam into his legs.

Tanner's little daughter Mia held up her
arms in a silent request to be picked up. Her
flowery pink dress had what looked like a

chocolate ice cream stain and her dark hair was escaping from her braid.

Rhett obliged, settling her on his hip. "What's wrong, sweet cheeks? Aren't there any horses around for you to practice Liberty on?" She may have only been a toddler, but she had an uncanny ability to sway horses—and heartbroken cowboys—to do her bidding.

"The boys won't let me." She pouted.

"Blame me." Shane appeared at Rhett's side, earning a half-sneer from Rhett. "I told the boys the horses had to stay in their stalls for the party."

"But Shane." Mia tugged more of her hair free. "I'm good with horses."

"I know you are, honey. But rules are rules." Shane gave her a tender smile, which might have fooled Mia, but Rhett knew better.

"Rhett?" Mia fiddled with a button on Rhett's shirt. "Are more kids coming? Little ones I can play with?"

"Sure, there are." Rhett spotted Gabby coming out the back door. Okay, she was twelve, but she carried a little baby girl. And Gabby's step-mother Laurel was two steps behind her, carrying another. Rhett pointed. "There are some right now."

Mia scrambled out of his arms and ran for

the pair, which had the unfortunate effect of leaving Rhett with Shane.

"I've been waiting for you to come by." Shane wore that smile again.

"I've been busy." Rhett clasped his cold beer in his left hand and shoved his right hand in his pocket, which kept him from balling it into a fist and popping Shane in the nose.

"Holden was looking forward to evaluating your business ideas." Shane continued to smile.

"Honey." Franny Clark, Shane's fiancée, took his arm. "I know business is important to you, but you need to respect the fact that Rhett is mourning."

Rhett choked on a swallow of beer. "Beg pardon."

"Sonny's told everyone in town about what happened," Franny said, going so far as to reach out and rub Rhett's arm consolingly.

"I never should have let Sonny borrow my truck," Rhett said under his breath. He tried to find the composure to smile at Franny. "It's not so much a mourning as a cool down period."

Four young cowboys charged out of the house and raced over to join them. They all stared at Rhett. The older two, Davey and Charlie, stood a little bit apart.

"What can I do for you, boys?" Rhett asked.

They'd all been in his roping classes more than a time or two.

"Ah, it ain't true." Six-year-old Adam stomped his boot into the ground.

"Is so." His partner in crime, Quinn, tipped back his dusty cowboy hat and looked Rhett up and down. "All we gotta do is find it."

"Find what?" Rhett asked, he looked to the older boys, who were both younger than ten as far as he recalled.

A pair of identical twin boys tumbled out of the house, nearly falling. They righted their cowboy hats and joined the circle around Rhett. Alex and Andy were also his students.

"Aunt Sophie said you were broken." Quinn grabbed one of Rhett's arms and gave it a good shake. "But you don't even have any bandages."

The older boys and Shane were chortling. Rhett glared at Shane, who stopped.

"Auntie Em says you need time to heal." Adam stared Rhett in the eye. "But you ain't got no stitches."

The boys fell on the grass, they were laughing so hard.

"He doesn't have any stitches," Franny corrected her son, giving Rhett an apologetic look.

"All right. All right. You've all had your fun,

but as you can see, I'm fine and dandy." Rhett stared at each boy in turn. "Now scoot before I get out my lasso and rope you."

"Roping lesson!" Quinn hopped up and down.

"Let's go get our lariats," Charlie said.

"And let's set up our targets," Davey said.

"Come on, Rhett." Adam tugged Rhett's hand. "Let's go have a roping lesson."

"Fine. Let's do this." It was better than standing around with Shane. And maybe then he could prove to Second Chance once and for all that he wasn't broken.

"I'M NOT MAKING another platform for Hester and Ester." Rhett was in Big Boy's stall. He slipped a halter over the black gelding's head and then led him out to the breezeway and tied a quick release knot with the lead rope to a hook on the wall.

"Goats need challenges, especially young ones." Sonny sat on a nearby bench. He wore his hot pink T-shirt that said: Be a Unicorn. "They've only got two little platforms in their play yard. No boulders. No steps. No tunnels."

"No dice." Rhett gave his horse a brief brush down, sliding his curry comb over his ticklish spot in his haunches too quick.

Big Boy kicked up his heels.

"Sorry, fella." Rhett slowed down. He'd been rushing through everything lately. It was as if he couldn't go at a regular pace.

Tanner's rodeo school had come and gone, which had given Rhett some much-needed cash. Cash he was going to use to pay his credit card bill, which had all those hotel rooms and food on it. Rhett had decided not to ask Shane or Holden to reimburse him. That just seemed wrong.

Now there was just normal ranch upkeep and chores to be done. But with Bentley around, there was less for Rhett to do. He almost felt... unneeded. On his own family's ranch!

"Look, Sonny. You know you aren't going to start your goat farm here. It makes no sense to build some epic goat playground when you aren't staying."

Sonny made no comment.

Rhett craned his neck over Big Boy's back to check on the old guy.

He was pouting.

"I'm not kicking you out. I'm just reminding you of reality." And reality was that every day Rhett didn't hear from Olivia, his hopes of her returning diminished. Sometimes, late at night, he felt as if she was never coming back.

"Reality is that Olivia's going to come back and she's going to have a plan for us."

"For *us*." This was news to Rhett. Kind of. He supposed if Olivia wanted him back that she and Sonny were a package deal. "You know, I could head into town tomorrow and talk to Holden about starting my business here."

Sonny nodded. "That's what you said yesterday."

Disgusted with himself, Rhett picked up Big Boy's hooves one-at-a-time.

"And the day before," Sonny added.

Rhett bit his bottom lip to keep from saying anything foolish, because his actions were doing just fine at creating that impression.

"And the day before that." Sonny sounded pleased, not disappointed. "Why do you think you've been unable to move yourself forward?"

"I'm not one of your clients," Rhett snapped.

Sonny chuckled.

Rhett stomped into the tack room for Big Boy's saddle and bridle. They rode farther up the mountain every day, stalling for time until Olivia returned. But every time Rhett came back to the Bar D, Olivia hadn't come back. Or called. Or provided the town with any gossip via her family.

That was starting to hurt.

Patience.

Rhett used to have that in spades.

He saddled Big Boy, mounted up and left Sonny to play with his goats.

They walked through the south pasture. His horse's long stride was a contrast to Rhett's racing thoughts. He shouldn't have agreed to deliver Olivia to Philadelphia, obviously. Or challenged her to do all those things, obviously.

What kind of man pushed a woman to step out of her shell?

He had to dismount to open the gate and lead Big Boy through. In the saddle once more, he brought the gelding to a slow canter. It was during this part of the ride that he replayed their late night conversations in hotel lobbies, feeling again the rush of attraction and the pleasure of their banter. He rode the fence for half a mile before reaching the lake on the south side.

The old homestead was on the other side of the lake.

Rhett always averted his gaze. Besides, there was an old dirt road that ran straight through the trees. It was perfect for an all-out gallop.

He could ride so fast, all his mistakes with Olivia would be left in the dust.

Including his flat-footed reaction to her telling him she loved him.

Rhett leaned farther over Big Boy's neck, urging him to run faster, fast enough to leave the painful past behind.

A blue jay swooped in front of them.

Big Boy leaped, landed, spun around, kicking like a bucking bronco.

Rhett hung on, using all his skill to reassert control. "Easy boy. Easy. E—"

Crack.

Rhett hit his head on something solid and then everything went black.

CHAPTER TWENTY-ONE

SLEIGH BELLS JINGLED.

Rhett always thought they'd jingle contin-
uously, like the song. But this was a jingle.
Silence. Jingle-jingle. Silence.

Someone gave his arm a bath.

"Ow." He swatted them away.

Jingle-jingle.

Bleth-th-th-th.

"Aw, come on." Someone had blown a raspberry in his face.

I should be seeing this.

Rhett cracked open his eyes. The world was
a tunnel of fuzzy light and—something big
and black approached his face. Rhett's eyes
flew all the way open just as Big Boy nudged
his nose against Rhett's chin.

"Don't." Rhett flinched from the love tap.

Big Boy shook his head as if Rhett wasn't
moving fast enough, sending his bridle jin-
gling a little.

A wind whistled through the tree tops overhead.

Rhett's head pounded, somewhere near his crown. "Double ow."

Above him, a blue jay scolded them both.

"Give me a break, would ya." Rhett rolled over to all fours, because even a lovesick fool cowboy knew that you didn't leap to your feet after hitting your head and taking a tumble. He didn't vomit. Always a good sign.

The jay continued to scold.

"You're lucky I don't hold a grudge." Rhett got to his knees and reached around to assess the damage on the back of what he hoped was a hard head. There was a big bump. His pulse pounded in his temples to the same tempo as in the rising bruise.

Big Boy stomped a hoof.

"Sure, you can be impatient. You probably don't have a scratch." Rhett got to his feet to check his companion just in case. "Nothin'," he declared.

His hat was nearly as flat as a pancake underneath the jay's pine tree.

Rhett decided to leave it for now because his limbs were beginning to do the post-adrenaline hokey-pokey and he didn't trust himself not to keel over if he bent down to get it.

Big Boy stomped his hoof again.

"Ah, yes. You want the ride over with so you can get some oats." Rhett grabbed on to the saddle horn, fully expecting to swing himself up. His legs, however, had other ideas. They were the consistency of hot porridge.

The jay swooped again, spooking Big Boy, who practically leaped three feet sideways, taking Rhett out like a bowling ball striking a lone pin. Luckily, he didn't hit any ancient pine trees. He just rolled across some old pine cones.

"This just isn't my day." *Understatement.* Rhett picked himself up, thinking about the long trek back to the ranch.

The jay kept trash talking.

"What say we walk home, fella?" Holding on to the saddle horn, Rhett set off at a slow pace, leaving the jay behind.

Big Boy had some big strides, plus they were heading for home so the gelding had incentive to hurry. He kept outpacing Rhett and practically dragging his feet out from under him.

"Olivia would have something to say about this," Rhett muttered. He just couldn't think what it would have been. And then it came to him, so clear and vividly, he had to share with Big Boy. "She'd say 'Know your limits.'"

Rhett chuckled. "She should say 'Know your blue jay.' Ha!"

Big Boy walked on without comment.

"Sonny would say I'm joking to hide my hurt." Rhett's head was pounding good and hard now, and the sun was going down behind him. "He'd want me to reframe this into something positive."

Head hurting, pride hurting, heart hurting, Rhett couldn't think of anything positive to say.

He reached the gate and managed to get them through, but the world was looking all fuzzy and it felt like Big Boy was dragging Rhett along.

And then people were crowding him, tugging his arms over their shoulders and asking him all sorts of questions he couldn't make out or begin to answer.

All he kept repeating was one thing, "Don't tell her. I don't want her to worry."

CONCUSSIONS WERE A beast to recover from.

And anytime one's health was in question, people were a beast about being kind.

That was Rhett's opinion, and during his recovery, he was sticking to it.

In other words, Concussion Rhett was as

ornery as a hungry bear stung by a bee in springtime.

For weeks, he wasn't allowed to ride or do chores. He had nothing much to fill his days but to hold baby goats and keep Sonny company.

There were some problems with that.

First, Sonny wasn't the company he wanted. The old man enjoyed talking about two things—goats and feelings. The last thing Rhett wanted to talk about was his feelings. At least not with Sonny.

Olivia, do you still love me?

And second, the baby goats weren't babies anymore. It was easier to hold Ajax in his lap. But large high-energy herding dogs weren't very cuddly. Which had Rhett eyeing Millie, the barn cat, not that she was into cuddling either. She viewed Rhett as a plaything since he sat in the barn all day, moping about. The gray cat reveled in leaping out from behind feed bins and hay bales—*hay bales!*—and wrapping her paws around his boots.

Olivia, when are you coming home?

His questions went unanswered.

Time passed. October rolled around. Rhett had the all-clear to ride again but he couldn't quite bring himself to do it. He put Big Boy through his paces on a lunge line or turned him out for a day in the pasture.

Rhett had put off making plans to open an adventure tour company, too. If he saw Holden in town, he went the other way. The weather was turning. In another month or so, the snow would come down so thick that the passes would be closed.

Rhett tried thinking about the future. The production crew for the movie being made in town had contacted him about scheduling and availability in April. He still hadn't cashed his advance check. How could he? He'd thought Olivia might find it in her heart to forgive him. But one day bled into another and he was still at the Bar D, still alone.

Rhett stood at Big Boy's stall door rubbing the gelding behind his ears and trying to work up the energy to ride. Gray clouds were gathering outside, heavy with the promise of snow. He'd put on a thick jacket this morning, feeling the coming of winter like a chill in his lonely bones.

Sonny joined him at Big Boy's stall. "I see those gears in your head spinning. You're overthinking. It's just a ride. You don't have to gallop through the woods."

"The jay has gone south for the winter," Rhett said testily. "I have nothing to fear."

"That's right." Sonny's yellow T-shirt was covered in brown goat hair, not that it blocked his message: One Step at a Time. "But it isn't fear that's stopping you."

"And here we go." Headfirst into Rhett's own personal life coaching session.

Sonny clapped a hand on Rhett's shoulder. "What's stopping you is a broken heart."

Rhett tipped up the brim of his new black cowboy hat and gave Sonny a hard look designed to encourage him to step off that platform of his and let Rhett be.

"You need to get out more," Sonny continued, fingers brushing through his beard. "Find your own swath of blue sky."

"A new significant other, you mean?" Rhett scoffed, not backing off even if his stock-in-trade glare wasn't working on the old man. "What happened to finding my own special dessert and never wanting another again?"

Sonny looked perplexed.

"You don't remember? Seriously?" Rhett shook his head. "You may have forgotten you love pineapple upside down cake, but I haven't forgotten my cinnamon roll with extra icing."

He turned on his heel and headed toward the door, pulling his hat brim low.

Someone stood at the breezeway entrance, the setting sun at their back. A woman.

Rhett marched closer, thinking it was his sister, Cassie.

Except Cassie didn't wear baggy cargo shorts and untucked polo shirts. Nor did she have sun-kissed, brown curly hair.

His steps slowed and faltered. His mouth became parched—thirsting for words, thirsting for emotion, thirsting for passionate kisses.

"Sounds like you two have been scoring some serious desserts while I've been gone." Olivia's voice filled his ears the way the memory of it had filled his head for over two months.

Five minutes ago, he'd wanted nothing more than to see Olivia, to know that she was okay and to hold her in his arms for longer than thirty seconds. He'd been thinking in terms of forever.

Maybe it was the injury he'd done to his head.

Maybe it was how she'd shown up without any warning.

Maybe it was any number of excuses that

suddenly filled his cowboy pride with the strength to raise his head, square his shoulders and walk on by.

CHAPTER TWENTY-TWO

HEART IN HER THROAT, Olivia watched the man she loved walk away from her.

Of all the ways she'd imagined coming back to him, of all the receptions she'd played out in her head, this wasn't one of them.

"It's been a long time." Sonny came to stand next to her, tone chiding. "No postcard. No email. No text messages."

"You know I avoid difficult emotions," she said, throat thick with a myriad of the same. "I knew I couldn't just…call." Or communicate through any of the other methods he'd mentioned.

"He's been hoping you'd come back." There was a chill in that statement. "We both have."

Olivia's chest felt tight, each breath a battle as hope was squeezed out of her heart. "I thought you'd understand." He'd known her better than anyone.

The wintry mountain wind pushed through

the barn, tried to push her away, back down the mountain.

Sonny tsked. "Funny thing about understanding, Olivia. It requires knowing what the other person is feeling and going through."

They don't want me here.

She'd returned to Second Chance and Rhett and Sonny feeling strong and capable. She'd returned with forgiveness and love in her heart. She'd returned and found they wanted her to apologize.

The wind pushed harder.

Standing her ground, Olivia drew a deep breath. "I spent time working on myself. I didn't think you'd take issue with that." She'd thought he'd be proud.

"I bought some baby goats on the trip back from Philadelphia." Sonny splayed his fingers through his white beard, almost irritably. "For weeks, while I held Ester, I'd meditate on how to be a blessing to Rhett and his broken heart. And while I held Hester, I'd meditate on my behavior with you and what I could have done differently. Forgiveness was on the forefront of my mind."

She'd bet there had been tears shed.

"And then one night as I was checking social media for some lighthearted posts about

baby goats, I saw something Kendall posted."
His blue eyes connected with hers, so full of
disapproval. "She chronicled your adventure
tour experiences."

"Did Rhett see?" Olivia whispered.

"I was proud of your progress…your ini-
tiative…your joy. But…" He shook his head.
"…as the weeks went on, I began to realize
there was something missing from those pictures. Heartbreak."

"Did Rhett see?" Olivia asked louder.

"After that, when I held Hester, I reviewed
the memories I had of you and Rhett together,
playing at being a couple and I started to
second-guess the impressions I had and the
words I'd heard you say to him." Sonny shifted
his stance and in that small change, Olivia saw
the hurt and the doubt she'd caused.

"Did Rhett see?" Olivia demanded, chest
heaving. "Did he see any of her social media
posts?"

Sonny made her wait for his answer and
even then, it wasn't what she wanted to hear.
"I didn't show him, but I can't say if he saw
any on his own."

"I'm sorry." Olivia threw her arms around
Sonny. "I had to do things my way."

"The hard way, as usual," Sonny grumbled, arms circling her tentatively.

She squeezed him tight. "I'll explain everything later. Right now, I have to find Rhett."

Because if Sonny, her strongest supporter, had doubted her love and purpose, she could only imagine how Rhett's heart had turned away from her.

AFTER BEING TOLD by Cassie that Rhett wasn't home, Olivia ran all the way to the old homestead and the lake, hoping she'd find Rhett there.

With his back to her, he sat in the little dinghy, floating about five feet from shore.

Olivia didn't hesitate. She kicked off her flip-flops, waded into the frigid lake water, grabbed hold of the boat's side and tumbled in.

Rhett turned to look at her, eyes flat.

"Hi." Olivia sat on the narrow bench seat across from him. Her feet stung from the cold and her heart stung from Rhett's frigid reception. She took stock of him. Of that strong chin, thrust out as if looking for a fight. At those high cheekbones that seemed hollower than the last time she'd seen him. At that five-o'clock shadow making him seem worn out and in need of a hug.

Olivia's heart went out to him, and she hated herself for being selfish. She should have realized what she'd put him and Sonny through.

Her gaze flicked upward. "I like your new hat."

That made him frown, as well as made her wonder about the reason for a new hat.

They stared at each other in silence as snow began to fall.

Olivia, who'd spent two days driving up from Phoenix, realized she hadn't been prepared for her reception or dressed for the weather. In an attempt to keep warm, she folded her knees up to her chest, crossed her ankles and hooked her elbows around her legs. "I owe you an explanation."

He might have nodded.

Olivia assumed so. But permission or not, she wasn't sure where to start. She latched on to Sonny's advice from when they'd first met—start at the beginning. "You were right to box me in and make me sail."

His lips thinned to a hard line.

"I wouldn't have chosen it. In fact, as soon as I realized where you were taking me, I wanted to tell you that I'd chosen sailboarding." She swallowed thickly, reliving the mixture of panic and longing that short drive had given her. "But I couldn't get the words out. Me, who'd barked commands at the first sign of an emergency, couldn't tell you what was on my mind." She drew in a cold breath, swallowing a snowflake or two. Snow dotted Rhett's black cowboy hat and his broad shoulders. "And when we parked, I fell into the role of Captain Olivia Monroe." The tough talker no one questioned. "After the sail, a new reality set in because the two men I loved, the ones who had my back, were gone."

Rhett didn't move. His elbows were resting on his knees, hands clasped before him. His black leather cowboy boots were dry and planted firmly on the dinghy's deck.

"It was then that I realized that without anger driving me forward, I'd leaned on others." Her voice lost some of its certainty. "I knew that I had to take time for myself. I needed to create the wind behind my own sails, not let that fall on you and Sonny."

The wind blew the dinghy out toward the center of the lake. Snowflakes thickened, both in size and in intensity.

Olivia suppressed a shudder, hugging her legs close. "And because I was trying to do things on my own...*not*...I took Kendall with me for the first two weeks."

Rhett frowned.

"We approached a road trip the way you might have." Despite the dour mood between them, Olivia managed to smile. "We found lots of adventures to go on. Kendall being Kendall, she took plenty of pictures." Enough to provide fodder for social media posts for more than a month. Olivia took stock of Rhett's expression. He was frowning... Had he seen any of Kendall's posts and been under the impression that she'd been out whooping it up all this time, he'd have been scowling. "But after two weeks, I realized what I'd been doing, and I sent her home. When I looked around, I was in Arizona, standing in the parking lot of a mountain bike rental place. There was a help wanted sign." She shrugged, which was more of a shiver. "So I went in and applied for the job."

Snowflakes were beginning to melt and sink past her curls to her scalp. They'd also dotted her eyelashes. Her toes felt like ice and Rhett's heart didn't seem to be melting.

"I spent the past six weeks or so working there, learning how to ride trails, and run a sports rental business." It was humbling how little she knew about something that wasn't sailing. "And I wanted to call you...but I didn't want to talk if you weren't within reaching distance." Which was ironic given he was now within reaching distance and she felt so very far away. "Every day, I'd wake up and think I needed to call you. And Sonny," she added. "And every night, I'd fall into bed thinking it was too late to call you, but I was determined to do it in the morning."

"What held you back?" His voice creaked through the air.

She shrugged, blinking back tears. "Knowing how we left things. Not wanting to know if you'd given up on me. Hating myself for every harsh word I ever said to you. Hating myself for lacking the courage to pick up the phone and call anyway."

"I know how that feels," he said gruffly.

If it hadn't been for his tone, she might have held out hope that he still loved her.

Instead, her head bobbed like a life preserver on rough seas, and she held herself together by two frozen elbows and a tight hand clasp.

"In the meantime…" Her voice hardened. "Kendall has been posting pictures from our two weeks together on social media. Sonny thought I was out and about having a grand old time."

Worry about Sonny later.

It was Rhett she wanted to make peace with. Rhett she wanted to forge a future with.

If he still loves me.

The snow was falling so thickly, she couldn't see shore.

Olivia refused to ask him to row toward the dock. She had a feeling that this was her last chance with Rhett and she had more to get off her chest. "All my life, people have been telling me what I can and can't do. And when the 'can't' annoyed me, I tried to find the means to do it anyway. And if I fell flat on my face trying, my father would tell me in no uncertain terms to pick myself up and try again, which annoyed me. But then Grandpa Harlan would tell me that 'can' was like a rocket, leaving the *t* behind on lift-off." She'd forgotten about that. Grandpa Harlan had been a lot like Sonny. "He believed I could overcome anything, any objection, any fear. But as I grew up, I often succeeded more than I failed. And when I did something, everyone noticed and applauded. So, I kept on launching off *can't* into *yes-I-can*. But I kept doing it to show them, whoever they were. I didn't try things for me." She clenched her jaw, willing her teeth not to chatter. "Do you understand?"

He stood, rocking the boat as he removed his jacket and put it around her. "I think so."

The jacket offered his warmth, but it did nothing to give life to her broken heart. At least not until he sat down next to her and put his arm around her.

There was hope! Even if he was only preventing her from freezing.

She laid her head on his shoulder. "I didn't do things the way you do—to celebrate life. I did things to earn accolades and approval."

"And endorsements and sponsorships." He tried to brush snow from her short curls, only to give up and plunk his hat on her head.

She nodded. "I'm a sell-out. I don't deserve to be a role model or a spokesperson."

"Just another reason for you to blaze a new trail and start your second act." Rhett stared deep into her eyes and for a moment Olivia forgot about wrongs and cold temperatures. "Do you have any ideas about that?" His gaze dipped to her lips and one corner of his mouth tipped up.

"For a small town cowboy, you're very obtuse." She shamelessly snuggled closer.

"Sonny would disagree, I'm sure." He was having none of her snuggling. He reached for the oars and began rowing. "He's decided I need his life coaching."

She recalled Sonny's words about Rhett's broken heart. "I'm sorry for that."

"Don't be. We have an understanding. He babbles on until I can't take it anymore and then I stomp away thinking about what he's said."

Olivia smiled up at him. But then her smile faded.

He noticed, of course. "What's wrong?"

"Everyone's been telling me that I *can't* be with you because of whatever reason they feel is valid—that you're a cowboy and that you never play it safe."

"If I played it safe, I'd never have let you tell the whole town that I was your man." Rhett spared her a glance, dark brows raised. His black hair was blanketed with a dusting of snow.

"You gave me the adventure of a lifetime, Rhett. And instead of taking it slow, I took the word *can't* and took a giant leap forward into *can*. I can love you. I do love you." And she hoped that he felt the same.

The little boat slid to a stop on shore where it was normally beached. Rhett hopped over the edge into what must have been icy water.

He turned and reached for her. "Come on. I've got you. All of you. For now and evermore."

She took that to mean he didn't just have her under his protection—for warmth and a lift to safety. But that he loved her.

For now and evermore.

This was what Olivia had wanted for months. And yet, she hesitated. She hesitated because she'd gone through so much to find her independence, her courage and what she wanted for her second act. She wanted to come into this relationship with Rhett as a partner on all levels.

She stood on the cold planks of the boat bottom. "Rhett Diaz, I love you and want to marry you."

His grin broadened and he beckoned her closer. "The water's starting to ooze through my boots, my little hay bale. How about we finish this discussion under a roof somewhere? Preferably in front of a fire."

"Rhett Diaz, I just told you I loved you and asked you to marry me." She stomped her heel a little, sending the boat rocking.

He leaned forward and plucked her into his arms. "Honey, first off, you didn't ask me anything. Captain Olivia Monroe told me she wanted to marry me, like a command to hoist the sails."

"Sorry. Old habits." She nestled into his warmth as he carried her toward the old homestead. "Will you marry me, Rhett? Or am I still moving too fast for you?" She hoped not.

"Honey, I'm not a sailor on your racing team."

"And I'm not a mountain person." And she'd much prefer it if he'd call her his little hay bale again. "But I have an idea that involves compromise."

"Do tell." He opened the homestead door without dropping her and carried her inside, depositing her on the couch and covering her with a brown and orange crocheted blanket.

"There's a property for sale next to the Flying T on the banks of the mighty Mississippi River." She held up her hands, inviting him to be by her side.

"There is?" Rhett feigned surprise.

"There is." Olivia nodded, shedding his jacket and hat and slipping into his lap. "You told me Tad was worried about whether he'd be able to run the hang-gliding business while also shuttling Jazzy around to compete in rodeos. If we buy the neighboring property—"

"It's on the Mississippi River. You could still

go out on the water sometimes." He looked deep into her eyes. "That is, if you had a mind to sail."

"I might." She'd been learning to slow down and a nice classic sailboat as Rhett would say might fit the bill. "We'd need a barn so you could bring Big Boy."

"And… You're going to think this is weird, but I'd like to have some goats." He shrugged. "And Sonny. Heaven help me, the man's grown on me like lichen on an old tree."

"He'd like that," Olivia agreed. "We might host a retreat there for athletes who've lost their confidence."

"Or cowboys who get stuck in a rut." He gave her a rueful smile. "For one reason or another."

"I think we've got it all figured out." Olivia loved him so very, very much. She took his face in both her hands. "Except for one thing. You haven't told me you love me or if you've agreed to get married."

"Are you sure?" Despite his question, Rhett pressed a kiss to her palm. "This is happening awfully fast. People might say I caught you when you were down."

Olivia found it easy to joke because the look he gave her was filled with love. "Cowboy, we have a life plan. All that you need to do is say yes and we'll be well set to start a new life together."

"Olivia… Liv…" He began to slowly close the distance between his lips and hers. "Do you remember that day you grabbed me in a parking lot and kissed me? I didn't tell you no then, and I'm not telling you no now. I love you. And I'm always willing to give you space to go out and find yourself, as long as you call me and tell me that you love me, too."

"I will." Although Olivia doubted that she'd ever need space to spread her wings again. "And I promise not to be overly bossy."

Rhett raised an eyebrow in apparent disbelief. "I think we both know that's not going to be a promise you can easily keep."

Olivia gasped.

Rhett pressed his fingers over her lips. "Now, my little hay bale. I just want you to make note of this so we can tell our kids someday." He rested his forehead on hers. "You were the one who came around asking me to marry you. Finally. You need to show me the respect and love I've shown you. Always."

"Your wish is my command, my devoted, adorable cowboy." Olivia chuckled, safe in the knowledge that they understood each other perfectly. "Now kiss me."

Because it had been a long time coming and they both deserved some tender loving care.

EPILOGUE

"ARE YOU DONE hugging the goats?" Olivia entered Sonny's goat barn and came to stand near Rhett.

He held a small brown baby goat. "I needed a moment to chase away my trepidation. Isn't that what you say every time I take you on a new adventure?"

"It is." Olivia smiled and sat down next to him on the bench. She took the baby goat from his arms and set it in the pen with its mama. And then she took Rhett's hands. "When I was racing, I'd never have guessed this was where I'd end up."

"That we'd be living on a ranch in Minnesota on the Mississippi River?" He was teasing, of course.

She played along. "That I'd be helping you run a multi-experience adventure tour company?" They'd been in Minnesota for two years and had built a few beginner mountain biking trails on their ranch. They planned to break ground on a zipline experience next spring.

"And that you'd be helping Sonny run a goat farm and emotional retreat?" Rhett squeezed her hands tight. "Not to mention how we've partnered with Tad and Sharon to run the hang-gliding business."

"And the water jetpack experience. We're busy," she agreed, since he needed to hear it said out loud. "But we've hired some good people."

Nancy from her former racing team and her teenage son, Van. They lived in town several miles down the road.

"We need to hire a few more. That sailboat you bought…" His hold on her hands was becoming tighter, giving away his stress.

"It's in need of refurbishing, but I'm not averse to putting in some elbow grease."

The baby goat bleated, walking back toward them on unsteady feet. It was darling. Sonny had been right about the goats relieving stress and bringing people joy.

The alarm on her phone went off.

"It's time to start dinner." Olivia had insisted Sonny teach her how to cook, but the only way she got food on the table when it was her night to make dinner was if she set reminders for herself.

Sonny had a small room inside the bunkhouse they'd built to house his retreat clients, who came to get away from it all and recenter themselves. Sonny was good at that. He was also thriving with Rhett and Olivia in Minnesota. They ate together almost every night. They were their own little family unit and considered Tad's family an extension of their own.

Olivia drew Rhett to his feet. He still took long rides on his big horse, weather permitting, although they didn't gallop as if the devil was on their heels. And he still enjoyed prodding Olivia when she took herself too seriously and grew bossy.

But today was different.

"I love you, but I scared you," she told Rhett. "You need a hug."

Rhett scoffed, but his dark eyes betrayed the truth.

Olivia enfolded her husband into her arms and began to count to thirty. When she was done, she drew back to look at her strong, hardworking cowboy. The man who'd stolen her heart and took time to get used to the idea of change, big or small.

"I love you, too," he said simply, because

he wasn't a man of fancy words, unless you counted the creative nicknames he found for her.

Hay bale was still her favorite.

"We're pregnant," Olivia told him again, repeating the words that had sent him out to find a baby goat.

Rhett nodded, giving her that slightly lopsided grin as his gaze drifted down to her mouth. He wanted a kiss. "I'm good with that now. We always talked about having kids...not the goat kind. And it's...time?" He looked deep into her eyes. "What aren't you telling me?"

She drew him down to the bench. "It's twins."

* * * * *

For more great romances in
The Mountain Monroes miniseries from
Melinda Curtis and Harlequin Heartwarming,
visit www.Harlequin.com today!

HARLEQUIN SELECTS COLLECTION

19 FREE BOOKS IN ALL!

From Robyn Carr to RaeAnne Thayne to Linda Lael Miller and Sherryl Woods we promise (actually, GUARANTEE!) each author in the Harlequin Selects collection has seen their name on the *New York Times* or *USA TODAY* bestseller lists!

YES! Please send me the **Harlequin Selects Collection**. This collection begins with 3 FREE books and 2 FREE gifts in the first shipment. Along with my 3 free books, I'll also get 4 more books from the Harlequin Selects Collection, which I may either return and owe nothing or keep for the low price of $24.14 U.S./$28.82 CAN. each plus $2.99 U.S./$7.49 CAN. for shipping and handling per shipment*.If I decide to continue, I will get 6 or 7 more books (about once a month for 7 months) but will only need to pay for 4. That means 2 or 3 books in every shipment will be FREE! If I decide to keep the entire collection, I'll have paid for only 32 books because 19 were FREE! I understand that accepting the 3 free books and gifts places me under no obligation to buy anything. I can always return a shipment and cancel at any time. My free books and gifts are mine to keep no matter what I decide.

☐ 262 HCN 5576 ☐ 462 HCN 5576

Name (please print)

Address   Apt. #

City   State/Province   Zip/Postal Code

Mail to the **Harlequin Reader Service:**
IN U.S.A.: P.O. Box 1341, Buffalo, NY 14240-8531
IN CANADA: P.O. Box 603, Fort Erie, Ontario L2A 5X3

*Terms and prices subject to change without notice. Prices do not include sales taxes, which will be charged (if applicable) based on your state or country of residence. Canadian residents will be charged applicable taxes. Offer not valid in Quebec. All orders subject to approval. Credit or debit balances in a customer's account(s) may be offset by any other outstanding balance owed by or to the customer. Please allow 3 to 4 weeks for delivery. Offer available while quantities last. © 2020 Harlequin Enterprises ULC. ® and ™ are trademarks owned by Harlequin Enterprises ULC.

Your Privacy—Your information is being collected by Harlequin Enterprises ULC, operating as Harlequin Reader Service. To see how we collect and use this information visit https://corporate.harlequin.com/privacy-notice. From time to time we may also exchange your personal information with reputable third parties. If you wish to opt out of this sharing of your personal information, please visit www.readerservice.com/consumerschoice or call 1-800-873-8635. Notice to California Residents—Under California law, you have specific rights to control and access your data. For more information visit https://corporate.harlequin.com/california-privacy.

50BOOKHS22R

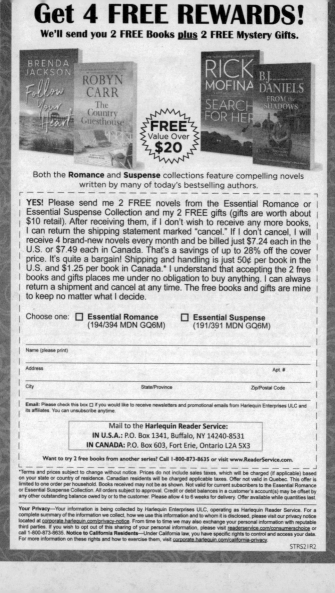

#415 THE COWBOY'S UNLIKELY MATCH
Bachelor Cowboys • by Lisa Childs

Having grown up in foster care, schoolteacher Emily Trent readily moves to Ranch Haven to help three local orphans—just not their playboy uncle, Ben Haven. The charming cowboy mayor didn't get her vote and won't get her heart!

#416 THE PARAMEDIC'S FOREVER FAMILY
Smoky Mountain First Responders • by Tanya Agler

Horticulturist and single mom Lindsay Hudson looks forward to neighborly chats with paramedic Mason Ruddick. He was her late husband's best friend, but he can't be anything more. Unless love can bloom in her own backyard?

#417 THE RANCHER'S WYOMING TWINS
Back to Adelaide Creek • by Virginia McCullough

Heather Stanhope wants to hate the rancher who bought her family's land. Instead, she's falling for sweet Matt Burton and his adorable twin nieces. Could the place she longs to call home be big enough for all of them?

#418 THEIR TOGETHER PROMISE
The Montgomerys of Spirit Lake
by M. K. Stelmack

Mara Montgomery is determined to face her vision loss without any help—particularly from the stubbornly optimistic Connor Flanagan. Can Connor open Mara's eyes to a lifetime of love from one of his service dogs...and him?

Visit ReaderService.com Today!

As a valued member of the Harlequin Reader Service, you'll find these benefits and more at ReaderService.com:

- Try 2 free books from any series
- Access risk-free special offers
- View your account history & manage payments
- Browse the latest Bonus Bucks catalog

Don't miss out!

If you want to stay up-to-date on the latest at the Harlequin Reader Service and enjoy more content, make sure you've signed up for our monthly News & Notes email newsletter. Sign up online at ReaderService.com or by calling Customer Service at 1-800-873-8635.

RS20